"How big is this cabin?" Ella asked when Noah came out and found her pacing the length of one wall. "Twenty-eight by twenty-eight?"

He looked at her crosswise. "Is this part of your inventory?"

She nodded.

Noah's brows lowered. "I feel like the rug is about to be yanked out from under my butt."

"Why?"

"I live here, for one." He held up his injured hand. "And where else can I practice with this? You're going to give me more than thirty days' notice before you evict me, aren't you?"

"Calm down." Ella could relate to the anxious feeling uncertainty brought, but she had to put her young daughter's needs—and the family's—first. "I don't know what's going to happen to this town at the end of the year. None of us do. The family is divided." Was that saying too much?

"And waiting on your valuation to make a decision?"

She nodded again.

He stroked his beard, considering her. "I can help with that."

"How?" she asked, eyeing him with a big dose of suspicion.

Dear Reader,

My dad was an impulsive businessman. If he was shown an investment property and was driving through town and saw great interest rates posted in a bank window, he went in and opened an account. If I operated like that, I'd be bankrupt, but Lady Luck smiled on Dad and made him a wealthy man, although you wouldn't know it by his lifestyle. Quirky? Yes. And after he passed, we found several quirky bequeaths in his will.

When I began talking to Harlequin about creating a new series for Heartwarming, Dad and his last wishes were still very much on my mind. And so Harlan Monroe was born, a man who'd created quite an empire but had unusual ideas about money and how to pass on the important aspects of his legacy to his twelve grandchildren.

Kissed by the Country Doc introduces some of the twelve as seen through the eyes of Ella Bowman Monroe. Three years ago, orphaned Ella fell in love with one of Harlan's grandchildren instantly—not that any of the other Monroes believed in love at first sight. Now widowed, Ella doesn't know how she fits in with the Monroe clan. Enter jaded Dr. Noah Bishop. There's something about Ella he can't resist. Is it love at first sight? I'll leave it up to you to decide.

I hope you come to love The Mountain Monroes as much as I do. Happy reading!

Melinda Curtis

HEARTWARMING

Kissed by the Country Doc

USA TODAY Bestselling Author

Melinda Curtis

HARLEQUIN® HEARTWARMING™

ISBN-13: 978-1-335-51054-9

Kissed by the Country Doc

Printed in U.S.A.

Prior to writing romance, award-winning *USA TODAY* bestseller **Melinda Curtis** was a junior manager for a Fortune 500 company, which meant when she flew on the private jet, she was relegated to the jump seat. After grabbing her pen (and a parachute), she made the leap to full-time writer. Between writing clean romance for Harlequin and indie-pubbed romantic comedy, Melinda recently came to grips with the fact that she's an empty nester and a grandma. Brenda Novak says Melinda's book *Season of Change* "found a place on my keeper shelf."

Books by Melinda Curtis

Harlequin Heartwarming

A Harmony Valley Novel

Dandelion Wishes
Summer Kisses
Season of Change
A Perfect Year
Time for Love
A Memory Away
Marrying the Single Dad
Love, Special Delivery
Support Your Local Sheriff
Marrying the Wedding Crasher
A Heartwarming Thanksgiving
"Married by Thanksgiving"
Make Me a Match
"Baby, Baby"

Return of the Blackwell Brothers

The Rancher's Redemption

Visit the Author Profile page
at Harlequin.com for more titles.

THE MOUNTAIN MONROES FAMILY TREE

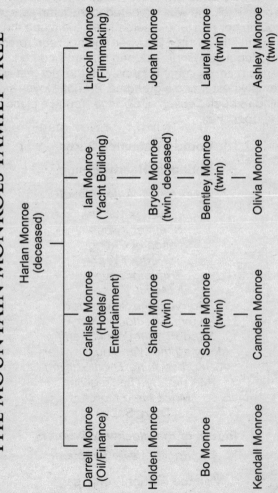

Harlan Monroe (deceased)

Darrell Monroe (Oil/Finance)
- Holden Monroe
- Bo Monroe
- Kendall Monroe

Carlisle Monroe (Hotels/Entertainment)
- Shane Monroe (twin)
- Sophie Monroe (twin)
- Camden Monroe

Ian Monroe (Yacht Building)
- Bryce Monroe (twin, deceased)
- Bentley Monroe (twin)
- Olivia Monroe

Lincoln Monroe (Filmmaking)
- Jonah Monroe
- Laurel Monroe (twin)
- Ashley Monroe (twin)

PROLOGUE

THERE WERE DAYS when Ella Bowman Monroe felt like life couldn't get any better—when her house was clean, when her little girl was clean and when she was surrounded by her large family of boisterous in-laws. On those days, this orphaned widow felt like singing as loudly as Grandpa Monroe.

Today wasn't shaping up to be a singing kind of day.

Chalk it up to her grandfather-in-law's funeral on this snowy January afternoon, the reading of his will and the Spanx she'd wiggled into that were so tight every breath was a struggle.

"Mom," two-year-old Penny whispered from her lap. "I go." And her daughter didn't mean she wanted to leave. The ripe smell of dirty diaper mushroomed around them in the dining room of the Monroe Philadelphia compound like an alien force field.

To Ella's right, her husband's cousin Sophie

spared Penny a glance and a nose tweak. "No more artichoke quiche for you."

To Ella's left, Sophie's twin brother, Shane, waved a hand in front of his nose. *"Penny la Pew."*

Penny giggled and grinned, glorying in their attention. "Kiss," she whispered, leaning to kiss first Sophie and then Shane, and then twisting to kiss Ella.

The smiles, teasing and kisses would have been normal—so very normal—except for the elderly lawyer wheezing through the legalese of the will and the black-clad Monroes ringing the formal dining-room table. They nodded at appropriate wheezes as if well-versed in legalese.

Near the head of the table, Ian Monroe, Ella's father-in-law, turned his somber face her way, his expression one of reluctant farewell.

Because his father just died.

No. That wasn't grief.

Ella had been on the receiving end of reluctant farewells before, most notably when she'd been transitioned out of one foster home and into another, repeatedly. Ian's expression wasn't rooted in grief. It was rooted in regret. The remorse of goodbye. She was suddenly certain of it. It made little sense—why now?—but she couldn't see past Ian's regret or her fear.

The Monroes were the only family she had. The only family Penny had. This couldn't be goodbye.

Don't panic. Don't pass out. Breathe.

Ella breathed deeply, despite the Spanx.

And then nearly gagged.

She'd inhaled too much eau de poopy pants.

Thankfully, the elderly lawyer with the rasping voice finished reading the first part of Grandpa Harlan's will and signaled a break. Ella carried Penny out of the lavishly decorated dining room and toward the bathroom down the hall, fighting the feeling that she was about to be excommunicated.

Two years ago, Ella had been an interloper in Ian's eyes, a woman who'd "trapped" his son, Bryce, into marriage by becoming pregnant a month after their first date. The Monroes were old money, old traditions, old school. In the Monroe world, nobody fell in love at first sight. You dated. You were vetted by the family and a private investigator. And after several years, you had a lavish wedding ceremony at the country club.

But she and Bryce had tumbled into love at

a charity ball. He'd swerved to avoid a passing waiter, bumped Ella, knocked her off her feet and into the shrubbery. She'd laughed—because what else could she do in her rented designer dress? He'd hurried to set down his drink and before he even reached to pull her up, their gazes collided and it was...*love.* It had hummed in her veins. He'd felt it, too. They'd both froze. They'd both laughed. And then Bryce had helped Ella out of the shrubbery and never let go.

When Ella had told Bryce she was pregnant, he hadn't blinked. He'd dropped to one knee, professed his love and enthusiastically asked her to marry him, as if her unplanned pregnancy was the best news in the world. A weekend trip to Vegas, and they were married, much to the chagrin of the family. But in time, Ella had won them over. She'd won them over before Bryce had died in a car accident a month before Penny was born.

The memory put an ache in her chest.

Ella was a Monroe now. It said so on her driver's license. No one could take this family away from her. She was expected at holidays and birthdays and any old day. She was included on trips to the family lake house and family business updates. She was a Monroe.

She. Was. Family.

So why had Ian's expression shaken her?

Because for fifteen years I had no family.

On their way back down the wide hall, with the Spanx now stuffed into the diaper bag, Ella and Penny stopped at a section of the wall devoted to memorializing the dearly departed Monroes. There were Grandpa Harlan's parents in 1950s faded photographs, Cousin Carl, who died storming Omaha Beach, Harlan's four wives—the actress, the pilot, the politician and the oil heiress—and, of course, Bryce.

Ella's heart hitched when she looked at her husband, at brown hair so dark it was almost black, at friendly bright green eyes, not to mention the smile he'd passed on to their daughter.

"Blow Daddy a kiss," Ella told Penny.

Together, they sent air kisses toward Bryce's handsome, worry-free face.

And then Penny wriggled free, running on her short sturdy legs toward the grand marble foyer outside the dining room. She wore a black dress with a white sash and her thin blond curls bobbed as she made her escape, clutching what looked like Ella's black Spanx in her small fist. She ran in circles around the plush red-and-black carpet, waving the Spanx like a flag.

"Mr. Quinby—" Ian's voice drifted from the dining room "—we have no need of Ella. Please proceed."

No need of Ella?

She wanted to protest, to charge inside and shout: *But I'm a Monroe.*

But… *Was she?*

Weak-kneed with doubt, Ella sank into an antique chair that was stiffer than her father-in-law's voice, a chair where she could watch the proceedings like the outsider she was.

At least she'd been asked to attend. Other partners and spouses were barred from the reading.

"And now for Harlan Monroe's personal message and family bequests." Mr. Quinby tugged his tie, cleared his throat and cast a sideways glance toward the much younger lawyer behind him. He lifted a sheet of paper with hands that shook. "I'm going to read a letter from the deceased. One that was written over two years ago, notarized and kept with his will. He wrote…"

Two years… Could this have anything to do with Ella falling in love with Bryce? The timing couldn't be a coincidence.

The old lawyer sucked in thready amounts of air. "'If you're hearing this, then I am dead. And if you want an inheritance, you'll have to listen to my lawyer without any back talk.'" Mr. Quinby did a quick visual survey of his audience.

He was anxious for good reason. The Monroes were an expressive, explosive bunch. But this time, there were no outbursts, no questions, no challenges. Or, as Grandpa Harlan put it, no back talk.

The old lawyer heaved a sigh of relief and resumed his oratory. "'I was born into a home with nothing but love. I was raised in hand-me-downs and nourished by leftovers. I played unsupervised and ran barefoot until it was too dark to catch a baseball or to fish. Those humble beginnings gave me an appreciation for life, a drive to succeed and, most importantly, a love of my fellow man. I was unable to give the latter to my children. It's my fault my sons consider themselves superior to others, that they consider their wealth a form of entitlement.'"

That was Grandpa Harlan, calling a diamond-studded spade a diamond-studded spade.

"You, my girl, have gumption," he'd told Ella the first time he'd met her as he'd grabbed onto her hand from his wheelchair. "Don't let the Monroes take that away from you. You've got to greet every day with a happy song." He'd given her hand a squeeze and then raised his arms in the air and goofed, *"Are you ready, Hezzie?"* It was a favorite line of his that had been popular when he was a young man. And then he'd burst into song, uncaring of his surroundings or the audience.

Grandpa Harlan hadn't had a pretentious or self-conscious bone in his body.

Penny did a slow-motion, near-silent fall to her rump on the plush carpet, and then lay down on her back and pretended to make a snow angel. One hand still clutching black Spanx. She turned her sweet face toward Ella and whispered, *"Mom. Mom. Mom."*

How could Ella worry about anything with a daughter like that? And yet, how could she not? She had no family apart from the Monroes. Without them, who would Penny have if anything happened to Ella?

Ella peeked in the dining room, her gaze connecting with Ian's. Her father-in-law gave her that farewell look once more. It roiled the artichoke quiche in her stomach.

"'I made my first fortune in Texas oil before I ever married,'" the lawyer went on. "'I was also a lucky man who found love four times over. My wives were drawn to my sense of adventure and my charm.'"

Someone chuckled. Grandpa Harlan was a straight-shooter with a good heart, but he forgot to mention he had a wandering eye.

"'My four sons were raised in the lap of luxury, never worrying about having a roof over their heads, where their next meal would come from, or how to pay for their college education.'"

So true. Those four millionaires had never balanced the need for rent money against the cost of a new pair of shoes.

"Hep." Penny struggled to sit up—the Spanx was pulled over her head like a stocking cap half covering a bank robber's face. "Mom, hep."

Ella reclaimed possession of her undergarment and then her seat outside the dining room, hoping she hadn't been noticed. Thankfully, all attention was being given to the lawyer reading Grandpa Harlan's letter.

Freed, Penny lay back down and began to sing a soft, wordless song, while she made another snow angel in the carpet.

"'My four sons…'" Mr. Quinby cleared his throat, nervous once more, perhaps because he was delivering Harlan's barbs without cover against return fire. "'My four sons are too old to unlearn the privilege of the silver spoon, too busy to enjoy the priceless beauty of a mountain sunrise, too calloused to appreciate the comfort that comes from loyalty, or the joy that love for love's sake can bring.'"

"Beautiful," Ella murmured.

Maybe he wrote that after Bryce and I fell in love.

"'To those coldhearted fools, I leave the Monroe Holding Corporation and all its entities on one condition.'"

Everyone leaned forward in their seats, even Ella.

"'As for my grandchildren…'" The elderly lawyer ran a finger beneath his collar.

"Wait," Holden, the oldest grandchild, said.

He managed the Monroe assets. "What condition?"

"I'm getting to that," Mr. Quinby said defensively. He rattled the letter. "It's right here." And then he spent a moment trying to find his place. "'As for my grandchildren, there is hope for their moral fiber. But only if they break free of the influence of my four failures and learn there is more to life than the bottom line. Therefore, for the good of my grandchildren, as a condition of their inheritance, my sons will immediately fire said grandchildren and terminate their contracts with any and all entities under the ownership of the Monroe Holding Corporation. Also, it is my further stipulation that within the next thirty days, my grandchildren will vacate all residences, homes, apartments and penthouses that are owned by the Monroe Holding Corporation.'"

Yikes. All the grandchildren lived in corporately owned housing.

"'In the meantime—'"

"He left us nothing?" Holden demanded. His gray eyes seemed colder than the ice frosting the pristine landscaping outside.

Mr. Quinby sat back warily, as if this had been the reaction he'd feared all along.

Ella sat back, too, thinking that everything was going to be all right. She wasn't a Monroe grandchild. For her, nothing would change. Ian's regretful expression from before must have been regarding his conditional inheritance and that of his children.

"I'm supposed to move out of my home?" Bentley was Bryce's twin brother and designed luxury yachts for Monroe Shipworks.

"Grandpa is firing me?" Shane spit. He ran the family's hotel chain based in Las Vegas. "From the *grave*?"

"Let him finish." Sophie adjusted her glasses, presumably so she could better see the lawyer if he ever got the chance to continue.

"Yes, please." The junior lawyer behind Mr. Quinby spoke up. His name was Daniel Something-or-other and he had a kind look about him. "Your questions will be answered if you just let Mr. Quinby finish."

"Thank you, Daniel." The senior lawyer cleared his throat, sounding like an old car reluctant to start on a chilly morning. He acknowledged Shane with a wave of his hand. "Technically, *your father* has to fire you—" his hand swung toward Bentley "—and *your father* has to evict you. That is, if he wants to inherit twenty-five percent of your grandfather's assets." He turned to Holden. "Harlan did, in fact, leave his grandchildren something." Mr. Quinby ran his finger down the page slowly. "Ah! Here it is. 'By each of them standing on their own two feet, my grandchildren, I hope, will discover their moral compass, which will guide them to the lives they *should* choose to lead. Not the ones that would most benefit the Monroe Holding Corporation. To that end, I leave the town of Second Chance, Idaho, to my grandchildren and great grandchildren.'"

"You're not really going to go along with this—this...*farce*?" Holden leaned forward, black eyebrows drawn low in disbelief. "Grandpa Harlan clearly wasn't in his right mind when he wrote this."

Several pairs of eyes swung toward Ian and his three brothers. Chairs creaked. Ella held her breath, worried for her husband's siblings and cousins. Not because of the fortune they weren't getting, but because their fathers might choose money over family.

Ella didn't blame Bryce's cousins and siblings for being upset. They'd been groomed since birth to work in one of the family businesses—oil, finance, luxury-yacht building, hotels or filmmaking. They didn't have trust funds, but they'd been given everything they'd ever needed—the finest educations, mortgage-free homes and generous salaries. All with the expectation that they'd benefit from their commitment to the family someday. They just hadn't expected that benefit to be a town.

Ella's glance swung to Penny and then back to the others in the dining room. All the while, she was wondering: *Who inherits a town?* For that matter, who *owned* a town to begin with?

Harlan's lawyer wasn't finished yet. Quinby cleared his gravelly throat. "Again, I'd like to repeat to Harlan's four sons that their inheritance is contingent upon the condition being met." Meaning mass layoffs and evictions for their children.

No one in the dining room moved. No one seemed to breathe. Ella had been shuttled from foster home to foster home for many reasons. She'd never been moved along so someone could fatten their bank account. The thought was crushing.

"Dad?" Shane asked in a low voice. "Don't say you're considering this. That letter won't hold up in a court of law."

Daniel, the younger lawyer, jumped up. "I'll

remind everyone of the clause we read before the break regarding challenges to the will. If you challenge and lose—" he stared at Shane "—your share goes to charity. If you refuse to abide by the terms of the will—" his gaze swept Harlan's four sons "—your share goes to charity."

Daniel's expression was no longer kind. It was firm and lawyerly. He was suddenly the most hated person in the room.

As one, Harlan's sons, ranging in age from fifty to seventy, stood. They were men who loved their children. They wouldn't cut them loose. And yet, they surveyed their progeny with odd looks—shocked, saddened, resolute— similar to how Ella imagined she'd stared at Bryce's face before they'd closed the coffin one last time.

Ella began to doubt.

The four brothers exchanged glances. Nodded. Stepped clear of their chairs.

Ian raised his chin. "You're all fired, evicted and all contracts with the Monroe Holding Corporation and its entities are revoked."

The chaos that erupted had the old lawyer cringing and everyone talking at once.

This wasn't her fight. Ella scooped up her

daughter and then immediately retreated to their small house at the rear of the family compound, where she put Penny down for a nap, checked the weather report to see how much snow was expected and did a quick inventory of her refrigerator and pantry to make sure she had enough food to last the storm.

The younger lawyer and her father-in-law found her an hour later.

She made Ian a Scotch on the rocks and asked Daniel repeatedly if she could get him something to drink. He refused every time.

Daniel was probably a good lawyer. He had a calm voice and a placating manner that softened the blow of his words. "Mrs. Monroe, the stipulations of the will apply to you, as well."

Ella sat down on the arm of her sofa. Hard.

She'd planned to return to the main house and check on the cousins once Penny woke from her nap. The terms of the will were shocking to say the least, and she wanted to be a shoulder to lean on. But apparently, she had a shock of her own to deal with.

Her gaze drifted to a high table by the door and a glass bowl that contained a scuffed baseball, a silver dollar, a turquoise tie tack and a smooth, flat rock. Every time she was cast aside, she took something to remember the place, the home, the people she'd loved. Familiar questions bombarded her: *Why can't I stay? What can I do to change your mind? What will I take to remember you by?*

Surely, it hasn't come to that. I'm a Monroe.

The fact that they were here talking about Harlan's will stipulations proved it.

Small consolation.

"I don't understand." Ella forced her gaze back to the lawyer. "I don't work for the Monroes and I'm only Harlan's grandchild by marriage."

"The clause that applies to you is about your daughter *living* in a Monroe Holding Corporation property." How could Daniel look so kind and deliver such devastating news?

"This cabin is owned by the family's holding company?" Ella glanced around the log-cabin home Grandpa Harlan had built with modern amenities after a trip to the mountains over a decade before. Her gaze landed on the smiling photo of Bryce on the mantel.

Ella's cabin was a simple rectangle with two bedrooms and one bath, one of four homes in the Monroe compound. She'd been living here rent- and utility-free since Bryce had died.

Staying in the house had made her feel like one of the family. She'd been surviving on Bryce's life insurance, which she was trying to make last until Penny started school in three years, at which point she'd return to work as a real-estate agent. She could afford to live elsewhere. It was just…

Her gaze connected with Ian's. "You knew about this beforehand." Not a question. He'd had that look.

Ian set down his drink and stood, drawing Ella to her feet. "Eleanor, I'm sorry, but you have thirty days to figure out what to do." His bright green gaze was reassuring and reminiscent of Bryce's, even if his smile wasn't.

He'd said nothing about her remaining a part of the family, now and forever.

She felt a sense of panic rising in her chest and wished she had the courage to run. *But he was family. Her family.* Bryce had promised her she'd always be a Monroe. She had to ask the question. "Am I still a part of this family? I…"

Ian's smile hardened. "You're the mother of my grandchild."

So she had her answer. Her temples pounded. Daniel looked away.

Ian no longer sounded like the caring father-in-law. His expression was once more reminiscent of regretful goodbyes. "I know you'll land on your feet. Probably somewhere in the vicinity of a new man." Ian no longer sounded like the caring father-in-law. His expression was once more reminiscent of regretful goodbyes. "You won't inherit anything if Penny doesn't move out."

Ella sat down again. Harder this time. The wood frame jarred her backside and fear jarred her insides. She should have realized she was just as expendable as the blooded Monroes.

If he was willing to fire and evict his own children, or do whatever needed to be done, she never stood a chance. "I'll be fine. I'm fully capable of supporting Penny." Of holding on to her dignity if she couldn't exactly hold on to her status as one of the Monroes.

Orphaned again? She wanted to cry.

She'd lived in four foster homes in six years. When she'd married Bryce, she'd thought she'd never lose a family again. She'd invested herself in the Monroes, let herself love and trust. And now this.

Someone knocked on the door.

Without waiting for an answer, three of the

Monroe cousins trundled in, stomping their boots and shaking their winter jackets to shed the snow that had fallen on their way over.

Sophie pushed her glasses up her nose and scowled at the lawyer. "Has he told you the details regarding our property?"

Ella had been about to offer them food and drink, but… *Our property?* "The town in Idaho?"

"Two thousand mostly undeveloped acres in the middle of nowhere." Sophie's twin, Shane, filled in Ella. Their branch of the family had light brown hair and dark brown eyes. "Fifty or so structures mostly built before the 1950s."

"Some of which are leased," Laurel added, distracted by Ella's gray knit poncho hanging by the door. The Hollywood Monroes had bright red hair and blue eyes. Laurel had been a costume designer at Monroe Studios in Hollywood up until an hour ago. She held the poncho up to the light, inspecting the stitches.

"Leases mean income." Ella tried to sound optimistic as she wondered what the cousins wanted from her.

"Not in this case." Shane scowled at the lawyer now, too. "Grandpa Harlan offered leases for one dollar a year."

Holden barged in without knocking. He hadn't bothered with a heavy coat and wore only his black wool suit, which was dusted with snow. "We didn't get your vote, Ella. You have to vote for Penny."

"Oh, for the love of…" Sophie shook her head. "She's a single mom, like me. She's not going to support you."

"Part of a town is better than nothing." Laurel turned away from the poncho. "Isn't that right, Ella?"

Everything was coming at Ella at a dizzying pace. Everyone was looking at her to follow their lead.

"Let Ella make up her own mind." Holden stood with his hands on his hips and fixed Ella with a firm, obey-me stare. He was cut from the same cloth as Ian and his brothers. "I've got six votes for challenging the will. If you vote with me, the tide will turn, and the others will realize there's power in solidarity."

"Ignore him." Shane moved to stand next to Ella. "At the very least, we can divide the town into parcels and sell to buyers interested in luxury ranchettes. Jonah and Cam are with us on this."

"Is there a market for that near this town?"

Ella's dusty real-estate savvy reawakened with a yawn.

"You can't sell the town until one year after the anniversary of your grandfather's death," Daniel pointed out, like a referee who'd sneaked up behind you during a big game to blow his whistle.

"Why would Eleanor go to Idaho?" Ian put his hand on the door handle and stared at Ella as if she didn't deserve to go with the other Monroes. The "real" Monroes.

Ella's vision tunneled.

"You should join the smart Monroe cousins and challenge the will as Penny's guardian." Holden's strong chin was up, daring others to take a shot at his logic. "It's risky, but—"

"It's too risky. She's coming with us." Sophie flanked Ella, opposite her twin. "We're going to Second Chance and we're going to evaluate it for sale. We need a Realtor for that."

Ella assumed she was the Realtor, although her license in Pennsylvania had lapsed and she didn't have one in Idaho. She tried to think of what Bryce would have wanted and what was best for Penny.

Holden only wanted a vote to swing momentum to his cause, one that risked Penny's inheritance, small though it was. And what Grandpa Harlan had wanted, what he'd written suspiciously near the time Bryce had died... A tug of responsibility pulled at Ella. She should do what the old man wanted.

"Grandpa Harlan wanted the family to go." Laurel stood between Ella and Holden, crossing her arms. "And Ella's part of this family."

Family.

Family was all Ella had ever wanted after her mother died. Family was the people standing by her side, the ones who'd care for Penny if need be, the ones declaring she was one of them, even though deep down Ella knew she wasn't.

She met Ian's gaze, and then Holden's. "I've made my decision."

She was siding with family.

CHAPTER ONE

SNOW DRAPED THE Sawtooth mountain range, carpeted the Colter Valley and frosted the Salmon River like a blue-tinged Christmas card.

And more snow was coming.

Second Chance residents, like Dr. Noah Bishop, knew it. This was the calm before the next storm. It was there in the biting, building wind at dawn, and at midday, when the sky was heavy with gray clouds that descended below the mountaintops.

Trudging through the drifts from his home office to the Bent Nickel diner, the taste of snow punched the air and clung to Noah's lungs like icicles to a metal roof. This time last year, he'd been operating on the shoulder of a football league's MVP. His one patient today had complained of an ingrown toenail.

Oh, how the mighty has tumbled from his pedestal.

Noah's inner voice hadn't adjusted to life in the mountains as a country doctor.

He slogged his way around the side of the inn to the cleared sidewalk. Farther down, the parking stalls in front of the grocery store and gas station were empty. The old, white steepled church, the boxy schoolhouse, the brick mercantile and log-cabin fur-trading post stood above the road, windows dark and empty. The buildings and a dozen or so smaller cabins made up the heart of the roadside town located where two narrow highways met in the Idaho high country. The rest of the residents were spread out around the bends of the Salmon River.

A snowplow rumbled by from the south and turned at the fork to the west, a last-ditch effort by the state to keep the roads open as long as possible.

Heads whipped around when Noah entered the Bent Nickel, all faces of citizens of Second Chance who hadn't gone south for the winter. Town residents were jumpy. There was more than a storm coming.

The Monroes were coming.

Folks had seen the announcements in the media about Harlan Monroe's death. He'd owned the town, lock, stock and barrel. According to those in the know, it was only a matter of time before some of his heirs showed up. The locals had made a pool as to what was going to go down.

The Clark sisters from the Bucking Bull Ranch sunk twenty dollars on the Monroes sending a real-estate agent to evaluate the place. Mitch Kincaid, mayor and innkeeper, put in ten dollars toward at least two Monroes showing up expecting a five-star hotel. Eli Garland, the homeschooling coordinator for the county, put his money on the Monroes not showing up until summer. Mackenzie and Ivy, who ran the grocery and diner respectively, plunked ten apiece on the Monroes arriving in a stretch limo. Their bet inspired Roy Stout, the town handyman, to wager they'd pull up in a Hummer, because how else was anyone supposed to get up to Second Chance in January without four-wheel drive?

Noah was among the residents who hadn't bet. Luck hadn't been kind to him lately.

"I'm making French fries and milk shakes for the kids," Ivy called to Noah from the diner's kitchen. She pampered the town's handful of children and encouraged Eli to hold home-study sessions in the diner. "Can I get you anything, Doc?"

"No, thanks."

Ivy served food that could only be classified as fuel. Unlike the fancy meals Noah had enjoyed in New York, there were no culinary delights to be had on any of her plates. But the coffee was strong and cheap, and the price of hanging out for a few hours was a mere armload of firewood for the fireplace, which meant it was the warmest building in Second Chance.

Noah set his logs on the woodpile and then began to shed layers—parka, knit cap, muffler. The black leather gloves he kept on, a fact several children noticed. He had no idea why the kids were still here. If he'd known they'd be lingering, he would've stayed in his cabin. He shoved a couple dollars in the coffee jar and poured himself a cup.

Mitch pulled out a chair at his table for Noah. They'd met at DePaul University when Mitch was prelaw and Noah was premed. They'd kept in touch on social media and through a fantasy football league. Mitch had hired Noah after his accident.

"I was just saying we need to be united when the Monroes get here," Mitch said. "I know I don't have to remind anyone about our non-disclosure agreement with Harlan."

Noah nodded, because Mitch was looking at him. He'd signed a nondisclosure agreement about the old man, but he'd only been here six months and had never met Harlan Monroe in person. He couldn't have picked his benefactor out of a police lineup. Unlike other residents who'd sold their property to the millionaire and might have been privy to something important about the old man, Noah had no secrets to divulge.

"Moving forward," Mitch went on, "it'll help if we negotiate as one entity. Ideally, we keep our low leases. Worst case, we buy back our places for less than we sold them to Harlan. In either case, don't make this easy on them. We don't want Harlan's heirs thinking this is the next Idaho town to be developed for Hollywood vacation homes."

There were worried head nods of approval and agreement. Nobody wanted Second Chance real estate to skyrocket or for it to become a soulless haven for celebrities.

Noah didn't nod. He sat. Unlike the other residents, the small home Noah lived in was rent-free. It was a stipulation of his contract as the town doctor. Granted, it wasn't where he thought he'd be, but if he couldn't be an orthopedic surgeon to sports superstars, it was better to be a nobody from nowhere.

Aptly put, his snarky inner voice whispered.

"You ready for a blizzard, Doc?" Roy sat at the next table over, facing the highway. He wore stained blue coveralls over a pair of yellowed long johns. His wiry, knubby elbows rested on the white Formica tabletop. A fringe of peppery hair was visible beneath his blue ball cap.

Noah shrugged. "Will it really be any worse than the storms we've already had?"

"Yep." Roy chuckled, revealing his gap-toothed smile. "More snow. More wind. More freezing temperatures."

More boredom.

Noah squashed that thought. He wasn't here for the intellectual challenge or the thrill of new, emergency limb-saving techniques. He wasn't here for experimental procedures or medical accolades. He wasn't even here for a research sabbatical. He'd accepted Mitch's invitation to become the town doctor because he could no longer be the surgeon who could perform miracles.

"Storm after storm after storm," Roy murmured happily. "I love winter."

Up here, winter lasted six months or more.

Mitch straightened, running a hand through his dark hair. "There's a car pulling in."

Mackenzie, who owned the grocery store and garage, moved to the front window along with Roy. "Maybe they're just passing through and need a bathroom."

"Or something to eat." Ivy was craning her neck, trying to see over the cook's counter.

"That's no car." Roy slapped his skinny thigh. "It's one of those Humdingers!"

A long black Hummer parked in front of the diner.

"It's them Monroes." Heedless of his audience on the other side of the window, Roy pointed and raised his voice. "I knew it. I just knew it."

"We don't know anything yet," Mitch said in a put-out voice.

A man in his thirties opened the diner's door for the carload. He had wavy brown hair in a neatly styled haircut and was inappropriately dressed for the mountains—slacks, leather loafers, a light winter jacket. No cap. No gloves.

A case of frostbite in the making.

Noah hid a smile behind a sip of his coffee.

A woman hurried inside. Bright red hair. Pale complexion. Black leather jacket over a black tunic sweater, black leggings and black boots. Something about her seemed familiar. She spotted the restroom sign and hurried toward it.

Carsick.

Whether they were the Monroes or not, they were providing Noah with some much-needed entertainment.

Another woman scurried in. She had wavy brown hair, pointy features and frazzled brown eyes shaded by dark circles that her glasses did nothing to conceal. She held the hands of two twin toddler boys, who clumped in wearing matching dark green unzipped jackets and white sneakers that flashed bright red beams from the heels as they walked. She followed the first woman to the restrooms.

Single mom in need of a good night's sleep and proper hydration.

A third woman entered, stepping to the side so the man could close the door behind her. Her hair was blond, her eyes a bright blue. She had a sprinkling of freckles and the kind of glowing skin that never tanned. She was the only sensibly dressed one of the lot in a navy stadium jacket, snow boots and a knit cap. The toddler she carried had the same coloring and wore a pink snowsuit.

She set down the little girl and proceeded to shed layers—hers and the toddler's—plopping their gear and a diaper bag in a booth. She wiped the toddler's runny nose with a crumpled tissue, straightened and took a good look around, while Noah took a good look at her.

She didn't seem like a millionaire. She seemed like the kindhearted girl next door. The one who blushed when you asked her to help you with your English homework, and was happy for you when you told her you'd asked the cheerleading captain to prom.

Not that I was that guy.

She made him feel guilty all the same.

"I'm looking for Mitch Kincaid." The man took up a wide stance. Hands on hips. An expectation of respect in his dark eyes. "I'm Shane Monroe."

Something crashed in the kitchen.

"Well, I'll be." Roy grabbed Shane's hand and shook it like he was pumping water from a well. "Good to meet you."

"Mitch?" Who knew what Shane had been expecting, but it wasn't the town handyman and his gap-toothed grin.

"Nope. I'm Roy." The old man kept pumping. "Harlan was my—"

"I'm Mitch." The mayor got out of his chair and introduced himself, shaking Shane's hand in a classy one-and-done.

Something crashed into Noah's thigh.

The toddler wiped her nose on Noah's black ski pants and then looked up at him with a mischievous grin and said, *"Hi,"* before fleeing with a squeal and a giggle across the diner.

"Penny." The girl next door snatched a napkin from the holder on the table and wiped at the streak of snot on Noah's ski pants. And then she froze, her hands inches from Noah's thigh.

Noah's ears filled with white noise, not caused by any head cold or sinus infection. This was one of those surreal moments where a beauty had unwittingly touched a beast. Noah's heart went out of rhythm. He felt light-headed.

Heart attack? Negative.

Low blood sugar? Negative.

High-altitude dehydration? Likely.

Despite his diagnosis, Noah reached for his

dehydrating coffee. But his eyes... His eyes couldn't turn away from her.

"My apologies. That was inappropriate." The woman's cheeks bloomed with color. Her bright blue gaze bounced to Noah's and away before she, too, made a run for it. "Penelope Arlene, you come back here."

Penny's laughter drowned out the white noise in Noah's head, and sent others in the room chuckling, breaking the tension that the arrival of the Monroes had caused. Noah breathed easier.

"We thought we'd come down and stay a few days," Shane Monroe was saying, still on his high horse.

Not that Noah was one to judge. As an orthopedic surgeon, he'd taken many a ride on a high horse.

And look where that's gotten me.

Noah clenched his gloved fists, his left hand more than his right.

The pale redhead emerged from the bathroom and collapsed on a stool at the counter with a croak for water.

Ivy was quick to serve her, looking slightly out of her element. "Are you Ashley?"

Ashley Monroe? The actress? Was that why she looked familiar?

"She's my twin."

"Oh." Ivy sounded disappointed, but not as disappointed as the redhead.

"You wanna stay here? Now?" That was Roy. Unfiltered. "In Second Chance?"

Mitch tried to hide a laugh behind a cough. "What Roy means is, there's a storm coming. Many storms, in fact. We usually get snowed in five to ten days during the winter. Passes close. No getting in or out." He gave Shane the kind of look a New York doorman gives a tenant while explaining it's impossible to get a taxi on New Year's Eve. "You might be better off heading down to Hailey, or the other way, to Boise."

"Better off?" Shane's dark eyes narrowed. "Is there something you don't want us to see?"

"Three to five feet of snow," Roy answered, smacking his gums. "It's a-comin' tonight. Six or more a day after. And so on."

Penny was playing keep-away-from-mama, running on chubby legs between tables in the middle of the room. Not that the girl next door was trying hard to catch her. More likely, she was trying to keep Penny from wiping her nose on another unsuspecting Second Chance resident.

"All we're saying is—" Mitch was a former lawyer and proficient at clarifying an issue "—you might be more comfortable in a place with accommodations you're used to because the passes might close."

Shane was just as tall as Mitch but managed to look down his nose at him. "You have beds?" At his nod, Shane added, "Then we'll be fine."

So much for the five-star expectations of Mitch's bet.

"You like snow, do you?" Roy asked.

"We'll be fine," Shane repeated.

Based on the thinness of Shane's coat and his fine leather loafers, Noah highly doubted he'd be fine. You could get away with thin jackets in cities like Chicago or New York, because you were only in the elements for a few blocks between the subway and whatever building you were darting into. In the mountains of Idaho, cold penetrated layers of clothing quicker than heat melted ice cream on a hot summer day.

The toddler boys raced into the dining room and joined Penny. The three of them ran around a table as if they were playing musical chairs or training to be track stars.

"Someone." Shane waved toward the spectacle. *"Please."*

The girl next door and the harried mom of twins moved in.

Sensing her freedom was about to end, Penny veered and crashed into Noah, giggling nonstop. She gave a wet snuffle and turned her face to Noah's knee.

This time, Noah was ready for her and swiped her nose with a napkin. "Gotcha."

She looked up at him, aghast, lower lip trembling.

"Come here, Penny." The girl next door crouched in front of Noah and held out her hands, just far enough away that she couldn't touch him again.

"No-o-o." Penny wasn't just an athlete in the making. She was also a bit of a drama queen. She clutched Noah's calf and shook her blond curls. *"No-o-o."*

Penny's mom raised those blue eyes to Noah's once more, causing a heart-stuttering, equilibrium-shaking, white-noise-in-the-ears relapse.

"Given the way my daughter clings to you, we should be on a first-name basis. I'm Ella." Her glance caught on Noah's black gloves.

And just like that, Noah was reminded why he didn't want a woman's interest.

The world self-corrected. Stabilized.

"Mom." Penny made a raspberry noise against Noah's knee, negating her mother having any name other than… *"Mom. Mom. Mom."*

"I'm Noah." He ruffled Penny's blond curls with his left hand. "Your daughter is what? Two?"

"I two," Penny confirmed, holding up four fingers.

The twins ran by, followed by their mother, who said, "No one told me the terrible twos lasted long after the age of four." She snatched a boy in each arm and gave them a playful growl as she stood, glasses sliding down her thin nose. "Only boys who behave get French fries."

The boys stopped struggling and allowed their mother to carry them to the lunch counter, where she deposited each on a stool and ordered French fries from Ivy.

"Fesh fies?" Penny toddled forward into Ella's arms.

"Apple fries?" Ella countered, then whispered conspiratorially to Noah, "So much healthier, and in my bag."

His mother would have said, "She's as adorable as her daughter."

I've never liked adorable.

His sister would have said, "She's not wearing a wedding ring."

A fact I noticed completely by accident.

"Fesh fies!" Penny cried, pointing at the boys.

"But apple fries just aren't the same," Noah murmured. He caught Ella's eye. "You should head back down the mountain before the storm hits. At Penny's age, a case of the sniffles can turn serious overnight." There. Spoken like a country doctor who only had a little girl's best interests at heart.

Mitch gave Noah an approving nod, the kind of gesture that said, *You're one of us.*

Noah clenched his teeth.

I have nothing in common with these people.

Worry flashed in Ella's eyes. She'd no doubt weathered illnesses with her daughter before. Little kids picked up every germ.

"It's just a cold." Shane made light of Noah's concern.

Ella's gaze shuttered. She gave Noah a small smile. "Thanks, but it looks like we're staying."

"That's too bad," Noah murmured, staring at his gloved right hand and wishing Ella Monroe would leave town quickly.

A woman like Ella made a man remember he'd once had lofty dreams, made him think he could still be somebody important, made him try to regain ground when the odds were embarrassingly, impossibly stacked against him.

Well, what do you know. His inner cynic chuckled.

Turns out, Noah did have something in common with the other residents of Second Chance.

He wanted the Monroes gone.

CHAPTER TWO

ELLA SHARED BOTH potato and apple fries with Penny at the counter of the Bent Nickel and tried not to stare the entire time at Noah and his gloves.

It was chilly inside the coffee shop and Ella hated being cold, but when she'd wiped baby snot off Noah's pant leg his gaze had heated her right up.

All due to embarrassment, naturally.

She sneaked a glance at Noah, testing her embarrassment theory.

His black hair was long and pushed back from his face, brushing his collar in loose waves. He had a full, short, dark beard and broad shoulders. His brow had been furrowed since she'd walked in and his eyebrows were on permanent ground patrol over his blue eyes. He'd seemed different than the rest of the men in the coffee shop. Or maybe it was just that he held himself stiffly, as if he considered himself an outsider.

Ella could relate. She'd spent most of her middle and high-school years feeling like an outsider, a foster child with a few friends and a drawer of hand-me-down clothes. She'd since filled her closet, but after what had happened at the reading of Harlan's will, she wasn't sure of her future as a Monroe. If she couldn't make a market assessment Bryce's cousins approved of would they shut her out of the family, too?

Her attention drifted to Noah. His clothes were new. That wasn't what kept him apart from the others. It was the black leather gloves, she decided. That, and the soulful look in his eyes.

Their gazes connected, and Ella lost track of her breath. The lack of oxygen combined with awkwardness heated her cheeks. The embarrassment theory was holding water.

Embarrassment and the fact that he's gorgeous and looks at me as if I wasn't the kind of woman to eat a package of Penny's cheese and crackers for breakfast.

The Bent Nickel diner was a throwback to a simpler time. Green-and-white checked linoleum tiles. Chrome bar stools with mint-green vinyl seats. Forest green vinyl booths and worn white Formica tabletops. Framed photos crowded the walls, mostly black-and-white pictures of people in front of cabins and vintage cars.

There were elementary-age kids gathered around the L-shaped counter and a booth beside it. Schoolbooks, notebooks and laptops were stacked or open. Tall milk-shake glasses and baskets of French fries were distributed among them. Between the chatter they spared amused glances toward Andrew and Alexander, Sophie's twin boys, who were holding a spinning race on their bar stools.

"Me, too." Penny patted Ella's arm and then pointed to the twins. "Me, too."

Penny didn't have the arm strength to spin herself. Ella turned Penny's bar stool in a slow circle.

"Whoa." Penny's eyes got huge. When her back was to the counter she had nothing to hold on to, particularly when she had an apple fry in one hand and a potato fry in the other. That didn't stop her from saying, "Again," when she'd completed one circuit.

Ella turned her stool a second time, aware of Noah's gaze upon them.

"Woof." Penny was halfway around on the

stool. She pointed out the window and dropped the potato fry. "Uh-oh."

Ella stopped spinning as she realized what Penny had seen—a yellow dog with an uneven gait. "Someone's dog is outside."

"That's a Labrasnoodle." Roy moved toward the window. "Does it belong to one of you Monroes? It's one of them designer dogs. A Labrapoo or Doodledoo or something."

"We brought kids," Shane said loftily. "Not dogs."

"The dog's limping." Roy peered to the side. "Come on, Doc. Looks like someone dumped a dog out here again." Roy glanced back at Noah.

Ella and Sophie exchanged raised-eyebrow glances, as if thinking the same thing: *What was a young veterinarian doing in an old town like this?*

Noah didn't get up. "I'm a surgeon, not a vet." His fingers flexed.

Ella and Sophie continued to be perplexed: *What was a young* surgeon *doing in an old town like this?*

A yellow, curly-haired Labradoodle placed two large paws on the diner's window, peeked inside, barked once and then dropped back to all fours.

"Woof," Penny barked again.

Her antics made the twins giggle and a pre-teen girl with braces say, "Ahhh, how cute."

Roy opened the door and the dog burst in, along with a surge of cold air. His feet scrambled for purchase and he slipped and slid around the room, managing to gobble up Penny's fry on the floor before he crashed into Noah almost the same way Penny had done.

The dog put his big paws on Noah's sturdy thighs, then he exhibited a panting grin that passed over every human in the room before settling on Noah. Immediately, he was surrounded by eight schoolchildren eager to pet the dog and take a photo with their tablets.

"Isn't this against some kind of health code?" Shane asked from one of the dark green booths. He was nursing a cup of black coffee and reading a thin local pamphlet on real estate for sale in the area.

Ella made a mental note to get a copy for herself.

"In winter, the health codes are more like guidelines." Roy thrust his hands in his pockets and rocked back on his heels. "And in winter the Bent Nickel is more like Ivy's family room."

"Talk like that will get me shut down quicker than the wind whips down this stretch of road during a blizzard," Ivy snapped. And then her tone softened. "I'd prefer to report that Doc's therapy dog came in the diner today. Just keep him out of the kitchen."

"I'll get you a bag of dog food, Doc." A tall woman grabbed her coat and hurried out the door.

"He's not mine." Noah sounded put out.

Roy put his hands on his knees and bent to peer at the canine. "He's not putting any weight on that back foot. Why do you think that is, Doc?"

Noah shook his head. "Again, not a vet."

Mitch cut his way through the crowd and ran his hands around the dog's neck. "I saw this guy outside earlier. He wouldn't come to me and he doesn't have a collar."

Most of the kids drifted back to the counter and their food.

Laurel had recovered enough from being carsick to get up and go over to pet the dog. "He might be microchipped."

"Not likely if he don't have a collar." Roy sat down by the fire and whistled for the dog.

"We've had folks dump pets out here before. Sad way to treat a member of the family."

Ella's compassion for the dog increased.

"Woof." Penny's eyes were huge. She'd never seen such a large dog before.

The dog heard Penny and wagged his big tail, but he didn't move from his position in Noah's lap.

"Come on, boy." Roy whistled again, slapping his thin thighs. "Dogs love me."

The dog wasn't budging from Noah.

"Maybe he's deaf," Roy said brightly. He had the kind of attitude that nothing could bring down, not even a blizzard.

The dog turned his head to smile at Roy.

"He's made up his mind." Roy stood. "Dogs have a way of choosing people and he seems to have chosen you, Doc."

Noah sighed and stared into the dog's big brown eyes. "Are we really going to do this?"

The dog bumped his big nose against Noah's chin, making all the children laugh.

Noah ran his gloved hands over the dog's torso and down each of his front legs. And then he ran his hand down the leg the dog held off the ground.

The poor boy yelped and somehow—big as

he was—managed to climb completely into Noah's lap.

"Best take him to your clinic," Roy said. "He might need surgery."

Noah blanched.

"While you take care of the dog, Noah, I'll check in our guests." Mitch gestured that they should follow him, which was easier said than done. Everyone had to bundle up first.

Shane drove the SUV two businesses down from the diner and parked, while Laurel, Sophie and Ella ushered the kids along the shoveled walk.

The diner, the general store, with its two gas pumps and a single-bay garage, and the inn had all been built along the river and had enough space between the two-lane highway and the buildings for a vehicle to pull in and park perpendicular to the road. There was a narrow sidewalk from one building to another covered by a slanted roof to offer some protection against the elements, although not the cold.

There were small log-cabin houses up and down the highway, many of which looked forlorn and deserted. There were many buildings on the other side of the road, both new and old. A huge log cabin sat on the corner and butted against another small highway, across from which was a small church and a building with a cupola and bell.

Ella didn't relish doing a market assessment with so many buildings spread out and heavy snow in the forecast. Would she have to shovel her way to every door?

The icy wind blew strong enough to chafe Ella's cheeks and sweep Penny's feet out from under her.

Ella kept her daughter upright but shrugged deeper into her stadium jacket. "I hate cold."

"You should come live near me in Southern California." Laurel wrapped her thin leather jacket tighter around her chest. "Since you have to move."

"Don't take her away from me," Sophie countered. "I'm determined to get a job at the museum in downtown Philadelphia." Sophie had been the Monroes' art-collection curator.

Yes, the collection was so large it needed a manager.

"Cold, Mom." Penny raised her arms to be lifted into Ella's.

They hurried past the garage and then climbed the stairs onto the wood porch, which spanned the length of the inn, and went inside.

The Lodgepole Inn was a long, two-story log cabin wedged between the highway and a bend in the river. The logs used to build the cabin hadn't been planed. Their curving girth took an extra foot off the interior on every exterior wall, making the large space seem cozier somehow.

"How big is this place?" Ella asked while Mitch checked her in.

"The Lodgepole Inn has ten rooms upstairs and two suites downstairs." Mitch had thick black hair and a cautious smile, one that you didn't usually find in politicians or innkeepers. He swiped Ella's credit card and returned it to her. "My daughter and I run the place."

Penny and her cousins ran around the great room, which had a comfy couch covered in a blue-and-brown quilt, several high-backed chairs, a large TV on the wall and a big rock fireplace, the kind pioneers used to cook in but with hearth seats built into either side. The kids squealed and released pent-up energy from hours spent on a plane and in a vehicle.

"How charming," Sophie said, giving herself a tour of the main room.

"Our inn used to be a brothel for the miners." A preteen girl with pale strawberry-blond hair, braces and her father's cautious smile handed Ella a metal key attached to a thin strip of wood that had the words *Blue Bonnet* carved in it.

"Gabby," Mitch gently chastised. "That's not the way we market the Lodgepole Inn."

The preteen shrugged. "I did a paper on the history of the town."

"We don't know for sure it was a brothel," Mitch said apologetically, as if it might matter to the Monroes. "Some people say it was a barracks for the cavalry. I can tell from the architecture it was originally two large, two-story cabins with a stable in between. You'll see several different types of cabins in town—round-log, square-log and brick."

"Our round-log inn was a brothel." Gabby frowned at her father. "I even footnoted it in my report."

"I'd like to read it." Ella's interest was sincere. History added value to property. The information the lawyer had given her included when structures were built and what their exterior dimensions were, but not much else.

Mitch's smile hardened at her request. "Ella, if you need anything let us know." He waved a hand toward the stairs, which were made of pine and had a rustic lodgepole-pine railing.

"What we'd like to know," Shane said, handing over his credit card, "is why my grandfather purchased this town."

"Gabby, go get Shane the key to Sawtooth." Mitch waited until his daughter disappeared into the back room. "He didn't tell you?"

Shane shook his head.

"I don't know," Mitch said, not entirely believably.

"Really?" Shane rubbed his jaw and considered the innkeeper. "He bought this place from you a decade ago. You signed a lease for one dollar a year. You're telling me that somewhere along the line you didn't ask my grandfather why he was interested in your property?"

"You're facing a dead end." Gabby returned, placing the key and wooden key ring on the counter. "That's about as much as I've gotten out of him."

Mitch frowned. "Gabby, what have I told you about adult conversations?"

"I'm just trying to take on more responsibility in the family business, like you asked." The preteen held up her hands. "I guess you don't need help with check-in."

"That's not what I meant." Mitch sighed and smiled at Ella, gesturing from his daughter to Penny. "Take notes. This is your future." He turned to Shane. "If Harlan Monroe didn't tell his family why he bought the town, you can assume he didn't tell us, either." He consulted a map of the inn. "Let's put Laurel in the Meadow Room."

"Mom." Penny tugged at Ella's leg with both hands. Her cheeks were flushed. "Want cookie." She coughed.

Was that a productive cough? Or just an I-need-to-blow-my-nose cough? Ella dug in the diaper bag for a tissue and a small snack bag of bear-shaped graham crackers.

"In case you need anything to wash that cookie down with, there's a kitchenette around the corner with a small fridge, a microwave and a sink," Mitch said, using the interruption to gloss over Shane's dig for information. "Help yourself to coffee or water."

"I can store things in the refrigerator?" Ella thought about cheese sticks, milk and yogurt. "Is there a freezer?" For ice cream.

"No, sorry." Mitch seemed genuinely apologetic.

"This is really fine work." Laurel fingered

the blue-and-brown quilt on the couch. "Who made this?"

"Odette." Gabby bounded from behind the desk to the living room. "She's super old."

"Gabby."

"That's what *she* says," Gabby countered, defending herself with a put-upon huff. "She lives down the road. She tried to teach me how to knit and sew, but I'm kind of a lost cause."

"Meaning the knitting needles weren't as interesting as a video game," Mitch murmured half under his breath.

"I was just a kid when she tried to teach me before," Gabby said. "Are you really Ashley Monroe's twin? You look just like her."

Laurel nodded, smiling weakly as if her stomach was still upset. It was a burden to look exactly like her famous sister.

"You were eleven when she tried to teach you," Mitch said. "And you're still a kid."

"Dad. Don't mind him. His bark is worse than his bite." Gabby executed a disparaging eye roll to the ceiling before her glance landed on Laurel's nearby feet. "I love your boots."

"I got them at a vintage store in Hollywood." Laurel traced the quilt pattern with her finger. "I'd love to meet Odette."

Sophie was standing near the collection of items hanging on the inn's wall—an old ice pick, a washboard, a bed warmer.

"Odette's not much for strangers," Mitch cautioned. "Took her months to warm up to Noah."

Noah didn't look like a doctor. He looked like he'd been in the mountains for too long and had just come down for a cup of coffee for the first time in months.

"Is Noah new to town?" Ella asked casually, pouring a little water into a small plastic cup in the kitchenette.

"Noah came to us months ago when we needed a new doctor." Mitch answered Ella's question, but he was still having a who-will-blink-first face-off with Shane. "Second Chance is the county seat. We have the only doctor and homeschooling coordinator for a hundred miles."

"What happened to the old doctor?" Shane asked.

"Doc Carter?" Mitch's expression turned grim. "She died."

"This bed warmer is from Europe." Sophie adjusted her glasses and peered at the back of the piece hanging from the wall. "Antique and highly valuable."

"It was here when I bought the place eleven years ago," Mitch said, not sounding impressed. "And before you question me about what your grandfather bought, he paid for the land and the structures in town, not anything inside where people were still living. So, if the bed warmer is worth anything and you want it, you can make me an offer."

"That answers the question about why you sold this place to my grandfather." Shane pulled the keys to the SUV from his pocket. "Money."

"Shane," Sophie chastised.

Ella wanted to second Sophie's reprimand, but she wasn't sure it would be well-received now that her place in the family seemed to be in doubt.

"What about properties where people weren't living?" Laurel looked thoughtful. "And where businesses had gone under? There are a couple of vacant-looking buildings around here."

There were more than a couple.

"If it's vacant or the business went under, everything in it is yours." Mitch didn't seem happy to admit that. "Next." He waved Sophie to the desk.

His daughter glanced from her father to Shane, but said nothing.

After everyone was checked in, Laurel watched the kids while Shane, Sophie and Ella unloaded the luggage from the Hummer. It wasn't yet dinnertime, but the sky was darkening and the temperature was dropping noticeably.

"Be careful what you say to Mitch," Shane cautioned when they were outside. "I don't trust him."

"Is that your testosterone talking, brother dear?" Sophie slung cartoon-decorated backpacks over each shoulder.

"That's my business-sense talking, sister dear." Shane scowled, an expression that might have been amplified by the sudden gust of biting wind.

"He's defending his territory." Ella wrestled Laurel's huge, heavy suitcase to the ground, narrowly missing her toes. Laurel had also brought a large garment bag full to the seams. Wow. Did all costume designers pack for every contingency? "People get uncomfortable when there's uncertainty about their home."

It was the wrong thing to say. Shane's scowl deepened. "Remember you're a Monroe, Ella."

Sure, she thought, for now. But these past few days, she hadn't been proud of it.

CHAPTER THREE

NOAH TRUDGED THROUGH the deepening snow to his cabin carrying a bag of dog food.

The limping dog trailed behind him.

A dog. One everyone thought was cute. And no one else would take him? Because he was lame?

It figured.

Noah was reminded of his father's history of perfection. Every event in Noah's life that fell short of his standards was met with a pronouncement of the man's greatness.

You came in fourth in the relay race? My friends and I were state champs.

That's your SAT math score? My math mark was seventy points higher than that on my first try.

His father had the highest expectations. He'd have taken one look at the laboring dog and contacted the closest animal-rescue facility.

The joke's on you, Dad.

The truth was, the dog wouldn't go with anyone else.

Darn dog didn't know he'd made the wrong choice.

"Don't expect much," Noah told the dog when he reached the porch, because he'd been trained to have a polite bedside manner, even when he was in a foul mood.

The dog paused on the top step, panting. Snow clung to his shaggy golden hair as if it had been professionally frosted. His dark brown eyes, which peeked out from beneath overgrown bangs, were filled with things Noah didn't want—love and trust. With those eyes, he was exactly the kind of dog that should appeal to someone like Ella.

"And don't think this is permanent." Noah gave the canine a stern look. "It's just until you're back on your feet." He sighed, put his key in the lock and opened the door. "And now I'm talking to a dog." Which, on second thought, might be an improvement. He'd been talking to himself since he'd gotten here.

He hurried inside, closed the door quickly behind them and just as hastily hung up his outerwear on hooks—knit cap, scarf, jacket.

The dog sat at his feet, leg thrust out at an awkward angle.

"Did you forget we had an appointment, Doc?"

Noah jumped in the midst of removing his gloves. He quickly tugged them back in place and turned toward the corner, where the exam room was located. "I thought I locked the door."

"You did." A wiry old woman wearing a yellow knit cap over her coarse gray hair sat on the exam-room table, partially hidden by a privacy screen. "I know where the spare key is."

Why don't I know where the spare key is?

Noah's pulse rate peaked, then began its descent into normal. Thankfully, the important stuff—the medicines and equipment—was locked in cabinets. He doubted there was a spare key to those, but he made a mental note to ask Mitch about keys regardless. "Odette, you don't have an appointment today." Or any day, for that matter.

The dog hobbled over and sniffed Odette's feet, which were covered in red-and-blue hand-knit socks.

Odette patted the dog on the head. "Doc, dying patients need daily appointments."

"You're not dying." She was just old and in need of some company. "Go back to your arts and crafts."

She harrumphed, and then muttered, *"Arts and crafts,"* as if he'd referred to her quilting and knitting in a derogatory manner.

Which in hindsight, he might have. Her continued presence was getting on his nerves. His neighbor came by so often, she didn't comment on his gloves anymore.

The dog sat at the base of the table and wagged his tail, more than willing to accept a visitor. Why couldn't Noah have rescued a territorial guard dog?

"Doc Carter knew I was dying." Odette huffed, thin shoulders slumping. "She was nice to me."

Noah stalked over to the exam area, and grabbed the blood-pressure cuff and his stethoscope.

The canine panted and wagged his fluffy tail as if to say, *You have to be nice to her, too, because she's old and alone.*

He scowled at the dog. "I'm paid to keep Second Chance residents healthy. Kindness is extra."

The dog stopped panting, closed his mouth and stared at Noah in disbelief.

Noah shrugged and said to the dog, "Don't look at me like that. Kindness never healed anybody."

"Aha!" Odette fairly crowed with satisfaction. "You agree I'm down to my last days."

"No. I was…" *Talking to a dog because the isolation of Second Chance is getting to me?*

That admission wouldn't go over well. He wrapped the cuff around Odette's arm with difficulty, relying on his left hand to pull it snug. He had to hand-pump the unit, because every piece of medical equipment in the cabin was at least ten years old and behind in technological advances. He still had to use an oral thermometer to take a patient's temperature!

Odette went rigid, held her breath and leaned away from the cuff. "My brother always told me getting old was a chore."

"Don't tense up or we'll have to do this again."

"I'll just look at your therapy dog." Staring down, Odette visibly relaxed.

Noah felt her forehead—not hot—then relieved the pressure on the valve and watched the gauge fall.

"He has such sweet eyes. What's his name?"

"Dog." Noah removed the armband and picked up his stethoscope, instructing her to breathe deeply as he listened to her lungs. He checked her skin for elasticity. "Your blood pressure is normal. Your lungs are clear. You're hydrated." He retrieved her file from a drawer and dutifully logged the date, her numbers and his assessment—normal. Why did she insist she was on death's door? "Are you having hurtful thoughts? Are you depressed? Is it hard to get up in the morning?"

"No, no and no."

"Odette." He gave the old woman his most serious expression, the one he used to use when he told sports stars they had to agree to an intense postsurgery therapy regime if they wanted him to operate. "I think you'll live another day."

Odette fell back on the exam table as if this was the worst news ever. "How can you say that?"

"Because you have no history of any disease and you walked over here through two feet of snow, not to mention you ascended an incline." His was the highest cabin on this stretch of road. "If you were dying, the dog would've found you buried in a drift, not in here." He took hold of Odette's shoulder and raised her to a sitting position. "Come on. I'm sure you've got a project or two waiting for you at home."

"I do." She perked up, a smile revealing layers of wrinkles on her face. "I'm tackling homemaker quilt blocks today. Eight points plus four Y-seams. It's very challenging." She slid off the end of the table and walked to the bench where she'd left her snow boots and jacket, pausing to look out the big plate glass window to the buildings on the river side of the road. "There are visitors at the inn."

"Yes." He got out a towel and dried the dog off, taking his time before saying more. "The Monroes have arrived. Four of them. In a Hummer."

"Roy will be happy." Odette looked far from happy. "What are they like?"

"Why don't you go see for yourself? I'm busy." He picked up the paperback thriller he'd been reading for the last two months, sat down in his living room recliner and then glanced back at the dog.

As if released from the "stay" command, the shaggy beast came over and sat next to him, putting his muzzle on the arm of the chair and staring up at Noah with worshipful, big brown eyes.

There's nothing left to worship here, big fella.

"You aren't busy. You're going to hold that book and then stare out at the valley like you and Roy do every day." Because there were big picture windows in the north and east corners of the cabin, Odette had an unobstructed view of Noah's front room from her small cabin to the north, as well as Roy's, which was about fifty feet south of Noah's. "Tell me about the Monroes."

"If you're curious, you know where to get your answers." He extended the footrest on his recliner. "Or you can use those binoculars of yours."

The dog inched closer, put a paw on Noah's arm and kept moving forward, as if he'd inch his way right into Noah's lap.

"Don't even think about it." Noah blocked him with an elbow.

"I can't go down there with all those strangers." Odette paced with sturdy, healthy steps.

"Don't be such a drama queen. They're checking into the inn. Go ask Ivy or Roy their impressions if you don't want to see them."

"You're impossible. You and that dog. You'll both be happy just staring out the window while this old lady withers in front of your very eyes." Odette put on her jacket and her snow boots with vigor and then she was gone, slamming the door behind her.

Snow was beginning to fall. Noah watched Odette walk along the path she created to his cabin every day. She turned on her porch, made a rude gesture at him and then disappeared inside her home.

Then it was just Noah, the dog, the book whose plot he couldn't remember and silence. It was in the daily silence of Second Chance that Noah missed practicing orthopedics, missed solving the puzzle of a body's injury, missed the satisfaction of seeing patients hobble in and walk out months later.

His four-legged friend whined softly.

Noah wasn't sure if it was from the desire to be in his lap or if the dog was in pain.

That leg…

"Come on, dog." Noah removed his black gloves, went to the supply cabinet and rummaged around until he found a neoprene elbow brace with Velcro fasteners. He slid it clumsily on the dog's injured back leg because neither the dog nor his weak right hand cooperated. Finally, he got it in place.

"I know what you need, but that brace will make walking easier." Noah toggled through his phone until he pulled up a video of himself performing knee surgery on a basketball player, the basketball league's rookie of the year from two years ago. His own alma mater had requested the rights to film the surgery to use to teach doctors. In the film, Noah's hands moved with steady skill and smooth dexterity.

He tried to recreate the motions with his right hand—holding the knife, performing a precise cut, using a tendon stripper. His fingers felt feeble and clumsy, stretching the thick, jagged scars painfully. His hand curled into a shape Captain Hook would have been satisfied with, but one Noah hated.

Ella had acknowledged his gloved hands with nothing but a polite look. Such a nonreaction whereas every other woman he'd spent time with had made an issue of it.

Noah tossed his phone onto the coffee table and stared down at the dog. "What did it matter whether or not Ella made a big deal about the gloves?" She'd flinch away from the horrific scars on his hand, the same as any woman with any sense would.

The dog pushed his big head beneath Noah's scarred right hand, unfazed by the ugliness of Noah's flesh.

"I can't help you, mutt," Noah said, weaving his fingers into the soft golden fur at the back of the dog's neck. "You tore your ACL." And Noah was no longer a surgeon to the sports stars, not to mention he wasn't an orthopedic veterinarian.

He stared out the window toward what he could see of the Sawtooth mountain range beneath the low clouds, pet the lost dog and watched the snow make everything in Second Chance look idyllic, when in fact it was anything but.

"KIDS! KIDS!" PENNY CRIED, standing on her tiptoes and pressing her face to the frosted glass. She wore a footed pink sleeper and a severe case of blond bedhead. "Sed, Mom. Sed."

The road had disappeared beneath several feet of snow. The sun peeked through thinning gray clouds. Two stories below them, several children rode plastic sleds and inner tubes down a gentle slope beside the inn, one that plateaued long before reaching the river.

"Go see." Coughing, Penny tugged Ella's hand and faced the door, wanting out.

"We need clothes and food first." If not breakfast, at least something in her stomach.

"Cos." Penny dropped Ella's hand and turned her attention to the sleeper's zipper.

While she was occupied, Ella donned snow pants and a thick yellow sweatshirt, applying light makeup using the mirror in the cramped bathroom, which had barely enough space for a person to turn around in, but still managed to be charming. It had dark wood paneling and green fixtures from the forties—a pedestal sink, toilet and short bathtub-shower combo you could sit in if your knees were completely bent.

The log walls were similar to the walls of the home they'd be vacating in a few short weeks—round and yellow. The main room was small, too, with a queen bed framed with six-inch-diameter logs and dressed in a star quilt made with red and black blocks. The curtains were faded lace and didn't block out any sunlight. It was quaint.

The kids outside shouted with joy.

"Cos," Penny wailed, falling to her bottom on the thick carpet as she tried to peel herself out of the sleeper.

"I'll help." Ella made quick work of the sleeper, put a fresh diaper on her daughter and then dressed Penny in a pair of blue long johns to go under her pink snowsuit. "And now we brush hair and teeth."

"Want sed, Mom. Want kids." Penny ran back to the window to reassure herself the kids were still outside.

A half hour and a hurried start of coffee (for Ella), applesauce (for Penny) later, and the pair was outside in their snow gear, joined by Sophie and her two boys. The twins were already down at the bottom of the hill, having borrowed someone's inner tube. Penny had stopped to make a snow angel nearby.

"Can I take Penny for a ride?" Gabby asked. She wore a purple jacket that made her pale red hair look blond. At Ella's nod, the preteen put Penny in her lap and they tobogganed down the hill.

Penny's joyful shriek combined with the hill full of happy children and the cocoon of being with Monroes made Ella want to sing with happiness. She wasn't quite brave enough to belt out a tune in front of an audience, so she hummed, starting with Grandpa Harlan's call to action, *"Are you ready, Hezzie?"*

"Now that we're here, what's your plan of attack?" Sophie didn't take her eyes from her boys, who were prone to find trouble. "How are you going to evaluate the value of Second Chance in the middle of winter?"

"I have the plat map of the parcels before Grandpa Harlan purchased them and the deeds, but—" Ella waved to Penny "—I didn't count on everything being buried in snow. I have to look at the state of each roof, the electrical, the plumbing." And more. Ella sighed, not wanting to let down the family. "Do you think Shane will shovel a path to all the buildings for me?"

"He would if you told him we'd get out of town quicker." Sophie pushed her sunglasses higher on her nose. She'd braided her light brown hair into two short pigtails that stuck out from either side of her knit cap like dangling earrings.

The wind kicked up powder, sending it swirling around their feet.

"Sophie, did you notice Grandpa Harlan wrote that letter around the time Bryce died?"

"I did, but…" Sophie gripped Ella's arm. "What are you thinking?"

"That I… That Bryce's and my situation or the way we blindsided the family…"

Sophie squinted at her. "That you're the reason Grandpa Harlan had us all fired?"

Ella nodded.

"Just like a Monroe." Sophie hugged Ella fiercely. "Listen, Grandpa Harlan was Grandpa Harlan right up until the very end. He made sure we'd remember him forever." She released Ella, but held on to one of her hands. "You are *not* to blame. But it still stinks. It's times like these—when I'm unemployed and about to be homeless—that I wonder if I made the right decision getting a divorce."

"You did." Sophie's ex-husband had been a piece of work. Ella spared her a glance. "I meant to ask how your date went last week."

"What a disaster." Sophie shook her head. "The guy didn't know the difference between a Picasso and a Matisse. One of the boys swiped my lipstick out of my purse and left me a toy car instead. And my cell phone died so I couldn't even pretend to receive an emergency text from you."

"But…was there any chemistry between

you?" Ella tucked the memory of a chemical reaction to a doctor's soulful blue eyes to the back of her mind.

"Chemistry?" Sophie's bare hands fluttered in the crisp air before she stuck them back in her deep pockets. "I don't have the energy for chemistry or any of your love-at-first-sight luck. I'm just looking for someone who shares the same interests that I do."

A big gray truck with a snowplow attachment on the front stopped on the road nearby. Three boys tumbled out, dropped backpacks in the snow and raced to join their friends. The woman driving the truck waved and drove slowly on, clearing a path on the road and making a wide turn at the crossroads to return the way she'd come.

"Now there's a woman after my own heart." Sophie's cheeks were red from the cold. "She has three boys and she plowed a path to a sled hill to keep peace in the family."

"Your boys are angels." Ella stomped her feet to keep her toes warm, nearly missing Sophie's raised eyebrows. "Okay, they're angels *and* a caution."

Gabby took Penny's hand and began the climb back to the top, dragging her blue plastic sled behind her. The twins were trying to tug the inner tube away from one another.

"Alexander! Andrew!" Sophie yelled. "Share or we'll go inside."

The twins tried once more to wrest the inner tube free, and then climbed up the slope together, holding it between them.

"Mitch mentioned something about the passes to civilization being closed." Sophie's gaze was still on her boys. "What happens if someone needs the emergency room?"

"Maybe that's why they have a doctor in town." Ella had successfully avoided thinking about the handsome doctor for longer than ten seconds—thirty, tops—all morning. Now she recalled the firm muscle of his leg and blushed. "I was more worried about having enough food and heat if we were snowed in. How long did Mitch say the passes will be closed?"

"Five days." Sophie frowned. "Or was it ten?"

Ten days? Ella hoped Penny's cough went away.

Gabby and Penny reached the rise where Sophie and Ella stood just as a man rang a bell at the top of the hill. "Who's coming to school today?"

"You have optional school here?" Ella asked Gabby.

"We have independent study, but yeah, Mr. Garland is available to help us for a few hours every day, so it feels more like regular school." Gabby shrugged. "At least, what I expect regular school is like."

"You've never been to a traditional school?" Sophie asked, brown eyes wide behind her glasses.

"Nope. My dad moved me here when I was less than a year old." Gabby positioned the sled at the top for another ride down, sat on the blue plastic and then helped Penny into her lap. "Last ride before school, Penny."

"Schoo?" Penny rolled off Gabby's lap onto the packed snow. "I go schoo." She got to her feet and reached for the girl's hand. "I go."

"Okay." Gabby stood, braces on display as she smiled. "You can help me with math."

"I don't think so," Ella said gently. "Penny's too young for school." Not to mention she'd be a distraction to the learning environment.

Penny pouted, crossed her arms over her chest and muttered, "I go."

"No," Ella said, just as gently and firmly as the first time.

Sophie's twins leaped on the blue sled and barreled down the hill, screaming in delight. When they reached the bottom, they fell over sideways and tried to pelt each other with snow.

"I wish my boys were interested in school," Sophie murmured.

"Mr. Garland won't mind." Gabby swung Penny into her arms. "At least let her come see."

Penny stuck out her lip at Ella.

"Okay." Ella relented, clearly beaten. "Are you coming, Sophie?"

"Not yet." Sophie waved off Ella. "I'm going to stay and let the boys burn off some energy."

They stopped for Gabby's laptop and schoolbooks, and then followed the other children to the Bent Nickel, saying good morning to Mitch, who was clearing a path from the inn to the coffee shop with a snowblower.

Second Chance's schoolteacher was younger than Ella expected—in his midthirties—and attractive, although looking in his eyes didn't make Ella feel much of anything.

Penny claimed a seat at a table with Gabby, her chin level with the tabletop, her green eyes wide as she watched the other children.

"I'm working on the great American novel,"

Mr. Garland said to Ella. "In between hiking and fishing and teaching a bunch of bright kids, of course."

"Which means his book will never be finished." Gabby smiled widely when Mr. Garland raised his eyebrows at her. "Which is great, because I wouldn't want any other teacher. Don't you agree, guys?"

The other children, all younger than Gabby, agreed.

Mr. Garland smiled. "Gabby has great leadership qualities."

"Thank you, Mr. Garland," Gabby intoned as if by rote.

"And a healthy dose of sarcasm," her teacher added. "Which we love her for."

"Snark is free of charge." Gabby opened her laptop. "That's what my dad always says."

"Okay, Penny, honey. Let's go." Ella gave Mr. Garland an apologetic smile. "The kids have school."

"No." Penny's lower lip jutted out. She waved off Ella, which broke her heart. Her daughter rarely rejected her. "Go, Mom. Go."

The schoolteacher produced a coloring page and crayons. "She'll be fine here for a bit. It's good to foster some independence early."

"But…she hasn't even been to preschool." Which made Ella sound like one of those helicopter moms she'd heard so much about, hovering over her child 24/7.

The other children and Ivy reassured Ella they'd watch out for Penny.

"Thirty minutes," Ella said, relenting. Besides, Penny would need some independence when Ella returned to work. Now was as good a time as any to start. "And then we'll order a hot breakfast for you."

Ella hurried back to the inn to get her paperwork on the town properties. She'd looked at it a few times since receiving it and had told Shane she thought there were transaction documents missing. She didn't have any paperwork on a few of the buildings, most notably the fur-trading post and the mercantile. If Grandpa Harlan owned everything in town, why didn't she have recent documents for every property in Second Chance?

When she returned downstairs, Mitch was sitting behind the inn's check-in counter staring at his computer screen. Shane was drinking coffee in front of the fire. The fact that they weren't talking made the air crackle with tension.

"Where are you off to?" Shane sounded crankier than Penny when she'd been told she couldn't go to school. Having lived in Las Vegas and run hotels for years, she guessed he wasn't a morning person.

"I have twenty minutes to begin the property inventory before I have to pick up Penny." She waved the plat map and left before Shane could ask if he could come. She couldn't afford to lose time waiting for him to get moving. On the way out, she absently registered Mitch's odd, almost panicked expression. She chalked it up to something he'd seen on the computer screen.

Ella walked from the inn to the diner, getting her bearings on the map. And then she came upon a dead end. There was no more sidewalk. At least, not one that had been shoveled. There were at least four more buildings on her side of the highway, which... *Hey there*—the highway had been plowed. She slogged her way through knee-high drifts of snow to reach the cleared highway and then walked north.

The morning was still overcast, and the wind swirled around her like a champion skater.

The next building contained three small storefronts with large plate glass windows and signs that each posted a variation of Reopening in Spring. She'd have to walk through twenty feet of snow to reach the porch.

Um, no.

Best limit this trip to a scouting mission and use her impressions to form a plan of attack. She looked farther north. There were supposed to be four houses or cabins perched on the river side of the road.

Ella consulted the plat map and then surveyed the area. "Why are there only three?" Had she read the map wrong?

The wind tugged at the map.

She tried to hold the paper taut in the air, but doing so only made it billow like a sail. She switched tactics and tried holding it over her thighs, which worked better. Except… Where was she on the map again? She turned around slowly, trying to draw reference from snow-covered landmarks and—

A big gust of wind pushed her backward into a snowdrift, which, all things considered, wasn't as bad as it seemed. She was protected from the wind and realized the plot across from the missing home had a cabin perched high above the road.

"Aha!" She laughed and tried to stand.

Except, instead of getting to her feet, she sank deeper in the snow and then began to slide backward down the hill toward the river, her stadium coat acting like a soft-sided sled and her head cutting through nature's snow cone like a shark's fin cut through water. She didn't slide fast, but the incline was steep enough that her flailing arms and legs didn't stop her. Snow clung to the nape of her neck and pushed the knit cap off her head. She slid and slid and slid until her back connected with something solid and she came to a halt, although her heart kept beating as if she was running a race.

If not for the big cold rock at her back, Ella might have plunged in the river. She could hear its throaty gurgle alarmingly close. Her knit cap and property papers were halfway up the hill.

It had all happened so fast. Epiphany. Laughter. Disaster.

Her heart rate began to steady and the cold continued to spread, starting with her neck and her toes and working toward her core.

Cold. So hard to shake regardless of whether you were indoors without heat, or outdoors facing a locked door.

Panic had her jackknifing and scrambling

to get her boots beneath her. One leg sunk in the drift to her knee. The other got tangled in the long hem of her stadium jacket. Snow tumbled down the collar of her sweatshirt, making her shiver.

"Oh, good." A masculine voice. A face at the top of her snow slide forty feet above her. Dark beard. Black knit cap. *Noah.* "You're alive."

Ella laughed, a loud, sharp sound because relief and disbelief and get-a-grip were all tethered together inside her and needed an outlet.

"You are alive, right?" Noah's sarcasm was more welcome than any empathy he might have offered. It kept the tears at bay.

"Barely." The cold was seeping into her backbone and when she moved, snow slid beneath her waistband.

She crawled two steps, sinking in the powder, and slid toward the river until she was back where she'd started using the rock for leverage.

The big golden dog poked his head in her snow tunnel, gathering himself as if he was going to jump to her rescue.

"Not so fast, boy." Noah grabbed the dog. "Let's not make this worse than it already is."

Worse than it already is?

The reality of the steep slope and uncertain

footing hit Ella hard enough to bring tears to her eyes. If she died… If Penny was orphaned…

"Seriously, are you hurt?" Noah asked.

Are you hurt? The policeman had kneeled to ask the question to a twelve-year old Ella, his breath visible between them in the apartment.

"Are you hurt?" Noah repeated, impatiently this time.

If her childhood had taught Ella anything, it was that she could survive what life tossed her way. Or in this case, she could survive where life tossed her.

"I'm fine if you don't count my pride." Ella began the slow climb up, trying not to panic when her hands and feet sank, because they sank to something close to solid, if icy, footing. "I'll be fine." Pride made her add, "You can go about your business."

"My business is making sure people stay alive up here." Deadpan humor.

So different than Bryce's boisterous wit.

Grief pressed down on her lungs.

She didn't waste more breath arguing, not until she lost her footing again and slid several feet before catching herself. She was cold. Her limbs were trembling. And her spirits were lower than her feet in the deep snowdrift. "You wouldn't happen to have a rope, would you? A long shoestring? A ball of yarn?"

"Nope." Noah sounded cheerful. "You look like you exercise regularly. You can do this."

"The only exercise I get is running after Penny," Ella said through gritted teeth, resuming her climb. If she moved slowly, she didn't sink so deeply. And if she didn't look up, she didn't feel the climb was impossible. Or that *he* was impossible.

"Hey, when you get out of there—which at your pace might be tomorrow—don't tell the kids that your jacket made a good sled."

She had to look at him then, if only to muster a scowl and a comeback.

His hands were shoved in his jacket pockets. His bearded expression closed off. He looked cold. Not physically cold, but emotionally removed, as if he couldn't care if she lived or died. His demeanor contradicted his humor and the fact that the dog leaned against Noah's leg the same way Penny sometimes leaned against Ella's, as if the dog knew Noah was hard on the outside and soft on the inside.

Bryce had been soft on all sides, and cheerful.

"You need to work on your bedside manner," she said, resuming her climb. "It's bad. I mean, really bad."

"That's what people tell me." He paused. "But then again, you're not my patient...*yet*. So, it's really unfair that you're judging me."

"I'd play a tiny violin with my fingers, but I'm kind of busy right now."

He chuckled.

His laugh was as unexpectedly sexy as that soulful look in his eyes.

Her feet slid out from under her and she clawed at the snow to keep from sliding back down. "Can you just not be so..." *Annoyingly sexy!* She clamped her lips together.

"So... So what?"

Ella refused to answer. She reached her cap and the map and stuffed them both in her jacket, vowing to keep her mouth shut until she reached the top—a vow that lasted until she climbed within reach of his shadow and glanced up at him. "Didn't there used to be a building here?"

"Not since I've been in town." Noah bent down and extended his left hand. His grip was strong. He hauled her up as if she weighed no more than Penny. "I knew you could do it."

"You have a strange way of administering

pep talks." Ella stared back down the incline and shivered. Her slide had ended a few feet from the icy water. "I think I just aged five years."

"Only five?" Noah's blue eyes flashed with humor, even as they performed a perfunctory, clinical examination of her body. "Why not ten?"

"There's snow melting in my pants." She met his gaze levelly. "It makes me feel alive."

His mouth twitched at one corner. His eyebrows weren't drawn as low as yesterday, although the soulful slant to his eyes wasn't going anywhere.

She gave the dog a friendly pat. "As you can see, I'm fine." She pulled her knit cap and the plat map out of the neck of her jacket and backed up a step, prepared to turn around and seek warm shelter.

"Agreed."

That one word, filled with innuendo, stopped her feet, started her overactive imagination... and her mouth. "I was lucky you were just walking by."

"I saw you from my office." He pointed at the cabin high above the two-lane highway she'd used as a place marker on the map.

The snow between the cabin and the road had been pristine before her fall, but now it had a big two-footed track in it.

She gaped at him. "You slid through the snow to reach me?"

"Yep."

My hero.

Her heart ka-thumped in her chest. "You skidded almost as much as I did."

"But I was always on my feet." He scratched the dog behind his ears with his left hand. There was something about the way he held his right that gave the impression it was injured and hurting. "Unlike you."

"I should get bonus points for sliding down backward."

His lips twitched upward at both corners this time. "If we call it game, set and match, I won't have to worry about you trying that stunt again."

Ella could continue their banter all day. It felt that natural. And yet, it was odd.

They stood staring at each other, which should have been uncomfortable. So why did Ella have the strongest urge to smile and ask him if he could use a cup of coffee?

She didn't do either. "Well, I've got a toddler to pick up." And a market evaluation to figure out.

"And I've got to return to looking out my window, waiting for the next medical emergency." Noah's gaze dropped to the dog's before returning to hers. "Seems like a slow morning, other than you, I mean. Maybe I'll walk over to the Bent Nickel for some coffee instead."

"All that watching. You're like a fire spotter in the wilderness." Ella backed up a few steps, reluctant to break eye contact, but feeling that she needed to return to the coffee shop without him. Because… Because…

Something fluttered in her chest. Something more than attraction.

"Oh." She stopped in her tracks as the flutter took on meaning.

It was awareness. Of a man. Who wasn't Bryce.

And appreciation. Of a man. Who wasn't Bryce. Her humor clicked with his humor.

And appeal. Of a man. Who wasn't Bryce. He was a reluctant rescuer of dogs and women.

Well, maybe not a rescuer of women, but he had waited to make sure she was all right.

Her mouth went dry as the implication hit her. This wasn't just a reaction—*wow, that guy's gorgeous.* This was something deeper—*wow, I wonder if that man's a good kisser.*

Noah cocked a dark eyebrow. "Did you forget something?"

"Yes." She'd forgotten what it was like to be interested in a man. She'd forgotten how attraction fluttered and buzzed and made her feet feel light. Or how she stammered and stopped and stared as if she couldn't believe she felt that magnetism, that pull to gaze deeply into someone's eyes and sneak a glance at a man's mouth and wonder about compatibility.

This was exactly the way it'd started with Bryce. Eyes met. Held. A few witticisms exchanged. It was exactly the same... If you didn't count the sudden awkwardness, because the last time she'd followed her instincts she'd fallen in love, gotten pregnant and faced the repercussions with the Monroes.

She needed to ignore attraction, awareness and appeal, and focus on awkwardness. Which right now was Noah waiting for her to say something as intelligent and sparkly as she'd said before. If she'd been witty with him before. She could no longer remember.

"I have nothing clever left to say," she admitted baldly, before she turned and walked away, lecturing herself about men with soulful eyes, quick wit and quirking eyebrows. Men like that were the opposite of Bryce, which meant they weren't her type.

So why did she still feel flutterful?

She didn't realize Noah and the dog were following her until Noah spoke.

"Who cares if you're clever all the time? That's the thing about life in a small town. Sometimes you don't have to say anything at all."

His words didn't reassure her.

The flutters didn't go away.

If anything, they increased.

CHAPTER FOUR

"I NEED A FAVOR." Mitch stood next to Noah at the counter with the coffee dispenser at the Bent Nickel. He was whispering, which for Mitch was unusual. The man had a courtroom voice and wasn't apologetic about using it. "You'd be doing me a solid if you kept your eye on Ella."

"Why?" Noah asked, when he should have said, *No.* His gaze drifted to Ella, whose laughter he'd listened to as she told the schoolkids how she'd nearly been swallowed up by the snow and plunged into the river.

That sunny hair. That rich laughter. That ability to laugh at herself. She made him want to laugh, too.

What do you have to laugh about?

Exactly.

"Ella's doing a property inventory." Mitch lowered his voice. "And I have my hands full with Shane."

"But doesn't she own the property?" She and all the Monroes. And have every right to take inventory? Noah gave Mitch a hard look. "What exactly are you asking me to do?" A direct question to a former lawyer. What were the odds he'd answer directly?

"Talk to her. Keep tabs on what she's doing and..." Mitch's gaze shifted to his daughter, who leaned over to color with Penny.

"And then you want me to tell you." Reporting what Ella was doing didn't feel right. Noah's gaze caught on her bright blond hair and yellow sweatshirt. She laughed again. Everything about her was hopeful, like sunshine streaming through a window after a heavy rain. Apparently, he'd have no trouble with the keeping-his-eyes-on-her part of Mitch's request.

Earlier, he'd been watching Ella walk around the road as if referring to a map and thinking how small she looked in that long jacket of hers. One minute she'd been consulting the pages as if she was lost, and the next she'd nearly disappeared into the snow descending toward the river. He'd never put on his outdoor gear so fast. A sliding near-fall later, and he'd been ecstatic to discover she was okay.

Could she have used help getting up the slope? Sure, but she'd made it. Could he have refrained from teasing her? No way. There was something about being near her that wouldn't let him remain silent.

"Why?" Noah asked Mitch. "Why is it so important to abide by a nondisclosure agreement with a dead man and spy on the Monroes?"

"You ask too many questions," Mitch said darkly.

The Monroes had claimed three booths on one side of the Bent Nickel. The redhead who wasn't famous and Sophie sat with the twin boys. The redhead was having tea, while Sophie and her boys were eating oatmeal. Shane sat alone in a booth, attention on his phone. Ella stood drinking coffee near Penny, huddled over her cup as if she was still cold.

A couple of kids took note of Noah's gloves. Noah turned his back on them. There was a reason he didn't usually come in this early. He avoided the place when so many kids were clustered about. If they knew what was beneath the gloves, he'd be the town boogeyman.

If he wasn't already.

Mitch turned his attention back to Noah, a question in his eyes: *Will you do it or not?*

"I don't know…" Of course, Noah would do it. He was just trying to play it cool, as if being near this woman wasn't the universe's way of torturing him.

As if the universe hadn't tortured him enough.

He'd do it if only to relieve the boredom of practicing medicine in Second Chance. "Are you asking me to make sure Ella doesn't fall into the river and drown?" Like she almost had earlier?

Mitch stared at him long and hard before nodding. "Yeah. That's it. This town isn't safe enough in winter for folks to wander about unescorted."

Liar.

But if Mitch was lying, so was Noah. A fact corroborated by the bitter taste at the back of Noah's throat.

Ivy brought plates of food for Ella and Penny and they slid into a booth near the children.

"You know that excuse won't fly more than once," Noah said to Mitch before slurping his coffee to rid himself of liar's breath. "How long are they staying?"

"Indefinitely." Mitch stared at the back of Shane's head and frowned. "They refused to give a check-out date."

"Well." Ivy butted into the conversation. She'd been eavesdropping from behind the counter. "I, for one, am ecstatic they're staying, at least for now. I'm going to have a really strong January. That Shane is a great tipper." She leaned over the counter and whispered, "Do you know what they plan to do with the town?"

"No." Mitch's frown deepened.

"It's no big deal, right?" Noah sipped his black coffee. "Whatever they decide?"

The pair scowled at Noah.

"We have kids." Ivy smoothed the brown hair that had fallen free of her low bun behind her ears. "Stability is important. To me, whatever they decide is a big deal."

"We were paid money when Harlan bought the town, but most of us have been living on that payout ever since." Mitch topped off his coffee cup. "It's not like the inn is full every night."

"Or the Bent Nickel at every meal," Ivy added.

The town was a sleepy stop on the way to

Sun Valley from Boise to the west, or Challis to the north. The small shops that were open eight months out of the year were more a passing curiosity than a must-see.

Noah stared down at the dog, who stared back with wide eyes as if to say, *Show some compassion.*

Or maybe the dog was hoping for some of the bacon Penny was eating and meant to say, *Order me a second breakfast.*

Noah held back a sigh, managing not to look at Ella. "Why is this my problem?"

"Because…" Mitch blew the steam from his coffee before taking a sip, his courtroom expression giving away nothing. "If they don't renew our leases, you won't continue to receive a stipend or have a free place to live." Mitch gave Noah's right hand a significant look. He'd seen Noah's scars. Once.

Noah didn't have many options when it came to practicing medicine, at least not ones he preferred. Where else could he practice wearing a leather glove? Plus he liked food and a roof over his head.

"I guess I'll get right on that assignment you gave me." Noah turned and faced his fate—a cheerful blonde with a precocious toddler.

There must be an alternative, he groused.

There wasn't. All the same, Noah decided his coffee cup needed a refill first. And then the dog needed a pat on the head. And...

Mitch frowned at Noah.

All right, all right. Noah held up his left hand, capitulating. "Come on, dog."

His unsuspecting assignment pretended not to see Noah approach, pretended not to hear Noah greet her with a gruff "Hey."

Penny sat on her knees across from her mother, fork in hand. Her golden curls had been smashed beneath a knit cap and hung limply about her head. She'd eaten most of her scrambled eggs, although egg bits littered the table, bench seat and floor. She was currently working on a pancake. When she saw Noah and the dog, she grinned and said, "Woof!"

The dog said hello to Penny with a nose-butt to the leg, and then he began cleaning up the egg crumbs on the floor and bench seat.

"Woof," Penny said again, wiping at her runny nose. She laughed, but her laughter dissolved into a deep series of coughs.

"Blow." Ella was on the case immediately. She half stood on her side of the booth and covered Penny's nose with a napkin. "Now drink," she said when her daughter's airways had mostly cleared.

There was something awe-inspiring about a mother who knew what she was doing when it came to her daughter's health.

Penny obediently slurped water from a small plastic glass, attention so intent upon the dog that she spilled water on the neck of her blue long johns.

Ella stood again, blotting water with a napkin. She'd worked her way through part of a small green salad with grilled chicken strips, possibly not caring that Ivy had microwaved them. "Have you named your dog?"

"He's not mine."

The dog backed out from under the table and gave Noah a reproachful look.

"You're eating salad for breakfast?" The only time Noah had done that was when he'd been an intern and couldn't remember what time of day it was.

"Best get my vegetable intake started early." Ella also had a cup of coffee, so she wasn't a complete breakfast oddity. "I realize he's not your dog, but you have to call him something."

"Woof," Penny said.

The dog stared at her, thumping his tail against Noah's leg.

"Woof-woof." Penny giggled, not coughing this time.

The dog shuddered with contained excitement, tail moving at lightning speed.

"I think your dog's name is Woof." There was mischief in Ella's blue eyes. "And don't deny he's yours. You might hurt his feelings."

Noah patted Woof's broad head and pulled a chair near the booth, wondering when he was going to regret this.

He was sitting with Ella for the good of the town. And his peace of mind regarding staying in Second Chance, not because Ella made him feel more alive than he had in over six months.

Now who's lying?

"Can I help you?" Ella gave him a sly look that said he was in for some payback. "Throw you a lifeline? Oh, here." She handed him a napkin. "Perhaps this can help whatever predicament you're in."

Noah stroked his beard, dragging down the corners of his mouth that wanted to tip up in a smile. "I'm just checking in, looking for signs that you need medical care. Head wound, frostbite, shock."

"My head and my conscience are clear, thank you." She speared a spine of iceberg lettuce.

And…he was dismissed.

Anger pinched the back of his neck. Nobody dismissed Dr. Noah Bishop. Nurses and staff scuttled out of his way.

Or they had.

Breathing loudly, Penny grinned at Noah, as if she wanted him to try harder.

"You told the kids your coat was like a sled." He narrowed his eyes. "Whatever happens on Sled Hill is on you now."

"I'll take that chance. Now if you'll excuse—"

"This may be Second Chance," he said hurriedly. "But even cats only have nine lives. You can come clean. I'm your doctor. This wasn't the first time you cheated death, was it?"

Her lips made a soft *O*. Her freckles turned more prominent.

Noah was on to something. "Let's do the math. Say you were thirty-five—"

"I'm thirty."

"—you'd probably be close to using all nine lives." He held up his hands. "But thirty, you say? You might have two, maybe three lives, left."

Across the room, Mitch huffed and mumbled something that sounded like *I asked for a simple favor and it turned into this.*

Noah spared Ella a strained smile and tapped the map she'd laid on the table. "What's this all about?"

Her expression shuttered. She whisked the map off the table and into the folds of her big, puffy jacket. "It's an inventory of the town buildings."

If she was expecting Noah to be upset, she was going to be disappointed.

He shrugged. "You're entitled to know what you own." He should have said that louder.

"Thank you." Ella leaned back to scrutinize him. "It's such an odd thing, isn't it? To inherit a town. Although I didn't inherit anything." She nodded toward her daughter. "Penny has a share."

"You're not a Monroe?" Noah frowned and tried not to look at Mitch.

"Yes, she is," Sophie said from the next booth.

Ella's mouth spiked into a rueful smile.

Noah kept silent, waiting to hear more. In medical school, he'd been taught techniques to extract information from patients reluctant to divulge sensitive symptoms. One such technique was the pause. Everyone wanted to fill the silence. And Ella was apparently no exception.

"Legally, I'm a Monroe because I married one," Ella explained.

"Past tense?" he asked, trying not to look at her bare ring finger.

"Widowed. Bryce died in a car accident."

Accident. The memory of metal shrieking made Noah grimace.

"Wuv Daddy." Penny blew a kiss to the ceiling, presumably to heaven.

"Yes, we love Daddy." Ella's eyes were watery. "Anyway." She blew out a breath. "I used to work in real estate, so I was invited along."

"She's a Monroe," Sophie insisted with her back still turned. "She's welcome to go anywhere with the family, because she *is* family."

"I'm representing Penny's interests." Ella's cheeks turned an attractive pink, but she smiled as if Sophie had paid her a great compliment. "Harlan's grands and great-grands inherited the town. More will likely come to visit as soon as they tie up loose ends."

"So, you mean to sell?" Noah glanced around.

Folks in the diner had fallen silent. Not so

much as a fork clattered on a plate. Even the schoolkids were listening.

"Why the sudden interest, Doc?" Shane turned, resting his arm across the back of the booth.

"I'm here on retainer paid by the Monroes." Actually, his check came from a bank account in Boise labeled Second Chance, Inc. "I'm just wondering how long I'll be employed."

The Monroes fell silent. They either didn't know or weren't willing to share.

SHANE LOVED DAILY SCHEDULES.

Morning paper with his coffee. Stock reports. Travel trends. Occupancy figures.

Meetings. Hotel and restaurant inspections. Purchase-order approvals.

Power lunches. Networking. The occasional date, which might or might not be combined with a review of entertainment for the Monroe Resort in Las Vegas.

He planned every minute of every day.

He sat in the Bent Nickel, contemplating the lack of anything on his schedule the rest of the day and the rest of tomorrow and the rest of the year until he found a new job and refilled his calendar. Anything would be better than thinking about the look on his father's face when Uncle Ian announced they were all fired.

He'd busted his butt for the family for more than a decade and this was the thanks he got? His stomach churned every time he relived the betrayal. What kind of father chose money over family? Over his own children? Over he and Sophie and their younger brother, Cam, who'd been the hotel's executive chef? Shane tried to think of what he could have done differently over the years, something he could have said or done to make his grandfather realize he led a pretty okay life, one of his own choosing.

Mitch slid into the seat across from him. "Penny for your thoughts."

He'd need more than a cent to get Shane to open up.

The others had left for the inn a few minutes ago. The schoolchildren had dispersed, as well. It was just Mitch and Shane, and Ivy doing dishes in the back.

"What do you want, Kincaid?" Shane hated to admit the innkeeper was a welcome distraction.

That didn't mean he had to like him.

"How did you sleep last night?" Mitch laced

his fingers around his coffee cup. "I don't always sleep well in a new place."

"Are you fishing for compliments and a good online review?"

Mitch shook his head. "This is my customer-service program. Nobody likes to fill out feedback cards."

That much was true. Regardless, Shane gave Mitch a hard stare, the one he used on employees who'd let him down.

"Your room is above mine. I heard you pacing." Mitch hid a half smile behind his coffee mug. "What is it you do, Shane? When you're not living a life of leisure, that is."

Shane's jaw jutted. "I'm in hotels."

"Oh." Mitch perked up. "Maintenance? Hospitality?" He paused, then added slyly, "Housekeeping?"

This guy was a laugh a minute. Shane had to unclench his jaw to speak. "Management. I'm currently between jobs." And didn't that sting to admit?

"Did you go poco?" At Shane's blank look, Mitch clarified, "Pursuing other career opportunities?" He lowered his voice. "Or did you get the ax and a good severance?"

Mitch was only half-right. There'd been no

severance. No trust fund. No inheritance. Only an ax. One with a dull blade.

"Are you this nosy with all your guests?" Disbelief. Hurt. Anger. The emotions gnawed at Shane's gut, thriving on caffeine and painful memories. They bubbled into his words. He hadn't talked to his father since the reading of the will. He didn't want to talk to him, despite the texts and phone calls from his mother, urging him to do so. It was too soon. "Or do you just have a special interest in me?"

"Ah, you were fired." Mitch grinned happily. "My condolences."

Shane felt a rising well of dislike for the man.

"Can I assume your interest in Second Chance has to do with finding a new job?"

"No." Beneath the table, Shane popped his knuckles...and contemplated popping Mitch in the mouth. He hadn't hit anyone since the third grade, when Carlton Eckersley threw Sophie's backpack in a school trash can.

"Regardless, I'll keep my eye out if anything opens up." Mitch sipped his coffee. "In the meantime, the Bucking Bull hires extra ranch hands every spring to help with calving and branding."

Shane's jaw clenched. "Not a cowboy."

"There's a river-rafting company at the north end of town. They hire river guides for the summer."

"Rafting isn't in my wheelhouse."

"Hmm. Well, if you're interested in an honest day's work—"

Shane's knuckles cracked like popping popcorn.

"—you just ask." Mitch slid out of the booth.

"I'm curious." Shane's brain finally kicked into gear. "What is it you're afraid of when it comes to Monroes in your precious little town?"

Mitch hesitated only a moment before answering, but it was that tick in time that confirmed Shane's suspicions. "We've got nothing to hide." Mitch walked toward the back of the diner.

"That wasn't what I asked," Shane murmured.

He tossed some bills on the table and went in search of the family, finding them in Sophie's room, which was in the corner of the inn. It had two twin beds, a bureau and a desk, whereas his room had a full-size bed and three feet of space between the mattress and four walls.

Shane had to take a moment to control his uncharitable thoughts about their innkeeper before he spoke. "Do you remember when the lawyer was reading that letter from Grandpa Harlan? Do you remember the part about how we needed to learn to live our own lives?"

Sophie stared at him blankly from behind her stylish glasses. "I have mommy brain and have no idea what you're talking about."

"Soph…" he began.

"Don't you *Soph* me." She sat on the log footrail on one of the beds. "Yesterday, my little angels slept on the plane and in the car. They didn't go to sleep last night until after midnight. And they were up before the sun." She thrust a finger toward Alexander. "Stay awake, young man."

Alexander blinked sleep-heavy eyes.

"Alexander." Sophie gasped. "I swear, if you fall asleep I'll have Uncle Shane play the Tickle Monster."

Shane dutifully raised his hands in the shape of claws. "You are truly evil, sister dear."

"Only my twin would know that." Sophie narrowed her gaze at Alexander.

"And your cousins." Laurel was lying on the bed. She'd been carsick yesterday and hadn't shaken off the funk yet today. Her red hair was in a messy ponytail at her nape and she didn't have any makeup on.

Shane hadn't seen Laurel without her war paint since she was a preteen.

"I suppose you mean the part in the will about us...*you* living a life of your own choosing?" Ella sat cross-legged on the other twin bed with Penny in her lap, rocking side to side. "Mr. Quinby didn't use those exact words, but that was the gist. What are you getting at, Shane?"

Trust Ella to get right to the point. She was always trying to drill down to the heart of the matter. In between making sure everyone was fed and watered, that is.

"Grandpa Harlan wanted us to realize more than this town has a spectacular view." Shane gestured to the window and the sweeping, jagged tops of the Sawtooth mountain range. "He set everything up here as if he was stupid. Buying out residents, then charging them next to nothing for their leases. Putting a doctor on retainer."

"Kiss me." Penny coughed, the deep-chested kind of hack.

Ella frowned, kissed the top of Penny's head and pulled her closer.

Shane tucked a shaft of worry away for later. "And this Mitch, this ringleader—"

Sophie rolled her eyes.

"—he's hostile for no reason."

"Other than you might kick him out of his home," Laurel murmured.

Behind Sophie's back, Andrew snuggled next to Laurel and closed his eyes. Alexander was on the floor leaning against a bedpost as if he'd fallen asleep sitting up.

Shane picked up his nephew and deposited him on the bed with his brother. He waved off his twin's glare. "The boys can sleep with me tonight." Not that it wouldn't be a tight fit in the room and the bed. But if they jumped on Mitch's ceiling…

"My brother, the prince." Sophie sighed. "What is it you want from us?"

Penny scrambled from her mother's lap and climbed into the other bed with Laurel and the boys, lying down next to Alexander.

"I don't know," Shane admitted. "All I do know is that Mitch seems like he's hiding something. He has shifty eyes."

"He has gentle eyes," Laurel murmured, half-asleep.

"And the doctor is after something," Shane continued. "He singled you out, Ella."

"He didn't single me out with any ulterior motive," Ella said staunchly, but her cheeks had more than a hint of color.

"Please don't tell me he has gentle eyes." Shane rolled his.

"That would be Woof," Ella teased. "The dog."

"Agreed," Sophie said. "The doctor's eyes are more pained."

"Haunted," Ella corrected, looking thoughtful. "Though not all the time."

Shane didn't want to think about where that comment came from. "I can't stand it anymore." He shook his head and moved to the door. "When are Cam and Jonah coming?" Along with the family already in Second Chance, they were the other two cousins who'd voted not to challenge the will.

"Soon." Sophie turned and brushed a lock of thick dark hair from Alexander's forehead.

Ella nodded. "It was a nebulous soon."

Soon didn't feel like soon enough.

CHAPTER FIVE

PENNY WOKE UP congested and coughing the next morning, a shell of her bouncy self.

Ella sent a silent apology to Grandpa Harlan. She suspected there'd be little cause to sing today.

She administered child-strength cold medicine and thought about Noah, purely in a he's-a-doctor-and-I'm-a-worried-mother sense. Would he and his mournful eyes be at the Bent Nickel this morning?

She could deny it all she wanted to, but there was something about Noah that made her want to sit in an easy chair and study him in a way that would peel back those layers and reveal why he'd been hurt, why he wore those gloves and why she couldn't stop thinking about him.

There were no shrieking kids sledding outside their window this morning. When Ella spared a look outside she saw why. Another several feet of snow had fallen, piling up alongside the inn to the porch railing, which must have been six feet off the ground.

She carried Penny downstairs along with their jackets and gloves. They'd left their snow boots at the front door. Her little darling was hot in her arms.

Gabby sat at the hotel's front desk with a laptop open. Her pale red hair was in a messy bun at the back of her neck. "Dad's out shoveling, despite me telling him it's a lost cause. There's a blizzard coming later today."

Ella appreciated Mitch's efforts more than his daughter did. "I was hoping to get to the Bent Nickel for some soup for Penny." Her daughter's forehead felt warm. "And to see the doctor."

"If Dad doesn't get the walk cleared, we have ramen noodles and food stocked in the freezer." Gabby gestured toward the back.

The door to Mitch and Gabby's living quarters was open. Ella could see a Peg-Board mounted on the wall inside the doorway. It was covered with keys, and not the keys attached to wooden keychains with room names on them. Those were house keys.

"That's a lot of keys," Ella noted, as she set down Penny and put on her jacket.

"Dad can unlock nearly every building in town." Gabby shrugged, not taking her eyes from the laptop screen. "I guess that's something mayors of small towns do."

Ella didn't think so. If Mitch had the keys to everything, why hadn't he offered to give them a tour of the town when the snow had cleared? "What are you studying?"

"Latitude and longitude." Gabby heaved a put-upon sigh perfected by generations of teenagers. "Why do I need to know that when I have GPS on my phone?"

"GPS is based on latitude and longitude." Ella put Penny into her snow boots.

"Huh." Gabby maneuvered the computer mouse, sliding and clicking urgently. "I wonder if that will earn me extra points on my homework. It's due this morning. I always take the most allowable time to max out my grade."

"Ahh." She was an overachiever. "What kind of grade did your history paper on Second Chance earn?"

"An A." She flashed her braces in a smile. "But Mr. Garland's an easy grader."

"Or you're a good student." Ella put on her snow boots next. "I was serious when I said

I'd like to read your report. Can you print it out for me?"

"I'll give you my graded copy if you promise to return it." She hopped off the stool behind the desk and disappeared into the back room. She returned quickly with a thick, stapled sheaf of papers. "I could have done a better job of footnoting."

"I won't judge." Ella held out her hand, more excited than she ought to be. More than anything, she wanted to be helpful to the Monroes. Besides, new information about Second Chance might make Shane less stressed and make him see fewer conspiracies.

"I couldn't go into depth about the town's recent history." Gabby held on to her report with both hands. "No one seemed to know much about your grandfather."

"Grandfather-in-law." Ella lowered her empty hand so as not to appear rude. "Was there a page limit?"

Gabby nodded, looking relieved. "It's not my best work."

"But it did earn you an A," Ella said kindly, suspecting Gabby might be something of a perfectionist. "I'm not going to judge you or the report. I'm interested in the history and character of the town. I promise."

"Okay." The girl handed it over.

Ella tucked the report into her diaper bag, lifted a bundled Penny and carried her out the door, where it was windy and cold. And loud. Mitch was using a small snowblower and had nearly cleared the walk to the Bent Nickel. But the snow was coming down fast. It wouldn't be long before his efforts were for naught.

Ella darted inside the Bent Nickel as soon as Mitch moved beyond the door, grateful to be out of the cold. She set down Penny in their usual booth, removed their jackets and greeted Ivy. "Do you have any broth? Anything warm and steamy to help clear out Penny's nasal passages?"

"Oh, that poor dear. I have chicken noodle soup." Ivy banged around the kitchen cupboards. "Do you want another salad for breakfast?"

"Sure." Ella poured herself a cup of coffee. "What's the forecast for today?"

"Whiteout conditions. Best let me send you back to the inn with soup and sandwiches for later."

"That sounds like a plan." Ella slid into the booth next to Penny and drew her into her lap.

Penny wheezed with each breath.

"We're going to have to see the doctor today." She raised her voice and asked, "Is Noah coming in for coffee soon?"

"He doesn't usually come in until the afternoon, but I wouldn't expect him today. It's blowing something fierce. Mitch probably wouldn't have cleared the walk if you weren't here."

Ella glanced out the window. The snow was so thick, she couldn't see the buildings across the road, including Noah's cabin. With weather like this, how was she going to evaluate anything?

Penny slid down to lie across the bench seat, her head in Ella's lap.

While they waited for food, Ella took out Gabby's report. She was still reading it when Laurel joined her, shedding her black leather jacket—which couldn't be warm enough—and revealing a pale pink turtleneck beneath a baggy black tunic sweater. She hadn't put on a cap or a scarf. Her long red hair was windblown and her cheeks chafed from the cold.

Laurel tapped a picture in the report. "What a beautiful wedding dress. Whose is it?"

"Ruth Blickenderfer's from 1919. According to Gabby's report, she married Henri Blickenderfer and became town mayor a decade later." Ella flipped back a page and turned the report so Laurel could see. "Her father built a mercantile out of clay bricks next to the fur-trading post. You'd like the mercantile. They sold handwoven blankets and bolts of fabric." She flipped to another picture.

In the photo, the double doors to the mercantile were flung open and some of the goods inside could be seen.

Laurel leaned forward. "Look at the stacks of denim. That must have been when brands like Levi's were becoming popular."

"Is that what they are? Jeans?" Ella turned the photo sideways. "Honestly, the cans of food caught my eye, but this weather makes me think about stocking up." And cleaning her plate.

"It's across from the inn? Do you think anything is left behind in there?" Laurel looked almost as interested in the mercantile as she'd been in the reclusive Odette's quilt.

"I don't know." But Ella knew where to find

the key, vowing to go inside as soon as the weather allowed.

"What else does it say?" Laurel seemed genuinely interested. "Anything to help you?"

"No." Sadly. It was a sixth-grade report, after all. "The valley was originally a summer hunting ground for the Shoshone. There was a hot spring behind the trading post, which was where traders could buy a hot bath."

"I always feel better after a hot bath." Laurel shuddered and put her coat back on.

Ella flipped a page. "And then someone marketed the hot springs as a place of healing."

"That's the reason the brothel closed." Roy stomped snow from his boots at the door and then approached their table. He looked as if he wore the same blue coveralls and old long johns he'd had on the day they'd arrived. "They needed rooms for the tourists."

Ivy appeared with a salad and a bowl of soup. "That's all hearsay."

"It's the truth the way my grandfather remembered it." Roy put his nose in the air.

"Soup sounds heavenly, even if it is breakfast." Laurel glanced up at Ivy. "Is there any more? And hot water for tea?"

"Coming right up." Ivy hummed happily as she hurried back to the kitchen.

"Roy, did you grow up here?" Ella brought Penny to sit in her lap and crumbled some crackers in her soup.

"I did, along with several others, like Odette and Percy Clark. Takes a special kind of person to be happy in Second Chance through all its seasons." He pulled up a chair. "Winter here is invigorating."

Ella thought *invigorating* was a kind word. "I generally complain about the cold."

"There's a positive side to everything," Roy said. "The smooth beauty of the snow as you look across the valley. I could look at it all day."

"He means he could nap in front of his window facing the valley." Ivy set a bowl of soup, some hot water and a mug in front of Laurel. The diner owner scattered more cracker packets across the table.

"As the town handyman, I resent that remark." Roy's bushy white eyebrows made a landing over his eyes. "I'm on call, just like the doc. Never left anyone waiting. Arrive prompt is my motto. I didn't see you complaining when I came over and snaked your kitchen sink on a moment's notice, Ivy."

"That was last spring." Ivy patted his shoulder. "And I appreciated it. But now it's winter, the passes are closed and it's officially Roy's napping season."

The old man harrumphed as Ivy returned to the kitchen.

"How long will we be snowed in?" Laurel asked, steeping her tea.

"You're asking us to be Mother Nature's mind readers." Roy winced. "The passes are a good twenty-five hundred feet above us. If we get three feet of snow, they get six. These high peaks around us trap the weather here and when the snow gets higher than ten feet, you can bet it's going to take the state a long time to work their way up from their side of the mountains with their snowplows."

"Don't scare them, Roy." Ivy banged pots in the kitchen. "It's usually a few days at a time. Never longer than a week."

"A week?" Ella was suddenly ravenous. "What happens if you run out of food?"

"We all have deep freezers and deep pantries." Roy sat back in his chair and preened. "Life up here takes a bit of planning."

"Roy?" Ella tilted her head to look at him over Penny's curls. "Where do you live?"

"Across the road." He waved as if it was no big deal. "Next to Doc."

"But…the drifts are so deep." Ella looked out the window at a world thick with falling flakes. "How did you get across?"

"I shovel a path across the road just about every day." He pointed toward the highway. "That way, it won't matter if three feet falls because I'm only shoveling three feet, not the full six, eight or twelve."

"Twelve?" Laurel wrapped herself tighter in her leather jacket. "I'm from LA I don't do snow."

"You'll get used to it." Roy stood and went to grab a cup of coffee. "If we want to get somewhere after a blizzard like this, we get out our snowshoes or our snowmobiles."

"Or we go home." Laurel gave Ella a significant nod. "I'm not cut out for life in the snow. Let me know how I can help, Ella."

"Other than operating a snowplow, there's not much you can do." Ella needed a change of subject. "Laurel, have you thought about what you'll do now that you aren't working for Monroe Studios?"

"I run a celebrity stylist business on the side. I suppose I'll do that full-time. I'm kind of grateful. Working all day on movie shoots while networking on breaks and at night to find fashions for celebs—like Ashley—to wear to a premiere or special event was exhausting." Laurel stirred her soup. "I'm like Roy. I've been taking advantage of the break and catching up on sleep." She stopped stirring, forehead creasing. "But the future…" Laurel searched Ella's face. "Who am I kidding? I mostly style Ashley and she's not talking to me right now."

"I'm sorry to hear that."

"Fighting makes me sick to my stomach." Laurel stared at her soup. "It's good to get away and have some breathing room."

"Is that what this is?" Ella asked softly. "Will the family even survive this?"

"You'll see, it'll blow over and we'll *all* be one big happy family again." Laurel dipped her spoon into the soup and blew on it, adding with much less confidence, "Someday."

"Mom." Penny squirmed in Ella's lap. "Want potty."

Ella had been gently introducing the concept of using the toilet. Penny asking for the potty was the best news of the morning. Ella hurried to take her daughter to the restrooms.

Roy had told her about a way across the highway, through the snow, to reach Noah if need be. Laurel, like Sophie, reaffirmed that Ella was a Monroe. And now Penny was asking to use the potty.

Maybe this was going to be a singing day after all.

Are you ready, Hezzie?

CHAPTER SIX

"DON'T GET USED to this. I'm not a dog person."

Noah sat in his recliner, Woof in his lap. He ran his fingers through the dog's thick fur, surprised at how restful Woof was.

It wouldn't be fair to the animal, his father had said anytime the idea of a pet was brought up.

Noah felt as if he'd missed out.

The road, the Snake River and the Sawtooth mountain range weren't visible through the snow flurries and low-hanging clouds. Undoubtedly, Ella's snow tunnel, made when she fell backward down the hill, was filling. This late in the afternoon she and her family would be tucked into the inn, warm and dry, displaced doctors with deep scars the furthest thing from her mind.

Ella should be the furthest thing from his mind.

Noah closed his eyes, letting his mind take him back in time.

He was conducting an ACL reconstruction on the knee of a world-class soccer player. The notes of Coldplay's "Viva la Vida" filled the surgery theater. Everything was going as planned. Noah could see his patient would face a smooth recovery. Acknowledgement of his skill filled him with a sense of power and pride.

And then the unthinkable happened. Everything went to hell. His right hand seized up, fingers crimping on the scalpel. He fought to keep the scalpel still, to withdraw, to release. He couldn't move.

The music changed, turned loud and angry. Something by Linkin Park. And still, he couldn't pull back his hand. His patient...

Noah knew with one-hundred-percent certainty that one more tremor in his fingers and he'd slice his patient's tendon irreparably.

Noah cringed, startling himself awake.

Snow still fell in a gray curtain. The dog was still lying curled in his lap. Sweat dampened his spine.

The good news was he hadn't botched the surgery or destroyed a helpless man's career. History proved the procedure had gone off without a hitch. It was only in Noah's mind that he'd bungled the surgery. The bad news was he wasn't going to extend any more sports careers. This was his reality now. A sleepy practice. Not a surgery center. Patients with minor complaints. Not a patient whose body was insured for millions. Nothing high-risk or high-profile that would land him in the news.

Something scrabbled outside his front door. Woof's ears perked.

Nothing should be out in this storm.

Noah placed the dog on the floor and got to his feet. "Odette, if that's you…"

The old woman shouldn't be traipsing around in a blizzard so near dark. If it was Odette, he'd have to walk her home to make sure she didn't fall into a snowdrift or lose her way.

Woof reached the door ahead of Noah and gave it a sniff.

"What? No barking? Some watchdog you are." Noah opened the door, not to Odette, but to a small snowman in a navy stadium jacket holding a pinkish snow baby. Bright blue eyes stared at him from a muffler wrapped around a face.

Ella.

Woof danced back out of the wind as Noah tugged the pair inside. "What are you doing?"

"She's got a cough and a fever." Ella handed Penny to him and dropped her diaper bag to the floor. "The fever started last night, went down this morning and spiked this afternoon."

"Someone should have called me." Mitch or Ivy. Cell phones sometimes failed, but they had landlines in town.

"I was worried. I didn't ask. I…" Ella unwrapped her layers at record-breaking speed. "You have antibiotics, right?"

Noah nodded. "Not every cough needs antibiotics, but yes, I do have them." He set Penny on the floor and began removing her snowsuit. Her green eyes were dull, and her nose dripped white, not clear or yellow, mucus. She gave a worrisome, productive cough. With a child this age, things could get worse quickly, even if her symptoms weren't acute now. "You were right to think she needed medical care."

"Even if I was wrong to walk across the road in a snowstorm?" Ella shed snow pants and her stadium coat and joined him at the exam table. She wore navy leggings and a green hooded, knit sweater. "I'd do it again."

Only when she was standing next to Noah did he realize he wasn't wearing gloves. His stomach did a slow, sickening 360. He hurried to wash his hands and snap on a pair of latex gloves, forcing himself to check first to make sure Penny wasn't allergic to latex.

"You should have called." Noah let annoyance weigh down his words. He couldn't bring himself to look at Ella's face to see how repulsed she was. "The last time I checked the weather, the winds were supposed to be thirty-five to forty-five miles per hour. You could have been blown off your feet. You could have slid down a slope again and I'd never have known."

This last possibility sent his blood running cold. This woman needed a tracking beacon.

"I followed Roy's path. He showed it to me this morning." Ella didn't sound horrified at having seen the beast's true appearance. "We didn't get lost and I don't have your phone number."

"You shouldn't have taken Penny out in the cold." Noah was harping, but he couldn't help it. He hadn't quite shaken the shock of failure from his dream, much less the bitter embarrassment that came from exposing his scars. "It's dangerous. Too dangerous to go back." He gestured to the window. It was only four o'clock in the afternoon, but it was nearly pitch-black outside and all he could see was snow.

"I know, I—I panicked a little." Ella touched his arm. "I surprised you and I'm sorry." She nodded toward his gloved hand.

His scarred, nearly useless hand. She'd seen it and now the storm had trapped her here with a wounded beast, a fact that didn't seem to worry her. Or maybe it did, because she started babbling.

"I didn't want to infect Sophie's boys. Laurel hasn't been feeling herself and Shane means well but doesn't understand how quickly kids can get seriously ill. I just… It was quicker if I came by myself. I—I panic when she gets congested because my husband died from complications sustained in his car accident."

"What kind of complications?" Back to her, Noah rummaged in a drawer for his stethoscope, curious despite his dark mood.

"A punctured lung. It was so hard for Bryce to breathe. They said they were ventilating him, but there was air in his chest cavity where there shouldn't have been and he—he…"

She punctured Noah's defenses. "He went into cardiac arrest."

Ella nodded, swallowing thickly.

For most of Noah's adult life, performance and preparation had taken precedence over his personal life. He'd dated women because of their beauty, their renown, their willingness to sleep with him without expectations of a future—none of which was personal. None of which applied to his attraction to Ella. He wanted to soothe her fears with a gentle embrace. He wanted to brush the blond hair back from her face while she told him more about her past. He wanted to volley one-liners back and forth with her across the same pillow. He wanted to know what made her tick. He wanted her to open up to him about her past.

You're going soft.

He denied the thought because he didn't want to open up to her about *his* past.

Noah pressed his lips together, not speaking again until he was finished performing a thorough exam on Penny. "Her fever is low-grade. It's not viral, more like a mild case of bronchitis." For little ones, even a mild case could knock them out. "All I can do is treat her symptoms. Analgesic for the fever. Albuterol to loosen up the mucus in the brachia. You can ask Mitch for a humidifier. I'm sure he's got one from when Gabby was younger."

She gripped the exam table. "That's it? We don't need to medi-flight her out of here or—"

"In a few days, she'll be fine." Noah wasn't sure he could say the same. In a week, when the snow melted a bit and the pass reopened, Ella would conduct her inventory and the Monroes would leave. His days would go back to being predictable and no one in town would unsettle him.

Woof sat on Noah's foot and leaned against his leg, as if to say, *You'll have me.*

With Noah's luck, Woof's owner would show up with the county snowplows. If so, the dog would probably be better off.

He had no liquid albuterol, but he found an inhaler in the medicine cupboard and coaxed Penny to take in a small dose. Afterward, she curled up in a ball on the table and closed her eyes.

"Thank you," Ella said in a wrung-out voice. "We'll get out of your way."

"I told you before. You can't go back out there." Without thinking, he'd moved between Ella and the door. "It's a blizzard. It's dark. It's too risky."

As if on cue, the wind howled.

Woof scurried to Noah's side. Penny wasn't the only baby in here.

The dog's cautious.

Says the dull mountain doctor.

And now he was arguing with his alter ego.

"I'll just follow my footsteps back," Ella said, but then she looked out the window into the darkness and frowned.

"Not today, you won't. You should stay." To heck with soft. Both she and Woof stilled at Noah's harsh tone. "I'll make us dinner and in the morning we'll have—we'll have...waffles." Not salad.

"Thank you, but..." Ella blinked, and glanced toward the small L-shaped kitchen. "I have some snacks in the diaper bag. That'll get us through until morning. If the pass is closed, you'll need all your food."

It was Noah's turn to blink. He'd assumed she was going to argue that she couldn't stay, not that she couldn't eat his food. "We're not stranded on a deserted island. I'm not going to run out of food before the pass reopens." Not that he'd experienced a Second Chance winter before, but no one had given him dire predictions of snowbound starvation, either.

Ella nodded slowly. Whatever reason she had

to worry about food, she wasn't going to share it with him.

Penny coughed, deep and productive. Ella was by her side immediately, lifting her limp daughter into her arms. More coughing ensued.

Noah wished there was more he could do for her, but sometimes you had to let the body heal in its own time. For Penny, she needed rest, liquids, meds and humidity.

Humidity.

Noah darted in the bathroom and turned the shower on as hot as it would go, and then shut the door behind him. "When the bathroom gets steamy you can sit inside with her for ten minutes. That and the inhaler treatments should help."

While they waited for the bathroom to fill with steam, Ella paced, and Noah called Mitch on the landline, updating him on the situation and asking him to tell the Monroes.

"I hope Penny gets better soon," Mitch said. "And I hope you know what we need from you to—"

Noah hung up before Mitch could say anything more about him being the town's spy.

Penny went into another coughing fit and Ella disappeared into the bathroom with her, where the little girl's hacking eventually stopped. Ten minutes later, they emerged, moist and wilted.

Ella put Penny on the couch and turned to Noah. "We'll sleep here with Woof."

"It's a lumpy old couch. The bed is upstairs and…"

The dog hopped onto the couch next to Penny, curled up and laid his big head on her chubby little legs.

"And I've been outvoted." Noah went to the galley kitchen that was next to the living space. He started to take off his gloves to wash up and prep dinner, then hesitated.

"How did it happen?" Ella laid her hand above his right wrist.

He stiffened, not having noticed her come up beside him. The kitchen was so small she was not quite in it and not quite not.

"How did it happen?" she asked again, still holding him tenderly. Her blue eyes didn't shy away from his. "Your scars?"

He couldn't move. Hardly anyone but other doctors and medical staff had looked at or touched his right hand since the accident. No one had wanted to. Likewise, no one asked about the accident. Most people respected Noah's privacy.

Ella wasn't most people.

Her gaze swept the cabin. The small kitchen they were in, the small living space, the exam area, the sleeping loft above them and then finally her focus came back to Noah. She was waiting for his answer.

Noah couldn't seem to open his mouth, to form words, to ask her not to dig.

"I didn't mean to pry," she lied, not at all well.

"You did." That was Dr. Bishop's voice. Hard, egotistical, distance-setting. And no longer limited to conversations in Noah's head. "You were curious." But not repelled.

Why wasn't she repelled? Mitch had been. Hell, Noah was repelled every day.

Dr. Bishop's authoritative voice didn't deter her, either. She still held on to Noah, still probed for answers. "Do you wear gloves all the time in public?"

"Still curious, I see." There used to be safety behind the facade of Dr. Bishop. He used to be able to cow the most experienced staff. Now he couldn't even intimidate a toddler's mother.

She didn't flinch. "You know what they say about curiosity…"

A smile tugged at the corner of his mouth, tugged at his resolve to keep his scars from the world, tugged at the feeling that he should stay away from her for his own protection. A part of him was right. She made him soft.

Ella had a subtle confidence, an open way of looking at a person that made Noah feel as if he'd known her a long, long time, that they'd been friends forever, that he could joke and share stories. She wasn't as fragile as the girl next door he'd initially thought she was. But that wholesome, welcome quality seemed to span the distance between them, whether she was across the road or standing so close he could pull her into his arms and kiss her.

Kiss her.

He'd been avoiding that specific image since the moment she'd walked into the Bent Nickel. He could no longer avoid it when she touched him. The physical attraction beckoned like a warm heavy quilt on a cold winter's night. And boy, was the temperature ever dropping outside.

He couldn't move. He couldn't look away. He could only breathe. He was stuck the same way he'd been stuck during his distorted flash-back earlier. Only without the sense of dread and disaster. Strike that. She brought a different sense of dread and disaster. The kind a beast felt when dragged out of the shadows into the light.

"What good would it serve? This…curiosity?" Was that his voice? It was gruffer than Woof's growl.

That is, if Woof ever decided to be brave and growl at something.

"What good does it serve to pretend you haven't been hurt?" She tried to lighten the mood by smiling. "Your scars may affect you, but they don't define you."

The beast within him, the one that howled at rainbows and refused the possibility of any resemblance to his past life—that beast didn't want to smile. He wanted to glare at the world and women like Ella, warning them away.

And maybe he was glaring at her now, because her hold on him loosened.

"I…" She faltered then, her gaze dropping to his hand. "Lots of people bear scars, inside and out. Even me."

Her last words triggered the fury inside of him at the injustice of his injury. "When were you ever hurt as bad as this?" The words came snarling out of his mouth before he thought things through.

Ella yanked her hand away as if burned, backing off, taking most of his anger with her.

"I'm sorry. That was a visceral reaction." But he wasn't ready to apologize for it. "I... You're right that everyone has wounds of some kind." Just not as deep and life-altering as his. He stared at the latex glove on his hand, seeing the bumpy scars beneath. "Gloves make it possible for me to be..." *What? Kind?* He nearly laughed. No one in his old life would ever call him that. He finally settled on a reply. "*Civil.* Gloves help me be civil."

She looked dubious.

He wasn't going to dive into his messy emotions and try to explain. If she truly was the girl next door, she'd pat his shoulder and change the subject. And perhaps she might have if he'd answered her question.

How did it happen?

Flashes of light and darkness blinded him as images of the past pushed forward. The slow-motion drop through the air toward towering pine trees. The scream of metal and crack of glass. The amalgamation of noise that swallowed the horror.

Delicate hands clasped his forearms. "It's all right." Ella's voice. She faced him, square-on.

It wasn't all right. It would never be all right. *He* could never go back to who he'd been before the accident.

The here and now returned. Here being Ella and her gentle touch. Now being an ear-ringing silence punctuated by the howling wind.

"I used to be a surgeon in New York," he said, surprised it was his voice that filled the silence, no longer that of the cold, distant Dr. Bishop. "I specialized in orthopedics at a practice that served some of the highest-paid sports stars around. I repaired torn ACLs, performed Tommy John surgery, set stress fractures. I had a reputation for quick solutions and efficient rehab to get players back in the game as soon and as safely as possible."

Ella nodded the same way she would have nodded if he'd said he'd been a bus driver in Queens. Unimpressed. Not in awe.

A year ago, that would have gotten under Noah's skin like a stinging, thorny splinter.

But her gaze didn't say unimpressed or uninvolved. It said his story mattered. It said *he* mattered. To her.

So, he kept on talking. "One of my patients

was a professional golfer. He'd blown out his knee the year before and had slowly worked his way back onto the circuit. He wanted me to see him play and he wanted to fly me to the tournament in his plane." Noah's throat clogged with memories and regrets, about who he'd been back then and how he'd taken a little thing like hand dexterity for granted. "I went, because it was amazing to be invited." He would've bragged about that for years. "But...something happened." They'd barely begun their steep climb into the air before they'd plunged back down. "Crosswind. Wind shear. Whatever." It didn't matter. "We crashed in the trees just past the runway. I would've been fine if I'd gripped the seat belt. Instead, I reached for the dash."

She dug her fingers into his sweatshirt. "And the pilot?"

"My patient? The golfer?" Noah flexed his fingers and stared at a knot in a log on the wall behind her. "He died instantly." Gruesomely.

"And you're dying a slow death now," she surmised.

He startled at her words. But they rang true, resonating deep down in his chest, where the ache of loss resided.

"Let me see." Her grip on his arms eased.

Noah recoiled. *"Why?* No." Never.

"I've seen my share of scars, including my husband's, which were…not pretty." Ella's fingers flexed on his forearms as if in response to a stab of pain. She looked both a little nervous and a lot determined. "I think I can handle yours."

He shook his head.

Her eyes narrowed. Resolve was winning out. "Did I mention I delivered Penny naturally? I'm not squeamish about blood and such."

"You might be." After a good look at his hand.

"We all have scars, Noah. Don't be a baby about yours."

Stunned, he rocked back on his heels. She thought he was being childish? "I keep my hand covered because I don't want to—" *sicken* "—shock* other people." He did a quick inventory of her hands, neck and face. Her skin had nothing to reveal about her past but freckles from too much sun as a kid. "Your scars don't show."

"That's because my scars are internal." She tapped her chest over her heart, releasing him.

Every instinct urged him to console her. He

stood his ground. "Internal scars aren't the same."

"You're not doing a good job of fooling yourself, Noah. You've got deeper scars inside than on your hand."

The truth of her words chilled him.

The wind howled again. Woof's eyes flew to Noah. He snuggled closer to Penny, seeking comfort. Noah looked at Ella, who cast too much light on Noah's dark side with her bright blond hair and sprinkling of freckles. Her head was bowed, as if she sat in church praying.

"My mom had me when she was sixteen," Ella admitted quietly in a voice that could be barely heard above the storm. "Her parents kicked her out when they discovered she was pregnant. And my father... Who knows who he was."

Noah leaned forward, straining to hear her thin, wounded voice.

"It was hard for her. She held down two waitressing jobs to keep me. But somewhere along the line Mom developed a new love affair, this time with liquor and she..." Ella faltered. Frowned. "She was a good mom in the ways that counted."

Noah made a sound meant to agree even as

he realized her tone had turned defensive. He wondered if she was making a case to herself.

"When I was twelve, Mom went out on a Friday night, which wasn't unusual. When I got up the next morning she wasn't there." Ella still wasn't looking at Noah, still had her head bowed, still sounded brittle and un-Ella-like. "That wasn't unusual, either. But then Sunday came. And Monday. And..." She swallowed.

Noah couldn't swallow. He could barely breathe as he imagined a child dealing with an alcoholic mother, much less an alcoholic mother who'd gone missing.

"I couldn't call the police. I'd made that mistake before and Mom had to fight to get me back." She hesitated, just for a breath or two. "So, I didn't answer the door. I waited. And by waited, I mean I went to school and pretended everything was...the same." Her eyes came up far enough to meet Noah's. They were a deep, watery blue. "It was February in Philadelphia. The rent was overdue. The heating bill was overdue. There wasn't much in the refrigerator or the cupboards."

"How long?" he croaked, hurting so badly

for this child in a way he hadn't known existed. "How long was it before…?" *Before what?*

"A month." Her gaze slid to Penny. "They turned the heat off a few days after she disappeared." She shivered. "Our apartment wasn't well-insulated. I wore three layers of clothing and I still couldn't get warm."

Noah wanted to wrap her in a jacket, in a blanket, in his arms.

Ella's eyes were glazed and unseeing. "I ate everything in the house, including the mayonnaise in the jar. When there was nothing left, I stole packets of ketchup from the fast-food restaurant on the corner."

Her fight against starvation explained her prioritizing the need for food. He cursed in his head, feeling helpless and indignant and protective. He held on to her arms, although whether to steady himself or her…he wasn't sure.

"And finally…the landlord called the police, suspecting I'd been abandoned." She was staring at his chest without seeing anything. "It was a Saturday. I was buried in blankets reading a book I'd borrowed from the school library." She turned to look out the window. "And it was snowing."

Silence descended upon the cabin once more.

"What happened to her?" Noah had to ask twice before she answered.

"Mom got picked up for drunk driving that first night. They put her in the drunk tank to dry out. They didn't realize she lived on liquor. Busy shift. Change of staff. She went through withdrawals and died half a day after she was arrested."

The skin on Noah's arms pebbled. Ella had been twelve. She seemed so normal. He'd been thirty-five when he'd crash-landed and he...felt like a monster.

"And she didn't tell them to check on you? No one checked to see if she had a daughter or family?"

"Somehow..." Her voice sounded very small. "My existence slipped through the cracks."

As if she wasn't important enough to be remembered. *To be saved.*

"Do you tell this story to everyone?" Was that what he was going to have to do? Put on a brave face and pretend he was like everyone else? Make idle chitchat about his horrific scars with strangers? He didn't think he could do it.

"No." She chewed her bottom lip before continuing. "I told Bryce. I told Grandpa Harlan."

"What about Sophie? Shane?" The red-headed Monroe whose name he couldn't remember.

She shook her head. "I was going to tell the rest of the Monroes after Penny was born, but then Bryce died and…"

"You didn't want them to judge you," he guessed.

"No…yes." Life returned to her body in a passionate toss of her arms that forced him to step back. "I didn't want them to cast me aside. I didn't want to lose my family in case something happened to me."

"Why not just make a will and designate Sophie as Penny's guardian?" He'd noticed how well those two women got along.

"Sophie and I are close now because we both have young children and attend all the family functions. But if we drift apart…" Her gaze swept her daughter's face. "If for whatever reason I stop going or being invited to Monroe family functions and become more of an acquaintance… I never want Penny to be a taken in by a stranger, be it a Monroe or someone in the foster-care system."

Because that had been her fate.

"You're afraid."

"Like you aren't," she snapped back at him, fire in her eyes. "At least I can admit it. And I don't shy away from labels. *Orphan. Widow. Single mother.* You think those don't make me die a little inside to admit? Every one of those labels is a sign of failure."

"That's not true. You didn't fail at marriage or choose to be orphaned."

"What does it matter how any of it happened?" Ella chopped the air with her hand. "It feels like failure to me." She glared at him. "What label are you using to define yourself?" Her expression turned fierce. "And don't you dare say failure."

"I wasn't going to say that," he lied.

She raised her eyebrows, demanding the truth.

"Okay, I was going to say that. It's how I feel. Same as you." And, same as her, he'd earned it through no fault of his own. He cursed and ripped the latex from his hand, stinging his scars. He thrust his damaged appendage toward her. "Here. It looks like a pirate's hook. And it's about as useful."

"It looks like a hand," Ella said matter-of-factly as she stared at it. Her fingers hovered over his. "May I?"

She wanted to touch him? The beast?

Ella robbed him of breath. It took him a moment to nod.

Her fingers traced over the length of the scars. Three that traversed from the phalanges to the small metacarpals, fingertip to wrist. Her touch made them tingle. "How did your therapy go?"

He drew his hand away.

She searched his face. "You didn't do therapy."

"What would be the point?" Anger was rising from the ashes of loss. "I can't ever perform surgery again."

Ella chewed on his answer for a few moments as the wind howled outside. "Not all doctors are surgeons."

He made a noise that refuted her statement. "All I ever wanted to do was perform complex operations to heal people." With a skill that was looked up to.

Egotist, thy name is Dr. Noah Bishop.

"Oh, geez. You're one of *those*." Ella crossed the room to stand by the front window. Then she rubbed her arms and moved closer to the woodstove.

"One of *whats*?" He had to ask even though he was afraid he knew.

"One of those doctors who consider themselves godlike because they have skill superior to their peers."

Bingo. The accuracy of her barb cut open his chest, just over his heart. There was no defense against that.

"You know..." Ella flinched and then posed with her hands on her hips. "Sometimes Penny wants ice cream. She'll stand in the middle of the kitchen and scream, her entire body rigid because I've opened the freezer and she's seen the container."

"What a little angel," Noah murmured.

Ella went to sit next to her daughter and Woof on the couch. "And I'll try everything to distract her, including offering her a small cup of yogurt."

"Ice cream," Penny murmured, her sleepy eyes searching for the treat.

Noah made himself stare at his wounded hand. "You're saying I have the emotional maturity of a two-year-old." Good things. These were all good things. He wanted the intense glances they'd exchanged to end, the feeling of connection and attraction to go away. He wanted to be the useless, lonely beast.

"The world seems perfect when you eat ice cream, but it doesn't last. Nothing ever lasts." Ella rubbed her arms again.

He walked over, took the yellow-and-brown afghan Odette had crocheted from the back of the recliner and wrapped it around Ella.

Ella thanked him and pulled it tight across her shoulders. She was solid, independent, pragmatic. After every emotional blow, she'd pulled herself up and gone on with life.

It was shaming, really, to stand and face her when he was, by turn, a coward, like Woof.

"Think about it," she said in a quiet voice. "You can't trust ice cream to be there every day."

"Ella." It was the first time he'd said her name out loud.

She raised those blue eyes to his face. There was wariness in her gaze, but also something else. A feeling he couldn't quite name.

"Ella," he said again, relishing her name on his lips. "Why do you have ice cream in your freezer, if you won't let Penny have some?"

Ella brushed a stray curl from Penny's forehead. "She gets ice cream plenty of times, but she has to learn she can't always get what she wants."

Noah nodded.

That was a lesson they'd both learned the hard way.

CHAPTER SEVEN

TWO HOURS HAD passed since Ella had dumped her past in Noah's lap.

She'd let her curiosity about Noah get the best of her, let his obstinance and padlocked secrets pry open the door to her past. She hadn't wanted his sympathy any more than he'd wanted hers. Now they were both embarrassed and tight-lipped. There were at least twelve more hours until daybreak. And what if the storm hadn't passed by then?

Look at the bright side, Ella. Concierge doctor care for Penny.

That didn't remove the sting of confession. They'd been cordial through dinner—a tray of lasagna and bacon-roasted brussels sprouts, both defrosted—but things were uneasy between them. She missed Noah's teasing. She missed his bravado. She missed more warmth. A woodstove in the middle of the cabin was the only heat source.

Both Laurel and Sophie sent texts asking how Penny was doing. Shane sent a message asking for pictures of the cabin. Ella didn't want to take pictures in front of Noah, but she didn't want to sneak around behind his back, either. When she didn't immediately reply to Shane's text, he sent another. She'd be getting texts all night if she didn't do something.

Luckily, Noah went into the bathroom, giving Ella the opportunity to take a few photos with her phone. The cabin was a basic rectangle. Exam room in the back corner with a small desk and storage cabinets. The kitchen was located in the opposite corner. A ladder led to a sleeping loft. Everything was outdated—Formica countertops and bland light fixtures. But it had big windows on the front and sides that would let in plenty of natural light. If there'd been any light outside.

Ella sent Shane the photos.

Shane's response? *Market value?*

Did the man have nothing else to do but hound her for information?

Dutifully, she tugged a copy of the thin real-estate pamphlet from her diaper bag. She'd picked it up in the Bent Nickel to reference what other properties were selling for. Not that there were many old cabins in remote mountain towns for sale to pull as comps.

"How big is this cabin?" she asked when Noah came out and found her pacing the length of one wall. "Twenty-eight by twenty-eight?"

He looked at her crosswise. "Is this part of your inventory?"

She nodded.

Noah's eyebrows lowered. "I feel like the rug is about to be yanked out from under my bare-naked butt."

"Why?"

"I live here, for one." He held up his gloved hand. "And where else can I practice with this? You're going to give me more than thirty days' notice before you evict me, aren't you?"

"Calm down." Ella could relate to the discombobulating feeling uncertainty could bring, but she had to put Penny's needs—and the family's—first. "I don't know what's going to happen to this town at the end of the year. None of us do. The family is divided." Was that saying too much?

"And waiting on your work to make a decision?"

She nodded.

He stroked his beard, considering her. "I can help with that."

"How?" That was a big, suspicious "how."

"I've been snowshoeing. It's a great way to get around town."

Ella experienced a burst of fear that froze a trail from her head to her toes. She'd never gone snowshoeing and didn't trust herself not to fall into the snow again. "May I remind you this town is two thousand acres of land? Walking will take forever." She moved closer to the woodstove.

"Snowshoes are more efficient than you waiting for the snow to melt." He read her like a much-loved book, because she'd been wondering when the snow would disappear. "I'll be there if you get into trouble."

He'd be trouble.

"I'm not going to fall down another snowy slope." A meager promise, one she couldn't uphold.

Noah studied her in that way of his, the one that made her feel she had a mysterious illness he was trying to diagnose. "You've never experienced the great snowy out-of-doors, have you?"

"I live in Philly." She sniffed, rubbing her arms. "It snows. A lot."

"Not as much as here. Let me rephrase. Have you ever gone skiing or snowboarding?"

Ella shook her head.

"Snowshoeing isn't hard for a woman who clawed her way up a snowy slope." And there it was. The first grin since he'd flashed his scars.

It warmed Ella back up.

And then he had to ruin things when he added, "Mitch has a snowmobile we can use, too."

She flushed cold again. "This is where I admit I drive like a sedate grandma and hate roller coasters." At least roller coasters had rails. Snowmobiles sounded scary. She glanced at Penny, asleep on the couch, unaware that fate could take her mother from her in a moment's notice. "Snowmobiles are out."

Noah came to stand next to Ella, so close their arms almost touched. He pretended to be warming his hands—his gloved hands—but he was watching her out of the corner of his eye. "What happened to curiosity and the cat?"

"Snow is wet and cold." A huff worthy of

Gabby was in order. "I think that answers any question about cats you might have."

He stroked his beard, almost smiling. "How many properties do you need to see?"

"More than fifty." A daunting amount. Ella turned her back on the stove. "Do you think people will let me in their homes? Maybe Mitch could notify them I'm coming."

"I'd recommend the element of surprise." Noah turned with her, gaze intent upon her face.

Did he just sneak a peek at my lips?

Ella completed the circuit and faced the woodstove once more.

Noah followed her lead with a sigh. "Weather permitting, you could see what? Four properties outside the town proper a day? Maybe five depending upon snow conditions?"

Ten days. "You're depressing me." By the time she returned to Philadelphia she'd be rushing to pack her things and find a place to live.

"I'm offering options." Noah went into the kitchen and took a beer from the fridge. He opened it and leaned against the counter to drink. He had the lean body of an athlete.

Not that I care.

Ella tore away her gaze and checked on Penny, but her little darling was sleeping propped up on the couch pillows, exhausted from her day of coughing. Ella wandered around the small living room, wondering what people would think of her coming into their homes. She didn't want to be nosy, but it was a sure thing she'd look at their family photos when she was in their houses. Speaking of which...

Ella picked up a framed photo of Noah with three other people from the end table. "Is this your family?"

Noah glanced over to her. "Those are the Bishops." He took a sip of his beer, eyebrows on ground patrol. "My parents and my younger sister."

She'd been staring at the picture, but the details of what she'd been looking at finally sunk in. "You're all wearing stethoscopes. Are you... Are you all doctors?"

"It's kind of a Bishop tradition." There was an unexpected chill in his words. "A cliché, I know. Some men dream of producing athletes and some mini-mes in scrubs."

"Aren't people supposed to want a child as

an expression of their love and desire for family?" That was what Penny was for Ella.

Noah shrugged. Obviously, she'd come across another roadblock.

Ella decided to let it go. "No wonder you always wanted to be a surgeon." And no wonder he was taking his loss of career so hard. "What did your mom have to say about your accident?" And about him not going through physical therapy.

"I thought we were done being curious about each other." Noah crossed his arms, giving her a look that dared her to reopen the doors to their pasts.

"We didn't make a formal agreement of it," Ella mumbled. She brushed a finger down the photo frame. "I've always envied people their families. The Monroes were just the family I dreamed of having. Large. Supportive. At least they were until…" He didn't need to know how small Ian had made her feel.

Noah didn't pry. At least, not about her dangling sentence. "How did an orphaned daughter of a waitress marry into the wealthy Monroes?"

"How else?" She shrugged, setting the picture back. "I fell in love. It was one of those surreal moments. Our eyes met, and then I couldn't seem to look away because I knew deep down that he could be important to me." She didn't add she'd felt a similar shock when her gaze connected with Noah's. Whereas she'd felt comfortable immediately with Bryce, what she felt around Noah was more unsettling. It couldn't be love. "Thank you for dinner. And for doing the dishes." A treat for a single mother.

Noah hung a dish towel from the stove handle. "Don't tell Ivy, but I prefer my cooking to a lot of the things she makes."

"My lips are sealed." Ella smiled at him, daring the feeling of attraction to rise again. Which it did, forcing her to stare into Woof's worshipful eyes. "Did you ever figure out what was wrong with Woof's leg?"

"He needs surgery."

"And you can't…" She gestured toward his hand.

"No!" He scowled, curling his fingers into loose fists, at least on his right hand. "I can't grip anything for long, much less a scalpel. And the stress of holding something causes my fingers to convulse."

He did have some nasty-looking scars, just

not as nasty as he seemed to think. "Therapy wouldn't help?"

His scowl turned thunderous.

"I was just channeling your mother." Ella picked up the framed photo and turned it his way. "I bet she told you not to give up." His mother had a no-nonsense air about her.

Noah stalked over, took the picture and shoved it into the end table's drawer. "Next topic."

Was there a next topic? Her brain fumbled about as unsteadily as her gaze, which bounced from Noah to the kitchen.

The kitchen. Where Noah kept his food.

"When I'm able," Ella said firmly, "I'm going to replace the food we ate in your cupboard in case it's a long winter."

"I don't need it." He walked to the kitchen and opened a cupboard to show her. It was filled with dry goods and cans of food.

She followed him and poked around, lifting the lid on the deep freezer. "You, my friend, are Roy. He claims to have stocked up for the long haul, too."

"He and Mackenzie, who has the store, advised me, but I have to admit I thought they were being overly dramatic back in July." He tugged at the hem of his gloves, as if afraid she'd see something she shouldn't.

"Don't do that." She gave a half-hearted swat at the hand doing the tugging. "Let me see your hand again." When he didn't immediately comply, she held out her palm. "Come on. I'm feeling like we're dancing on a line between… *friendship*—"

"That's not the line we're dancing across," Noah murmured, looking at her lips.

"—and you shoving me out the door as soon as it's light tomorrow." Ella might have forgotten to breathe. A kiss? How she missed that.

She drew a much-needed breath.

There will be no kisses.

"I guess you're not going to give up until I show you again." Noah stripped the glove off his hand and held it out to her. "I should charge you admission."

"Stop it." She looked at his flesh. She guessed a craftsman like himself hadn't closed him up. Even Odette, rumored to have mad skills in the sewing department, could have done a better job. The scars were deep and jagged, both, she suspected, from the original wound and from the stitches. "You're lucky to have a hand, much less one in such good condition."

"Will the compliments never end," he said.

"Never." She traced the scar on his index finger with her index finger.

He sucked in a sharp breath and turned his hand over so he could curl his fingers gently around hers. "How can you not be sickened by me?"

"Me," not "my hand."

Noah was putting too much importance on what was a small part of him.

"What kind of person would I be if I was sickened?" She frowned, slipping her hand free and returning to her daughter. "The gloves give you a mystique, but I think I prefer you like this, with all your flaws out in the open."

Woof thumped his tail in agreement.

"You don't have to put the gloves back on." She lifted Penny into her lap without waking her, making enough room for them both on the couch. "I see a television in the corner and I'd really like to watch some mindless show that makes me forget I've been such a bad guest with all my *prying*."

"Good idea." Noah slid his hand back in the glove, earning a frown from Ella. "Do you like football? Hopefully, the storm hasn't knocked out the satellite feed."

"I prefer baseball or a sitcom. Football always puts me to sleep."

"Football it is."

"I DIDN'T MEAN to wake you," Ella whispered, having turned on the shower and closed the bathroom door, presumably to give Penny a steam treatment.

The little girl was propped between two pillows, snoring softly.

"Did I sleep?" Noah pried open his eyes, having spent the night on the recliner with Woof, since the dog had whined nonstop from the moment Noah climbed into the loft—something that was beginning to feel like routine, but not something he was willing to admit. "My body feels like I've been mummified."

Noah hadn't shifted near as much as Ella, who'd tossed and turned. He sat up and slid Woof to the floor quietly, trying not to wake his patient.

The sun was making a weak showing through the window. Snow blanketed everything and spilled through the porch railing onto the deck with the postcard-perfect brilliance he was coming to associate with winter in Second Chance. Inside, the world was anything but idyllic, if only because Ella and her probing questions were still here.

"You slept like the dead," Ella said softly, filling the coffeepot. Sunlight streamed through the front window, brightening her already bright hair and illuminating her subtle freckles. "Which annoyed me since I had trouble trying to get comfortable."

"I told you the couch was lumpy." Noah worked the kinks out of his back. "If we do this again, I'll take Penny and you take the dog."

Her blue eyes flew to his and for a moment all Noah could think about was nights spent with Ella in his arms and mornings greeted with sweet kisses.

What was he thinking? Beauty only fell for the Beast in fairy tales.

Mood sour, he turned to the door and discovered that Woof hadn't slept the night through. Noah picked up the shredded remains of Ella's leather snow boot. "This complicates things." He held it up for Ella to see.

"What?" She hurried to his side. "How am I supposed to get back to the inn without a boot?"

"As your doctor—"

She made an impatient noise.

"—I'd recommend you don't attempt the trip barefoot." A grin tugged at his jaw. "But if you did, it would be a great example for Penny later in life. You could honestly tell her you once walked a hundred yards in ten feet of snow... *barefoot.*"

She turned away, but not before he saw the beginnings of her smile. "I hate you right now."

Noah told Woof he was a bad dog before tossing the remains of Ella's boot in the trash. "I hate to break this to you, boy, but you're going to have to go outside." He put on a jacket and boots. "You're just lucky we're not making you stay outside in time-*out.*"

"You're going out, too?" Ella asked between angry huffs, fiddling with the coffeepot controls.

"Woof likes the company. If I don't go out with him, he doesn't go."

Ella chuckled softly, the sound reaching into Noah's chest and giving his sour mood a good dose of sweetness, one he ignored.

"You pretend to be coldhearted, Noah, but you're as caring as a kindergarten teacher."

What?

A boundary had been breached. Noah growled. It wasn't as if Woof was going to do it.

Ella wasn't fazed. In fact, she smiled. "By the way, if you go gloveless, it would better support your villainous image."

Not since he'd lived at home with his sister had anyone teased him like she did.

Noah took the dog to the porch, and then shoveled a path down the steps, wondering how long it would take him to shovel his way to the road so Ella could go back where she belonged. While he waited for the dog to do his business, he extended and flexed his fingers, testing the elasticity of his scars. For once, he didn't let the weakness of tissue deter him from trying.

"But what's the point?" he said to Woof when the dog bounded up the steps, dusted in snow.

Woof had no answer. He used Noah as a drying towel, rubbing the length of his body against Noah's jeans to remove the snow, and Noah's dark mood along with it.

Chuckling, Noah returned to the warm cabin and the welcome smell of coffee brewing. "It must have dumped six feet last night."

"On top of the three we had the other day.

Yikes." She was holding Penny and staring at the trim above the door. "Is that a date?"

He brushed off the layer of dust. "Eighteen ninety-five, Lee." Carved into the wood above the door.

"Do you think that's when it was built and the family name?"

Noah shrugged. "Does it matter?"

"I just didn't think any of these cabins were that old. This one seems so well-preserved."

"They told me Roy rechinked it before I got here."

The coffeemaker spit the last drops of caffeine into the pot with a gasp.

"At last." Ella put down Penny and hurried over to the kitchen. "Do you want some?"

"Mom!" Penny wailed in a hoarse, snot-filled voice from the floor.

Ella walked backward. "You know Mom needs her morning coffee, Pen." Her tone was chipper. "It's my one thing."

"Mo-om!" Penny stood in rigid indignation, breathing raggedly, green eyes filling with tears, as upset as if she'd been denied ice cream.

Instinctively, Noah bent to pick her up, sliding his hands under her arms. A few feet above the floor, his right grip gave way and he nearly dropped her. He managed to swing Penny to his hip using his wrist, drawing her close, more to reassure himself than her that she was safe.

Useless, useless hand.

Noah bit back a string of curses.

He and Penny exchanged wide-eyed stares.

Now what?

If she'd been older, she might have tattled on him. If he'd been wiser, he might have put her back down. As it was, neither one of them said or did a thing. They both turned to Ella, who'd poured steaming coffee into mugs and was searching the fridge for milk.

Only when she'd doctored her coffee to her liking and had cradled her mug with both hands did she turn to them, smiling warmly at the pair. "When do you think we can get out of your hair? I'd hate to eat all your frozen lasagna and drink all your coffee."

Noah opened his mouth to speak when three things silenced him.

Penny snuggled against Noah's neck with a snot-filled sigh, probably upset that she'd had to settle for her doctor's arms rather than her mother's.

Woof sat on his foot and leaned against his leg with a put-out sigh, probably upset that he had to settle for Noah's foot, not his lap.

Taking them in, Ella's expression softened, making Noah want to sigh.

Time crawled to a halt. Noah shifted to a different dimension, one where he was a much-loved family man with a wife who looked past all his flaws, not just the hideous one at the end of his arm. She wasn't fazed by his temper, his pessimism or his snark.

And then life blinked, rebooting the clock.

Penny sneezed and rubbed her nose clean on his T-shirt. Her sneeze startled Woof—tough canine that he was—off Noah's foot. The dog scrambled and shifted his leg in a way that hurt. He yelped. The yelp and sneeze startled Noah, and he tightened his grip on Penny, who pushed against his chest and tested the limits of his injured hand wrapped around her hip.

Ella was there before anything bad happened, soothing the dog, the child and Noah. She took back Penny, leaving Noah's arms feeling empty.

Sentimental mush, Dr. Bishop quipped, proverbial nose in the air.

"I think we all need breakfast," Ella said in a bright voice.

Dr. Bishop rolled his eyes. Noah's bad-tempered alter ego hadn't realized cynicism was no match for nothing-fazes-me Ella Monroe.

Noah didn't execute an eye roll. He moved past Ella to the refrigerator. "We are not having salad. Kibbles and waffles, coming right up."

Being painted with toddler mucus has softened you.

Ella came to stand next to Noah, doing a good one-armed job of getting Penny a glass of water and then encouraging her to drink. "Kibbles and waffles. That sounds tasty."

"To Woof." Noah removed a box of waffles from the freezer. "Get out of my kitchen."

"I can help. You wouldn't let me last night."

Helping, he acknowledged, was what drove Ella. Helping made her feel a connection and one of the family, just like her curiosity. "Get out of my kitchen."

"Regardless, you're spoiling us." She carried her child and her coffee and went to sit in his recliner. "And we're eating all your food."

"Not hardly." He put waffles in the toaster.

"When do you think we can get out of here?" she asked again.

Noah's jaw ticked. "I'm beginning to think you can't wait to leave." All her talk about his scars making no difference must have been just that—talk.

"You know... It's just... I need..."

"What?" Why wouldn't she just spit it out?

Ella's voice dropped to a low, scratchy whisper. "I need to go because there's this unnamed thing between us and it makes me uncomfortable."

Wasn't that just like Ella to lay all her cards on the table?

"Really?" Noah's chest swelled with masculine pride.

"But don't worry. I'm not going to do anything about it. I've got enough problems on my plate."

He was a problem? "As soon as you see Roy cross the road you can go. He's the bellwether of safe road conditions." Noah poured kibbles in the dog's bowl. "But if it snows again, you're stuck here."

With the Beast.

Out of the corner of his eye, he saw fresh flakes falling.

Ella's brow wrinkled. "What if I can't get out until tomorrow? Or the next day?"

"Would that be so bad?" Dr. Bishop huffed in disgust. "What are you? Afraid you can't keep your hands off me?"

Her silence spoke volumes.

CHAPTER EIGHT

"ROY'S OUTSIDE!" ELLA hurried to put on her jacket and Noah's boots, not fastening either.

It was almost lunchtime. Maybe she'd be able to gain some breathing room from Dr. Gorgeous, after all. She'd been cooped up with him so long, she was starting to imagine a look of interest in his eyes—all the time.

"Did Roy have a shovel in hand or his snowshoes?" Noah asked. He'd been holding a book, pretending to read while Penny sat on the floor and watched a child's program on TV.

"I didn't see." She'd been moving too fast. "Penny, I'll be right back." Ella burst onto the porch and was immediately disappointed.

It was snowing outside, and Roy didn't have a shovel. He stood on his narrow porch on the north side of his cabin smoking a cigar.

Maybe he was going to have a smoke before he dug his way across the road.

"Roy! Roy!" Ella waved, trying to be seen through the curtain of snow.

"Hey, there. I heard you took shelter with Doc." Roy wore blue coveralls and a jean jacket. He must have been freezing, but he took slow puffs from his cigar. "Nasty storm we had last night. This one is a baby storm by comparison."

Ella didn't care about the past. It was the future she was interested in. "Are you going to shovel your way across the road?"

"Nah. Not today." *Puff, puff.* "Not with the snow coming down."

"But—"

"Be patient, Ms. Monroe." Roy saluted her with his cigar. "We're getting snowshoe weather."

Noah stepped on the porch next to Ella, wearing a pair of sneakers and a black hooded sweatshirt. "Hey, Roy, do you have an extra pair of snowshoes Ella can borrow?"

"My daughter left a pair here. I'll bring them over tomorrow as soon as the snow stops." He stubbed his cigar out on the snowy porch railing and went back inside his cabin.

Ella's shoulders drooped. "Why can't he walk over here in his snowshoes, give me his daughter's pair and then I'll walk back to the inn?"

"Because it's dangerous. He could slip and fall." Noah tugged the ends of Ella's jacket closed and then rubbed her arms. "Roy may have game, but he's in his sixties. Don't ask him to go outside when it isn't life-threatening."

Ella hadn't realized she was cold until Noah touched her. He had that look in his eye again. The kissing look. She shivered, but not from the cold.

"I can make it to Roy's for the snowshoes," she blurted. It was all downhill.

"And then you'd have to come back here and take Penny. Why risk it?"

She stared up at him, at electric-blue eyes that were no longer haunted, at a mouth that looked ready to smile.

"Why?" *Because I'm falling for you.*

Ella gulped.

How could this be? She hadn't been looking for a man. Or love, for that matter.

Don't jump the gun again.

She gazed into Noah's eyes. He might want people to think he was uncaring, scaring them off with that haunted expression, but he had a big warm heart if a woman was willing to dig for it.

"You're pale." Noah hustled her back inside and removed her jacket. "Are you okay?"

"No."

Here she'd been telling herself that love at first sight happened once in a lifetime. And then she'd come to Second Chance and fallen for a stranger in less than a week.

Not that what she felt toward Noah was love, but it was more than a physical attraction. They were on the same wavelength.

I was on the same wavelength with Bryce. So, this must be love, too.

"No," Ella said again, denying it. She'd listened to the Monroes tell Bryce over and over that love at first sight didn't exist. This feeling couldn't be love.

But if it isn't... Then what I had with Bryce wasn't...

Her foundation was shifting. Ella needed to sit down. She sank on the recliner and put her head in her hands.

If what she'd had with Bryce had been insta-lust, not insta-love, then their marriage had been a sham.

"No," she said a third time, loud enough that Penny turned around to look at her. Ella sat up.

Noah removed a glove and placed his palm on her forehead.

Ella stared at him, but her mind's eye saw Bryce and his kind, loving expression. She and Bryce had been in love. They'd been in love from the start. She refused to doubt that.

Except...

"You need to rest and hydrate," Noah said. "I'll get you some water. You kick out the footrest and try to relax."

Ella did as the doctor ordered. She reached for the footrest handle, trying to ease back in the chair.

But there was nothing easy about the recliner. It jolted backward and the back fell completely off.

Ella stared at the ceiling behind her. And then at the topsy-turvy image of Noah hurrying to her rescue. "You have cobwebs in the corner."

"Who cares?" Noah helped her upright, taking her arm and guiding her to the couch. "Are you hurt?"

"The good news is, I didn't use one of my nine lives breaking your chair." But it wasn't exactly Ella's day, either. "Has the chair ever collapsed before? Or does it have something against me?"

"Never. It's a well-behaved chair." His fingers clinically probed the back of her head, her neck, her shoulders. And then their eyes connected, and his touch became anything but clinical—without ever leaving her shoulders.

"I'm good," she croaked, returning his hands to his space.

Noah blinked, and then left her, returning with a small toolbox. He turned the chair on its side, and poked around underneath. "I'm sure it's fixable."

Regardless, Ella wasn't trusting it again.

Woof sniffed the chair suspiciously while Penny coughed, squatted by the toolbox and then picked up a small wrench. She handed it to Noah.

"We make a good team." He ruffled Penny's curls.

Ella's heart melted. Noah was always so patient with her, even when Penny used him as a living tissue.

This isn't helping.

Ella stood and paced, making a list of all the ways Noah wasn't right for her and Penny, starting with he hadn't come to grips with his injury and ending with…

That one thing was her entire list.

She groaned.

"Are you sure you're okay?" Noah gave her the doc's clinical once-over. "Did you hit your head?"

"No." But that didn't mean she wasn't losing control of the situation.

He stripped off his gloves and reached into the guts of the chair once more.

Penny rummaged in the toolbox a few minutes more while Noah poked around beneath the back skirt of the recliner. Whatever he was doing made the chair innards clank.

"Mom." Penny beckoned. "Sit." She patted the carpet next to her, coughing briefly, although it was a drier cough than yesterday.

"Front-row seats." Ella did as asked, sitting on her knees on the thick carpet.

The cabin had hardwood floors. The gray-brown carpet was only in front of the chair and sofa.

"Kiss." Penny patted her cheek.

Ella may have been confused about her feelings toward Noah, but she had no doubt she loved

Penny to the moon and back. She kissed Penny's cheek. Her daughter returned the gesture.

"Kiss Woof." Penny opened her arms toward the dog.

Woof padded over to lick her face.

Penny giggled and kissed the side of the dog's big head. "Wuv Woof." She coughed some more.

Penny had a big heart for such a little girl.

But it was easy to love Woof. Ella couldn't imagine anyone dumping the big sweetheart in the middle of the road.

If you can fall for a dog in a day...

Ella's gaze drifted to Noah's broad shoulders.

"Got it." Noah rose to his knees and righted the chair. "The eyebolt on the stabilizer bar slipped out of its socket."

"Kiss No." Penny patted her cheek nearest Noah. "Kiss."

Noah gave Ella a questioning look.

"It's a game she plays sometimes," Ella explained. "Passing out kisses and receiving some, too."

Noah sat back on his knees and pecked Penny's cheek, receiving a kiss in return.

"Penny, you're going to be so much trouble when you turn sixteen."

"How can you say that?" But Ella smiled because Noah's hand was bare and he didn't seem to notice.

"Look at the signs." Noah tsked. "She's two and she plays a kissing game."

"Kiss. Kiss. Kiss." Penny passed out another round of smooches, much to Woof's delight and Noah's, too, if his bearded grin was any indication.

The dog rolled over so Penny could pat his tummy.

"Kiss Woof, Mom." Penny tugged Ella's hand toward the dog. She coughed, but only once.

Ella made a big show of kissing the dog's soft ear. Woof thumped his tail.

"Kiss Woof, No." Penny tugged Noah's hand toward the dog.

"How long does this game last?" Noah grumbled.

It was Ella's turn to tsk. "How hard is it to humor a child?"

With a belabored sigh, Noah kissed the top of Woof's front paw.

Penny made the rounds again, doling out

kisses to Ella, Woof and Noah. And then she latched onto Ella's hand once more. "Kiss No, Mom."

Ella's gaze flew to Noah's. A slow grin appeared on that darkly bearded face.

"Kiss. Kiss. Kiss." Penny grabbed Noah's hand and tugged him toward Ella.

Ella gulped. "We don't—"

"How hard is it to humor a child?" Noah's grin turned wicked as he leaned forward, across the dog, past Penny and within lip-locking distance of Ella's mouth. When she hesitated, he added in a gruff voice, "I may have scars, but I don't bite."

Knowing him, if she didn't kiss him, he'd blame his scars for scaring her away. She had news for him. His scars didn't bother her.

Ella closed the distance between them and touched her lips to his, intending to touch-and-go.

Noah had a different agenda.

His hand curled around her nape, holding her near. He turned the kiss from innocent to incendiary on a breath—his, because she wasn't breathing. The ever-present chill in the cabin dissipated, melting beneath the heat of his kiss.

Had she thought she could just talk to him all day? She should make room for kissing on that agenda.

"No, Mom." Penny's small hand pressed against Ella's shoulder, separating her from Noah. "No more kisses." A fit of coughing ensued.

Ella sat back and stared at Noah, who had a big, satisfied smile on his face. Without thinking, she smiled back.

She needed to be thinking.

Ella got up, forcing her lips down. "I need to get back to the inn."

Noah got to his feet, tugging on his gloves and scowling. "Do I scare you?"

"Yes." She had no qualms admitting it.

A NOISE AND a shadow startled Shane. He nearly poured coffee on his fingers instead of into his cup.

"Who are you and how did you get in here?" he demanded of the shadowy figure in the inn's downstairs hallway.

Sophie and Laurel were upstairs, as was Mitch. Gabby didn't skulk. She bounced.

"It's Mackenzie." The lithe brunette who ran the general store and gas station stood in blue jeans and a cheerful orange turtleneck sweater.

"I don't suppose you'd believe there are secret tunnels connecting the main buildings in town."

"Nope," Shane allowed, pulse returning to normal.

"And rightly so." She moved in to swipe a coffee cup. "I came out my service bay and dug my way to Mitch's kitchen door. It's only ten feet and protected by the eaves so the snow wasn't that deep."

"Why go to all that effort?"

"Because I saw Mitch upstairs making beds and he buys better coffee than I do." She poured herself a cup. "I hear you're a man down."

"What?"

"Ella and Penny are with Doc." Her hair was braided in neat pigtails, which, on first glance, made her look college age. "I guess that's a man and a half you're down. Why are you here, Mr. Monroe? I never did hear an explanation."

Shane's jaw ticked. If someone was honest with him, he had no qualms about being honest with them. But this woman had sneaked in the back door during a snowstorm. He moved to stand in front of the roaring fire. "Because we inherited the town."

"Let me rephrase." Mackenzie followed him, unperturbed by his ill humor. "Why are you here *now*? It's January. The snowbirds in town fly south after the Christmas holidays because no one wants to come up here in January—and often February, if I'm truthful—"

Which Shane hoped she was. No one had mentioned snowbirds to him.

"—because no one wants to get trapped. We usually get fifteen to twenty feet of snow these two months so if you live beyond this main drag, you might be snowed in for weeks." She looked at him expectantly, as if she'd given him information and now it was his turn.

He'd been focused on the snowbirds. And... Ah, yes. Somewhere in her diatribe was a question. "I'll admit we didn't do much pretrip planning." It'd been more of a whim. "Tell me about your snowbirds. Do you have a large retiree population?"

"Well..." She slurped her coffee. "There's Egbert. He runs the rental place up the road."

"Renting what exactly?"

"Snowmobiles. The meadow across the river is public land and perfectly flat. He rents inner tubes and fishing poles come spring and summer."

"But he's not here in winter to take advantage of the snowmobile season."

"He can go spend time with his grandkids rent-free in Houston, and with such a low lease…" She gave Shane a sideways glance. "Let's just say his overhead is very reasonable, so his hours of operation are loose."

Shane couldn't believe someone would pass up the opportunity to make money. But then again, he'd never had a one-dollar lease. "And there are others like this? People who run businesses but leave for part of the year?"

Mackenzie nodded. "We used to have a winter festival at the end of February, but no one's here to take advantage of the extra income visitors bring. Honestly, most of us struggled before your grandfather bought us all out, but some—like Egbert—used to be more invested in their businesses when their livelihoods depended upon it."

Shane's jaw ticked again. He didn't know who frustrated him more—his grandfather for being gullible or the snowbirds for their lack of drive. "What would it take to put on the winter festival this year? That would really put some juice back in this sleepy place." And make it more marketable for sale.

A heavy tread came down the stairs. "Mack. How nice of you to break into my home and steal my coffee." Mitch scowled, more toward Mackenzie than Shane.

"You know—" Mackenzie slurped her coffee "—I look the other way when you put your truck up on my garage lift without asking."

"You rarely use the lift." Mitch opened the door to his living quarters. "Shane, you were talking nostalgia, like the movies my mom used to watch with Judy Garland and Mickey Rooney, the ones where the kids were going to put on a show and save the town. Don't let me interrupt." He tromped off.

Shane hoped the *thwapping* noise was the door hitting him on the way out.

Mackenzie gave Shane a half smile. "He means well, but he prefers a sleepy town to strangers overtaking things because—"

"Mack! You left your wet snow gear all over my kitchen floor."

Mackenzie downed the rest of her coffee and hurried to clean up her mess.

But their conversation gave Shane ideas. He spent the rest of the afternoon searching for information regarding the town's winter festivals and wondering when the roads were going to be cleared.

"I…SCARE *YOU*?" Noah backed away from Ella, despite wanting to do the opposite. "I think it's the other way around."

She'd been gathering Penny's toys and things as if packing up to leave. She stopped and met his gaze squarely. "I've never frightened anyone in my life."

"I'm sure that's not true. You don't back down. And I'm quite good at getting people to keep their distance."

You used to be.

His gaze veered to the picture of his family. Ella must have taken it out of the end-table drawer. Noah had maintained a healthy distance from his family for years, unwilling to hear his father try to find ways to tell him how flawed he was. And that was before the accident.

Ella scoffed. "If you're trying to flatter me—"

He gave a shout of laughter that froze Penny and Woof. "You don't want my flattery." Suddenly, he was tired of feeling alone, of distance and separation. He inched closer, lowering his voice. "You want my kiss."

Her cheeks bloomed with color.

Noah reassured Penny with a tweak of her curls and Woof with a pat on the head. And then he fixed Ella with a look that wasn't filtered. "We can dance around this attraction all you want—"

"Yes, let's," she said too quickly.

"—but that won't change the fact that there's a spark between us."

She rolled her eyes. "So?"

"Exactly. So…" He pointed at his chest and then to her and back again.

"I'm not following."

"In the normal course of human events, when two people are attracted to each other they do something about it. They have dinner. They spend time together. They exchange a few kisses." He kneeled to Penny's level. "Don't you ever stop playing the kissing game, honey."

Ella was beside herself. "I thought you said the kissing game would make Penny a handful when she was a teenager!"

"Hey. If Penny doesn't stop, her game might encourage you to kiss me again." He grinned at Ella. He'd noticed his grin always got one in return.

"You're impossible." Ella stuffed toys in her

diaper bag, which held more items than Noah had imagined.

"I'm impossible? Because I want to kiss you again and you want to run away from—from…" He was very aware of a child at his feet. "The natural course of things?"

"I have to be logical. You live in the mountains of Idaho. I live in Philadelphia."

"For now. You should have added *for now*. You're here for at least another two weeks." Five cabin appraisals a day after the snow stopped. "We can play this out."

"To what purpose? I'm not moving here and you're not leaving."

Noah prided himself on his rational approach to life. Her arguments made sense. And yet, there was the easy rhythm to their banter and the sparks that flew from her touch. He should listen to reason, but he couldn't discount the feeling inside of him that wouldn't let him back away a safe distance, a persistent belief that a woman who didn't shy from wounds and prickly personalities like his was worth any price.

He glanced down at his gloved hand.

Impulsively, Noah jerked off his gloves and tossed them on the end table next to his family picture. He took Ella's cold hands in his. "Does this scare you?"

"No." Her body was still. Her eyes wide.

He hesitated, and then cupped her cheek in his injured hand. "Does this scare you?"

"No." Her response was barely more than a wisp of air.

"Does this?" He bent his head to kiss her cheek. "Or this?" He drew her close and kissed her properly—without dogs or toddlers between them. He kissed her tenderly. He kissed her deeply. And all the while he kept thinking: *Don't. Let. Go.*

"Kiss!" Penny scrambled to her feet and wrapped her arms around their legs. "Kiss me." She bobbed up and down in that awkward, endearing way toddlers had of showing enthusiasm without rhythm or grace.

Noah bent and scooped her up with his good arm, settling her on his hip, staying close to Ella.

Ella's cheeks were glowing bright pink. It made her hair seem yellower somehow.

"Kiss me," Noah said to Penny, touching his cheek with his disfigured fingers.

Penny was as unfazed by his scars as her mother. She kissed his cheek.

He kissed hers. "Now, kiss Mommy." Noah touched Ella's cheek lightly with his fingers.

Ella didn't flinch, either.

Penny obliged, happily doling out kisses.

Noah smiled. "And now—"

"It's time for lunch." Ella lifted Penny into her arms, still blushing.

"Coward," he accused, following Ella to the kitchen.

"Careful, Doc. I've got a strong sense of self-preservation. Any more threats of kisses, and I might steal your boots and use my jacket as a sled to get down to the road."

Noah leaned against the kitchen wall, enjoying the sight of Ella and Penny in his home, in his kitchen, sharing his space. "I wonder…"

"If I'd really do it?" She turned, blue eyes blazing.

"No," he said simply. "I wonder if you played the kissing game when you were a kid."

CHAPTER NINE

"IT STOPPED SNOWING!"

Ella made the joyous announcement when Noah stirred the morning after they'd kissed. She'd been tiptoeing around the cabin starting the shower and the coffeemaker. But the sun!

The sun bounced off pristine snow and leaped through the cabin windows with an energy Ella wasn't feeling. She was certain she hadn't slept a wink last night. Penny had woken early, her coughs not as wracking, unaffected by the bright morning and content to lie on the couch and talk quietly to Woof, who'd slid from Noah's lap to sit closer to Penny.

Ella had hoped the kiss yesterday would have cleared the air. It hadn't. After that kiss, she and Noah didn't talk, but they looked. They didn't touch, but they sighed with longing. They didn't kiss. They kept their distance. Or maybe all that detached mooning had been on

Ella's part. Noah had whistled while he cleaned the kitchen last night. *Whistled!*

"What a beautiful day," Ella said with forced cheer, taking a coffee mug from the cupboard.

"You say that like you can taste freedom." Noah tried to look wounded, but he just looked rumpled and cute, while Ella was convinced she looked as frumpy as she felt.

"In a few minutes, I'll be tasting coffee." The coffeemaker was heating up. Ella hoped that was the only heat exchange the cabin witnessed today. "Do you have shoes I can borrow so I can help you dig a path out of here?"

"Hiking boots and extra socks." He pointed to a pair of boots and thick socks near the door.

When had he put those there? She didn't remember them being there last night.

"But you won't be helping me clear a path." He got out of the recliner slowly. "I'll snowshoe to Roy's and then he and I will make a path to the coffee shop. If I know Mitch, he'll clear the sidewalk from the inn to the diner."

Both Noah and Woof shook out the kinks from a night spent in the recliner. Woof was more vigorous in his technique, but Noah got points in Ella's book for slow, languid movement. Plus, Noah still wasn't wearing his gloves.

The coffeemaker sputtered. Noah turned to look at Ella.

Why? Because she'd lost the thread of conversation. What had he been talking about?

He kept looking. She didn't look away.

This was where her brain should have been instructing her mouth on what words to say. But her brain was numbed by the snow-radiant sunshine and the man-hunk before her. And her mouth…

His gaze drifted to her lips. She felt dizzy.

Say something. Say something. Say something.

He kept looking. She couldn't look away.

She wanted his arms around her, if only to put a halt to the vertigo that was her tilting heart, and keep her on her feet. Only she feared she'd already fallen most of the way down. She feared she was falling under the spell of the attraction between them before she ever knew how he liked his eggs, how he spent the holidays, and what he was looking for when he trekked across the snow around Second Chance. Those were the kinds of things people said were important when you loved someone.

Her cheeks were heating. Her mouth was dry. And her lips seemed to be glued together.

She glanced at Penny. Her little girl's lips were wrinkled.

I need to put lip balm in the diaper bag.

She unstuck her lips and laughed, shaking her head.

Leave it to a single mom to break the mood with pragmatism.

Her feet pivoted. She reached for the coffee cup and the friend zone. "Do you want coffee? I can get you a cup. Or a shovel. I can help shovel. Just show me where you keep your equipment and I'll…"

Noah grinned, closing the distance between them like a cat who hadn't been fooled by a mouse trying to play dead. If she didn't move in the next ten seconds, he'd kiss her. She was certain of it. She should move. Seriously. Because she didn't want to kiss him… Er, him to kiss her.

Five.
Four.
Three.
Two.

"Here's your coffee." She thrust the coffee mug at him. "I always enjoy a cup in the morning, don't you?"

He looked down at her. He looked down at the mug. And then he leaned in…

Ella braced herself. She really didn't want that kiss, but if it was coming she'd take it like the trouper she was.

Noah reached past her for the coffeepot. "I do enjoy a cup in the morning. Just not an empty one." He filled the mug she'd given him and walked to the window, presumably to enjoy the view. "Say what you will about Second Chance, but the views are amazing."

Slug-brained Ella couldn't agree more.

Wake up, Ella. Single moms don't drool over their daughter's doctor.

Ella didn't move. Noah looked different this morning. Stronger. Taller. Prouder. She couldn't look away, certain this image was being implanted in her memory more permanently than if she'd taken a picture and put it in the slow scanner she had at home. At the Monroe home. Her temporary home.

Her father-in-law's stern face came to mind. *Ian…*

What would Ian say if he knew I'd been in

Second Chance a few days and was falling for a new man?

He'd wonder if Ella's love for Bryce had been real. He'd question the things he'd done to help her be a single, stay-at-home mother. He'd feel justified in kicking her out.

As would the rest of the Monroes.

Ella poured herself a cup of coffee.

"I appreciate the offer to help shovel snow," Noah said, the humor in his tone hard to miss. "But do you trust Penny in here unsupervised with Woof?" He pointed to the corner of the cabin.

Ella must have slept at some point last night because Woof had ripped up Ella's other boot.

At this point, she wouldn't trust the dog or her daughter unsupervised. "When you put it that way, it makes it easier to allow you to do all the manual labor."

And then the morning routine inserted itself. Sitting in the steamy bathroom with Penny. Waffles for breakfast. A brief shower.

Suddenly, Noah stood before her, brushing a lock of hair from her eyes. "I know you need space, but Second Chance is a small town and the three mountain passes are undoubtedly closed." He was taller than she was, broader than she was, more confident in what he wanted than she was. A trifecta of male magnetism.

"Noah—"

He pressed a finger to her lips. A scarred finger. "Let's not start the day with all the logical reasons why we should ignore this." He walked away, put on his snow gear, patted Woof and then kissed Penny. "Give that kiss to your mommy." He left Ella with a smoldering glance.

She collapsed on the couch, both disappointed and relieved he was gone, and was immediately joined by Penny and Woof, both of whom were eager to give her kisses.

TWO HOURS LATER, Ella and Penny were back at the inn.

She'd strapped modern snowshoes onto Noah's large boots and followed him across the packed path he, Roy and Mitch had made.

The process of creating a trail was intriguing. First Noah would make a square as a platform with his snowshoes. Then he'd walk sideways to tamp down the snow. He hadn't fallen. Not once. And he'd even carried Penny down the hill, across the highway and over the parking lot to the inn.

She'd returned his boots to him once she was inside the inn, but he'd refused to take the borrowed snowshoes and poles.

"We'll use them soon," he promised. "Besides, Roy said to keep them as long as you need them."

While he spoke, Ella's calves and hips were tightening. Someone needed to promote snowshoeing as the next big thing in fitness. Ella was sweaty. It didn't help that being with Noah was exhilarating and exhausting. Still, she had to thank him for his hospitality, so she said, "I may need to reconsider the snowmobile thing. I won't be able to walk up those stairs tomorrow."

"We'll see." He left.

She'd been half hoping he'd sweep her off her stocking feet and carry her upstairs.

The lobby was deserted. Ella took Penny by the hand and approached the stairs. "This will be good exercise for you since you had a ride home."

Penny coughed a few times, but gamely took the stairs.

Laurel, Sophie and the twins descended

upon them as Ella was unlocking the door to their room.

"Tell us everything," Sophie demanded, letting her boys climb on Ella's bed and bounce.

Ella plopped Penny on the bed in between two pillows. Her little munchkin giggled at the bouncy ride the twins gave her.

"You were snowed in with a hot doctor." Laurel sat on the edge of the bed. She wore slim-fitting overalls and an oatmeal-colored sweater that toned down her bright red hair. "Come on. Spill."

"Oh, that's not fair." Ella dug in her suitcase for a clean set of clothes and to hide her blush. "You were snowed in with a handsome innkeeper. You know, the one with kind eyes?"

"The one who's been hiding in his apartment downstairs?" Laurel murmured. Maybe it wasn't the oatmeal-colored sweater that muted her presence. She seemed washed out. "It's not like we shared living quarters."

"That Mitch is a cranky-pants." Sophie poked her head in Ella's bathroom and out again. She wore black leggings and a chunky fisherman's sweater. "Mitch shushed the boys yesterday afternoon like an old man whose nap was disturbed."

"Here we go again," Laurel murmured.

"You're going to defend him?" Sophie raised her voice, drawing sharp looks from her boys.

"The twins woke me up from my nap and I was upstairs. When I came down they were screaming like little heathens." Laurel smiled, but it was a wan smile. "At least, until Mitch told them to be quiet."

"Can I help it if my boys need an outlet?" Sophie adjusted her glasses, the better to glare at her cousin. "They're energetic."

"They never sit still," Laurel said. "That's for sure."

Sophie's eyes narrowed. "Just you wait until you have kids of your own. It's not so cut-and-dried."

"My kids will behave," Laurel insisted, in the tone naive people who didn't have kids spoke about overly energetic children.

"Are you saying I'm a bad mother?" Sophie drew herself up, looking like she was about to launch herself on Laurel. "How could you say my kids are heathens?"

"Don't say a word. There's no right answer here," Ella counseled Laurel. When Sophie gave her a defeated look, Ella added, "Laurel didn't mean it like that."

Laurel continued to be bounced on her corner of the mattress and raised her eyebrows as if to say, *The proof is bouncing on bedsprings*.

"I don't hear you defending my babies, Ella." Teary-eyed, Sophie swung her boys from the bed to the floor. "I thought single moms were supposed to stick together."

"I'm sorry. I'm tired." Ella stared longingly at her pile of clean clothes. "You know I love the boys." Sophie's ex-husband had spoiled the twins, doing no one any favors, especially now that he wanted little to do with them.

"You didn't say they weren't heathens," Sophie charged and hustled the boys to the open door. From the hallway, she shouted, "We're going to the sled hill, so the Hollywood princess can have quiet for her nap!" She slammed the door.

Penny's face crumbled. She began to cry. And then her sobs turned into coughs.

"Sophie," Ella called after her, but their footsteps echoed as if far away.

"What's wrong with Sophie?" Laurel picked up Penny, who was still coughing and crying at the same time. "Don't cry, little heathen."

"Well, you did call her boys heathens." Ella took Penny, resting her on her shoulder, and rubbed her back, not stopping even when the coughing subsided. "It's hurtful to a mom. We like to think our kids are perfect, not just in our eyes, but in the eyes of everyone else."

Laurel smirked. "Even when Sophie knew the twins were out of control?"

"*Especially* then." Ella kissed the top of Penny's head. "Meltdowns and wild behavior are going to happen, particularly when kids can't get outside to play. It's the people who say, *'That's all right,'* when you apologize for your child, who earn your unending gratitude."

"But the boys are just so...*destructive*." Laurel went to the window and stared at Sled Hill. "I can't trust them with anything."

"They'll grow out of it." As would Woof. "Try to be patient." Ella put down Penny. "I need to change and then we're going to lunch. Would you like to come along?"

"No. I'm still feeling funky." Lauren patted her abdomen.

Ella went into nurturer mode. "Have you been drinking enough water? You might have altitude sickness."

"I've got something." She sighed. "Besides, I should make my exit before I say something insensitive to you about Penny."

Penny lifted her head and gave Laurel a sad look as Bryce's cousin left the room.

"Laurel," Ella called, without hearing an answer. She looked at Penny. "Is everyone suffering from cabin fever?"

She hoped it wasn't that the family was disintegrating. If Grandpa Harlan had sent them here to map a new future and become closer knit, the exercise was turning into an epic fail.

On the way to lunch, Ella and Penny stopped at the general store. Ella needed another pair of snow boots if she was going to explore Second Chance's buildings.

"Can I help you, ladies?" Mackenzie glanced up from a large hardcover book she had open on the cashier counter.

"Snow boots?" Ella took in the cornucopia of items, from motor oil to fishing poles to candy and clothing.

"To your right." Mackenzie rested her blue-flannel-clad elbows on her book as she leaned forward. "I'm afraid I don't keep any quality boots. When travelers need boots, they want them cheap because they forgot theirs at home. When residents want boots, they order durable ones online."

"Can't rely on an online purchase when the

delivery truck can't get here." Ella wandered toward the section of snow gear.

While Ella poked her way through boot boxes, Penny grabbed a pink wool scarf and ran back and forth in the aisle with it trailing behind her like the tail of a kite.

If I buy that for her, am I spoiling her?

Penny giggled and coughed and giggled and coughed.

Ella decided then and there the wool scarf had found a new home.

The only pair of boots in Ella's size were neon pink with Velcro nylon tops. Woof had enjoyed expensive leather. If he got a chance at these boots—which he wouldn't—her thirty-dollar loss wouldn't sting as much as losing her good leather boots had.

"Did Doc talk to you while you were snowed in?" Mackenzie asked while ringing up the boots and scarf. The book she'd been reading was still open. It appeared to be a volume about restoring old truck engines. "Doc doesn't say more than two words to me—'yes, please' and 'no, thanks.'"

"We had long conversations." Ella was proud of that. "He has a great sense of humor."

"Really?" Mackenzie cut off the sales tags

from their items and the elastic joining Ella's pink boots together. "What did you talk about?"

Ella's mind went blank.

Oh, she could remember all of the kissing exchanges, but a verbal one?

"We, uh, talked about Penny's condition and—"

"No!" Penny pressed her face to the glass at the store's front door. "No-No-No." She turned to Ella and pointed outside.

Ella joined her at the door.

No, er, Noah and Woof were heading toward the highway and their cabin.

"It's all right, honey. We'll see them later." Much, much later if Ella had her way. After all, she had snowshoes and she knew how to use them.

"No!" Penny repeated his name and banged the door with her palms.

Noah turned and spotted them. He ambled over with the same deliberate steps he'd used to close the distance between them yesterday when he'd kissed her.

Ella's heart began to pound faster.

Penny danced. "No-No-No!" Happy cries this time.

Noah's eyes were bluer than the sky. Warmer,

too. He locked his gaze on Ella's until he stood just on the other side of the door.

"No!" Penny shouted, demanding his attention.

Woof licked the glass near Penny's face. Penny returned the sentiment, licking the glass in front of Woof's face.

Noah waved at Penny and then returned his focus to Ella, a question in his eyes: *Should I come in?*

Ella gave a little half shrug.

He quirked a dark eyebrow, which Ella interpreted as: *You don't know what you're missing.*

Ella crossed her arms, which would have communicated her dismissal if her gaze hadn't dipped—for one second—to his whisker-rimmed mouth.

He laughed, a booming sound that lightened every worry in Ella's chest. And then he turned and left.

"Bye, No," Penny said wistfully. "Bye, Woof."

Mackenzie grinned. "Now I know why you couldn't remember what you'd talked about. You guys have a language all your own. The language of *love.*"

"It's not like that," Ella protested, albeit

weakly as she watched Noah disappear into the snow hedge and cross the road.

But it could be, a small lonely voice in her head whispered. *It could be.*

THE CABIN WAS quiet when Noah and Woof returned. Noah fed wood to the stove and stared out at the beauty of the Colter Valley without seeing anything.

The cabin wasn't just quiet. It was empty.

There was no Ella filling it with her softly told truths and self-deprecating laughter. No Penny with her toothy grin and open affection. His refuge for the last six months didn't feel much like a refuge anymore. Not without those two.

Had they only been snowed in for a few days? It seemed much longer.

Where's your pride? Dr. Noah Bishop tried to gather his pride and rally. *Where's your independence?*

Independence? Noah laughed and removed his gloves. He flexed his right hand, willing it to close tight. When it didn't, Noah moved to the exam table, splaying his hand on top. He traced his scars with his left hand, much as Ella had done, except he applied pressure, trying to loosen the fascia and heat the muscles and tendons beneath. Everything was tight. It was painful.

And what was the point? He'd never pick up a scalpel again.

But I wouldn't drop Penny.

Noah pressed harder into the thin layer of tissue and groaned.

Woof came immediately to his side, his gaze sorrowful.

"That brace gives you a false sense of normalcy," Noah told him. "You'll need surgery to get better. But me? I need this." He pressed harder.

When he couldn't take it anymore and his hand ached like it was on fire, Noah glanced over to Odette's. It'd been days since he'd seen her.

She didn't answer her phone when he called, which wasn't unusual. Sometimes she got so caught up in her crafting she didn't communicate with anyone for days. Noah decided to snowshoe to her place. It was better than staring out his window hoping for a glimpse of Ella.

At Odette's cabin he removed his snowshoes, climbed her steps and rapped on the door, stamping his boots to rid himself of excess snow.

"Who is it?" Odette called primly.

Please. As if she hadn't seen Noah coming.

"Your doctor. Open up." The wind was chilling. More because he was sweating beneath his layers.

The old woman opened the door and he burst in, closing the door behind him.

Odette's coarse gray hair looked like she'd given herself a cut. It stuck out over her left eye and stood straight up in the back. But her skin color was good and she marched across the room to her chair by the window faster than Penny could have traveled the same distance.

Her cabin was awash in color. Quilts covered every surface—on the couch, on the chair, a quilted tablecloth, quilted kitchen towels, framed quilts on the walls. Fabric escaped from bags on the floor that surrounded her sewing machine station. Knitted scarves and caps hung from hooks on the wall.

Odette sat in her chair and picked up a pair of chunky knitting needles. The yarn she was using reminded Noah of sherbet. It was bright orange.

Despite being surrounded by color, the cabin was cold, which annoyed him. "Are you out of firewood?" Had she been so busy she hadn't noticed the chill?

"No. I'm just cheap." She wore several layers of socks and had a jacket on. "What's happened? Why are you here? Have I taken a turn for the worse?"

"I'm here to check on you because of the storm. And it's a good thing since you might freeze to death." He couldn't get her any more firewood. Her woodpile was buried under several feet of snow on the side of the cabin. But hers was a rare home in Second Chance, one with a treasured modern amenity—central heat. He turned her thermostat up a few degrees and when she grumbled, he pulled a twenty out of his wallet and slapped it on the table. "That's for the difference in your heating bill today. Now, do you have enough food?" Instead of waiting for an answer, he opened her pantry cupboard. She had more than enough canned food and more than enough sodium to clog her arteries.

"Doc, just because you like it hot doesn't mean you can come in here and jack up my thermostat." The cold hadn't diminished her cantankerous nature.

Noah removed his left glove and placed his palm on the back of her hand. "I know you aspire to be the ice queen, but if your hands are this cold when you're inside…"

She glared at him, knitting needles clacking discordantly. Knitting needles, not her small, sharp quilting needle.

Noah changed the course of his lecture. "If your hands are this cold you can't uphold the quality of your work."

She harrumphed. "Like you care?"

"Why are you so mad at the world?"

"Me?" She made a sound of disgust, plucked his empty glove from his right hand and shook it at him. *"We."*

"Odette—"

"We're the same, you and I." She set aside her knitting. "We're done. Worn out. Waiting for the inevitable end. Watching the world with envy."

He'd been about to refute Odette's claims when Ella's words came back to him: *And you're dying a slow death now.*

"I saw you kissing that Monroe girl." Odette's voice was as hard as the ice on the lake over the next rise. "Holding her baby like it was your own."

Anger welled inside him. Noah valued his privacy.

He snatched her binoculars from the window ledge and trained them on his window. Woof sat in a chair staring at Odette's cabin, one ear cocked up as if trying to listen to their conversation.

"In New York, they have a name for peepers like you." He set the binoculars on a table on the opposite wall, out of Odette's easy reach by the window.

She was unperturbed. "If you want privacy, hang some curtains."

"Maybe I will." He snatched back his glove and shoved his hand inside.

Odette grabbed his wrist above his right hand in the same place Ella had, only Odette squeezed. Hard. "Don't get attached to people. They always leave. And when they go, they take a piece of you with them until you feel like you're dying inside."

"I'm not going anywhere." But his words lacked conviction, because he thought of Ella and doubted she'd want to stay in town, so he added more firmly, "I *can't* go anywhere."

"It's a good place to die," Odette murmured as he stomped toward the door.

CHAPTER TEN

"I WANT TO go home," Sophie lamented a day after Ella had returned from Noah's. "I'm just an annoyance to everyone."

Meaning Laurel.

"You're not," Ella reassured Sophie, but she wasn't sure that was true.

Laurel hadn't emerged from her room at all this morning, claiming she still wasn't feeling well.

They sat in the corner on the floor of Sophie's room, backs against the wall, sharing a chocolate bar while the kids napped. They both wore leggings and sweaters, which seemed the only way to dress in Second Chance since leggings fit beneath snow pants.

Sophie unwrapped more of the candy bar. Her glasses had slipped to the tip of her nose, but she didn't seem to care. "Can't you just guess what this town is worth on the real-estate market?"

"No." Ella accepted a chocolate square. "Can't we just go home and come back when there's no snow on the ground?"

"No. Everyone either wants or needs this to happen now." Sophie popped another chocolate square in her mouth. "What about those snowshoes Roy gave you? The sun's out. The weather is clear. What's stopping you from using those?"

"Oh, not much. The freezing temperatures. My sore muscles. Fear of falling into a snowdrift never to be found again." Each admission pressed down on Ella's shoulders.

"Is that all?" Sophie chuckled softly. "That's nothing to a woman who's given birth." She nudged Ella's shoulder with her own. "Pretty please."

Add the pressure of family obligation to the weight on Ella's shoulders. But Sophie was right. She'd come here to get the assessments done. Now was as good a time as any to start. "You'll watch Penny?"

Sophie nodded. "Leave your door unlocked so I can get a diaper if she needs it."

Ella got to her feet, thinking about locked doors and keys. A few minutes later and she was skulking downstairs in snow pants, carrying her neon-pink boots and listening for any sound to indicate that Mitch or Gabby were in their living quarters.

All was quiet.

She opened the door to their home and scanned the pegboard keys, the ones without wooden keychains. Many had last names or names that made little sense to her, like Clapboard or Red Roof. And then she saw four keys on one ring with a large, curling paper tag—Fur Trading, Mercantile, Church, School. She snatched up the key ring with shaking hands, shoved it in her pocket and escaped to the porch.

It took Ella a couple of tries, but she managed to fasten the snowshoes on her boots. Knit cap, gloves, Penny's pink scarf wrapped around her neck, stadium jacket buttoned from her knees to her neck. She was ready to inspect buildings.

If only there wasn't a snowdrift higher than the porch in her way.

She moved to the edge of the porch, eyeing the drift that stretched to the mountain above her.

"Worst case," she muttered, "I slide to the bottom of Sled Hill."

That wasn't the worst case. But she clung to

the idea anyway as she stepped into the drift, sinking nearly to her knees.

"Make a square. Make a square," Ella muttered.

She stepped sideways, parallel to the road. Miraculously, she didn't fall or sink anymore. With mincing steps, she pointed her feet toward the mercantile. *"Now sidestep to the top."* That accomplished, she turned again, stepping up, sinking down, but always inching closer to the top of the drift, which was level with the porch eaves.

When she reached the top, she felt like shouting. For the sake of secrecy, she raised her arms to the sky in silent celebration, banged herself with the poles, wobbled and fell face first in powder.

Her scream was stifled by snow. And then she was practically swimming in the stuff, trying to get her feet back under her.

Once she was upright again, she glanced over at her snow staircase. Giving up would be so easy.

You, my girl, have gumption.

Grandpa Harlan may have thought so three years ago, but she'd lost it somewhere along the way. Maybe when she'd married Bryce and moved into the lap of luxury. Maybe after he'd died and she let Ian take care of everything while she grieved.

The Monroes could use a go-getter. Someone who'd climb any mountain for the good of the family. Ella needed gumption and the courage to face the world out on her own.

Ella looked at the snow-crusted bricks on the mercantile. They were big, uniquely shaped bricks that had been handmade a hundred or so years ago, not the oblong, straight-edged red ones. The mercantile had big front windows, like those in Noah's cabin, and a covered porch with a sloping roof. Who knew what materials had been used to build either of those. Who knew what kind of shape they were in. Doubt skittered along her spine.

You can tell if the roof leaks by looking underneath.

And it was only fifty feet away. A straight shot. An achievable goal.

Worst case, I can call for help if I get stuck.

A market assessment would give Ella something to sing about.

Are you ready, Hezzie?

A deep breath and a pledge to keep putting one foot in front of the other, and Ella was off.

Unlike the hike she'd made the day before, her route hadn't been packed down by Noah and Roy. Ella had to blaze her own path and occasionally sunk to her knees in the powder, which drove snow up her snow pants and then down into her inexpensive boots. Her long jacket hindered movement up the hill and soon became too warm for a sweaty, out-of-shape mom.

She reached the mercantile's front porch, also covered in snow—although only a few feet—and packed it down with her snowshoes, which she removed at the door. She paused to take in the view of Second Chance and the miles of uninterrupted snow on the valley floor. If the snow was plowed and the stores all open, the area would be a wonderland. It was probably just as charming when the snow melted.

All those stores... She counted at least twenty.

All her footprints... And she'd be making more trails to reach the other three buildings. There was no way Mitch wasn't going to find out she'd taken those keys.

She unlocked the door to the mercantile and peered inside, feeling a little creeped out.

The wood floors were in bad shape and in need of refinishing. The entire place was covered in cobwebs and smelled unfit for living in. Fluorescents had been installed overhead. Glass display cases lined one wall near built-in shelves, some still filled with dust-covered wares. There were bolts of cloth, a hat rack and an old dressmaker's mannequin in the far corner, surrounded by cardboard boxes. The ceiling didn't look to have any leaks, but Ella walked forward with careful steps anyway in case the floorboards were rotted, but they held firm beneath her feet.

If the floor gives way, there's no telling what's living underneath.

Maybe she'd find those missing documents about the purchase of this building. More likely, she'd find hibernating rodents.

Ella shivered and increased her pace. She found a small office and tiny restroom, both extremely outdated. She took pictures of everything with her phone and wrote pithy property descriptions in her head to make light of the creepiness: *High country fixer-upper with great views. Excellent business opportunity or convert to loftlike living.*

A mouse carcass rotted in the corner.

Perfect for the adventurous buyer.

"Where did you get those keys?"

Ella nearly jumped out of her snow boots. She whirled, expecting Mitch.

"The guilty always jump." Noah stood at the door, dark eyebrows raised on his handsome, bearded face. In his thick jacket, knit cap and snow pants, he looked sturdy and unshakable. The kind of man who'd sweep up varmint carcasses without complaint—although he might kibitz a little.

"The guilty always sneak up on you," Ella countered, as she marched toward him on shaky legs. "You scared me to death." She hadn't heard Noah approach or seen him snowshoeing her way when she'd been on the porch. And she wasn't going to admit his presence made the mercantile less spooky.

"Did you want me to knock?" Noah lowered his voice to a whisper. "Is that wise? Sound carries in the mountains and I get the feeling from the way you jumped that Mitch doesn't know you're here."

Ella wasn't buying his concern. Somehow he knew she'd "borrowed" Mitch's keys.

"Don't worry. My family owns this town." Best to keep that in mind. Maybe then her hands would stop trembling. She shoved them in her pockets and lifted her chin. "I can open up whatever door I want." As long as she stole the right key. "What are you doing here?"

"I saw you nosedive from my window." He tsked. "Remember me? My role in town is to keep people alive."

"I'm fine." She seemed to say that a lot when he was around.

"This time," Noah said with a reproachful look on his face. "Don't you know? Nobody snowshoes alone. That's a high-country rule."

Ella rolled her eyes. "I'm in town. Within shouting distance of everybody." As he'd been kind enough to point out.

"And the river is down, down, down that slope." Noah pointed. The river didn't seem an awfully long way away. "You know how a steep slope worked out for you last time."

Ella hadn't seen him for a day. A mere twenty-four hours. And yet, she'd missed their back-and-forth. She'd missed him.

Please don't tell him that.

Ella shooed him outside and was about to follow when she noticed a small plaque above the door. "Lee. Established 1905. Isn't Lee above your door, too?"

He nodded. "Maybe he built these buildings?"

"Maybe *she* owned these buildings?" The mercantile had items women might shop for. She imagined the ladies of Second Chance choosing dresses and matching hats there back in the day. Ella locked the door. "I don't suppose I can convince you to go home. I have work to do." And he was a distraction, plain and simple.

"Nope." His grin was infectious. "The buddy system is in effect."

"In that case, you go first and break that trail." Ella pointed to the fur-trading post and then strapped her snowshoes back on.

"Why not? It's a better workout than at a gym." He hadn't taken off his snowshoes and moved off the porch, being careful not to let his pole catch on the wood.

"Why do you only carry one pole?" She'd noticed yesterday that both he and Roy only employed one pole.

"Besides the obvious?" He held up his right hand and shrugged. "I can carry things like firewood or groceries."

Or little girls.

Penny. Her family. Their biases and expectations.

Bryce.

Ella hadn't moved, but she must have made a noise, because he glanced back at her, a trace of that distance in his eyes she'd seen on the first day they'd met. "What's wrong?"

"This." She gestured between them. "I can't do it."

Without taking a step, he moved miles away.

Ella's heart ached, but she had to say it. "I'm not ready."

His blue gaze took on a chill that had nothing to do with the wind blowing down the mountain.

"Not for hand-holding or kisses or…" She let the sentence go unfinished.

"The natural course of things," he finished for her sharply.

Ella nodded. "I fell in love too quickly with Bryce. Everyone questioned whether it was real."

"Everyone?" He'd been a successful surgeon. He knew she didn't have a family of her own. He could do the math himself, but he wanted her to say it.

"The Monroes," she whispered, wishing she

could fall into a snowdrift and disappear, because she'd never questioned her love for Bryce until Noah came into hers.

"And what did you think?" he demanded in a low, authoritative voice. "Because from what I know of love it's only the opinion of the two people involved that matters."

He was right, but that didn't mean she was ready to answer.

He turned his back on her and moved with athletic grace across the snow toward the large log cabin that had been the fur-trading post.

Ella assured herself she'd done the right thing by telling Noah where she was emotionally. She needed to protect her place in the Monroe family and not look like a woman who fell instantly for any man who paid her notice.

They reached the building quicker than if Ella had tracked through the snow by herself, possibly because Noah was angry and set a quick pace. More likely it was that he was better at walking in deep snow than she was.

He snapped off his snowshoes and leaned against the porch railing, staring out at the valley. His profile was as hard as the man himself, as unmoving as the thick, round logs forming the cabin.

"Your technique is improving," Noah said as she struggled with her straps. "Despite those hot-pink boots."

"Leave my boots alone." Ella was grateful he didn't resume their conversation about the natural course of things and true love. "They were the only pair Mackenzie carried in my size."

"They look like Woof treats."

"Woof has better taste than that." When Ella unlocked the door, she was unable to resist glancing over her shoulder at Noah. "Are we okay?"

His gaze swung to the inn across the road and then back to her. "We'll get there."

Not in the natural course of things.

The door swung inward on squeaky hinges. If she'd thought the mercantile was dark and creepy, the fur-trading post was positively hair-raising.

"Why aren't you going in?" Noah asked.

"I'm doing a mental recording of my first impression." Ella leaned back, bumping into his chest. "It's only got high tiny windows out here." She peered inside once more. "And two high tiny windows on each side wall."

Large cabin with lots of investment potential!

Noah brushed past Ella and into the darkness, although he couldn't go far. Someone had packed the building with stuff. "The windows are small enough to keep a bear or the boogeyman outside." He shot her a grim smile. "Hmm. A pretty girl. A dark, spooky cabin. If this was a horror movie, this is where the pretty girl would meet her fate."

Ella forced out a chuckle and forced her legs to move forward, trying to nudge him out of her way. "Let's hope that pretty girl chose the town hero and not the boogeyman to go exploring with. Otherwise, she'd be a goner."

"Wait." He held her back, producing a small flashlight from his pocket and illuminating the cabin inch by inch. There were boxes and barrels amid the counters and shelves, leaving trails to wander through. "One wrong move and we'll both be goners."

"Who would have left the place like this?" Curious, she glanced to the interior door frame, but it was too dark to see anything clearly. "Shine your light up there a minute."

He did, brushing his hand over the round log. "It might say Lee and there might be a date, but I can't be sure of either." Keeping the light above the door, Noah dropped his gaze to her. "Somebody's knife penmanship needed work."

Ella craned her neck. "I need to see more."

"Are you sure?" Noah ran the flashlight beam across the piles and stacks.

There were antlers mounted to the far wall and a counter made of unfinished wood. The bark was still clinging to it in spots. An old cash register sat on top, half buried by boot-size boxes. There were shelves from floor to ceiling along one wall and tables in the middle of the floor, every surface piled, every cranny stuffed. The ceilings were high and open-beamed without evidence of leakage. An old horse saddle straddled one of the beams. There were more cardboard boxes here than there had been in the mercantile.

"No, I'm not sure." Ella grimaced.

"This is packed tighter than the storage unit I left in New York." Noah ventured in a few steps, bumping his elbow on chains hanging from the wall, making them rattle. "But the ambiance is a bit different."

The chains were attached to a large trap.

"That's big enough to snap me." Ella shivered. The entire building reflected a feeling for the rugged mountain life. She much preferred the femininity of the mercantile. "I wonder who the last owner was." She nudged a box with her boot, not brave enough to look inside. "It's like they started to prepare for closing and then just left everything."

"The air... It's like breathing in sadness," Noah said, sounding surprised at the poetry of his observation.

Ella nodded. "Not even the town teenagers would sneak in here and make out in this place."

"There are no town teenagers." Noah's beam caught on a large stone fireplace with a hearth that rivaled the inn's in size.

Something scuttled in the corner.

Ella shimmied backward. "You should have brought Woof."

"That dog has a live-and-let-live policy." Noah turned, holding the flashlight beneath his face in an effort to look ghoulish. "Seen enough?"

Ella heaved a sigh. "No. I need to know when it was last updated. Roughly."

"How can you tell that?" He lowered the flashlight and clicked it off.

"The proper way to check would be to contact the county about a building permit. But

I've found I can generally date improvements within a decade by looking at the state of the bathroom or kitchen."

"That sounds like an exceedingly accurate way to put value on a property." He stood in shadow, but there was enough teasing sarcasm in his voice for her to know he wore a hint of a smile.

Ella couldn't find a comeback. She was too busy listening to the tiny voice in her head that whispered dire predictions of mice being attracted to pink boots.

There was a moment of silence where neither of them moved.

The wind whispered through the pines behind the cabin and somewhere in town a child laughed.

"What are you waiting for?" Noah asked.

"An exterminator." No lie.

Noah stepped into the light from the doorway, a tender look in his eyes. "I can beat back anything that tries to attack you."

Nervous laughter escaped her lips. "With what?"

"With this." Noah held up his flashlight, which was the size of four ballpoint pens taped together. "Come on." He reached for Ella's hand and tugged her inside, weaving through the debris. "The plucky heroine always makes it out alive in horror movies."

"At the cost of her brave boyfriend." She wasn't proud of the fact that she held on to Noah with both hands.

Her fears receded as they progressed through the trading post and she recognized cast-iron skillets, an old icebox, a lumberjack saw and a bench made of logs.

"Watch out." Noah slowed as they neared the far wall. "Ghost."

Four feet tall. Draped in canvas.

Ella laughed. "That'd be a short ghost." She was courageous enough to lift the canvas. It was another dress form.

Noah led her into a narrow hall, stopping at an open door.

Ella peered into a small bathroom, which had a green sink and toilet similar to her bathroom at the inn. "It's been winterized. There's no water in the toilet."

"That's Roy's job. He's always puttering around the old buildings."

"He's done a good job." That might explain why there'd been no roof leaks.

Beyond the hallway, there was a kitchen

with one high window and a narrow door. Ella didn't let go of Noah as she looked around.

"Black-and-white checkerboard flooring. The sink doesn't have any cabinetry around it and the counter space is more like tables with skirts to hide the shelves beneath. Based on this and the green colored fixtures in the bathroom, I'd say it was last updated in the nineteen thirties." She felt his gaze upon her and glanced up at him.

"That's an impressive parlor trick," Noah said in an intimate voice. He stroked her cheek.

It would be so easy to step into his arms, but the smart thing to do would be to say goodbye.

With difficulty, Ella held on to her resolve. She nodded. Assembled a smile. Backed away. "I like old buildings. Or, I used to think I did. They give me a feeling of home and permanence." She took her phone out of her jacket pocket and snapped some shadowy pictures, making sure to stay close enough to Noah that he could take a swing at any territorial critter should one appear. When she was done, she tucked away her phone and grabbed hold of him once more. "I'm ready to go now."

Noah waited until she glanced up at him before nodding and leading her back to the sunshine and snow. When they reached the porch and she'd locked up, he said, "I survived. Looks like we weren't in a horror movie after all."

"No boogeyman."

"No rodent of unusual size and touchy temperament."

Look at that. They could keep their hands off each other while she was here and enjoy a laugh the same way she joked with Sophie.

Ella allowed herself a small smile. "How about checking up on the church and schoolhouse?"

"Did you steal the keys from Mitch to those, too?" Noah gently tugged a lock of her hair. "You shouldn't be unsupervised. Ever."

"That's very judgmental of you, Doc." She snapped on her snowshoes, trying to ignore the flip and flutter in her chest at his touch. "Let's go."

"Quickly, before we're discovered." Noah was more proficient at putting on his snowshoes than she was. He was down the steps and heading out before Ella stood.

She huffed and puffed a good distance behind Noah down a gentle slope that led to the intersecting highway and up another to the white church.

"Tell the truth." Noah waited for her on the small side porch. "You hated phys ed in school."

Was he digging at her physical abilities?

"I might have mentioned the only exercise I get is run-walking after Penny." Ella reached the porch steps and plopped down on one. "But I didn't hate PE. I'll have you know my mother played softball in school. She taught me how to throw and catch."

"I liked lacrosse."

"Of course you did." She stuck her snowshoes in the nearest drift, next to his, so they wouldn't slide down the hill, and then got to her feet. "I bet you played all the country-club sports—golf, polo." She couldn't think of any others.

"If you're trying to set the stuffy standard at my door, I suggest you look to those Monroes of yours. I bet they host an annual charity golf tournament."

"And a yachting race," she admitted, stomping her boots on the porch. "I don't have the skill to participate in either."

It took some fumbling of gloved fingers, but she finally found the right key to open the door.

The church pews were still in place. The

altar was flanked on either side by two oblong stained-glass panels depicting doves. A clear glass window fit into the arch. So much light came through the windows that dust motes danced like a Broadway chorus line.

"It's beautiful." Ella snapped pictures while Noah poked around the rear of the building.

"There's nothing in here. No bathroom or kitchen for you to date this."

"Which means it's old. Really old." Ella went to stand on the altar. "The roof and the floors seem in good shape."

"You can tell a lot about a town by how well they keep up their place of worship." Noah ran a hand over the back of a wooden pew. "There's no sign saying this was built by Lee."

They locked up and plowed across the snow to the schoolhouse next door.

Ella unlocked the door and stopped. Had Woof been with them, he couldn't have gotten inside. It was stacked nearly to the ceiling with stuff. Boxes. A bicycle. Cans of oil. An old sewing machine. "I can't see anything."

Noah peered over her shoulder. "My grandfather used to have a shed in his backyard that looked like this."

"Was he a doctor, too?"

He nodded. "Pediatrics. Gramps loved kids almost as much as he loved accumulating stuff."

"Whose stuff is this?" Ella wondered aloud. "The schoolteacher's?"

"I've never seen Eli over this way."

Ella took pictures before she closed and locked the door.

They walked around the building, looking for a second door. There wasn't one. Or tall windows that might have hinted at a bathroom.

"Do you know what you should include in your market assessment?" Noah pointed to the view of the broad valley and the snowy Sawtooth mountain range.

"It's breathtaking."

"You steal my breath," he said artlessly, longing in his eyes.

They were on the south side of the schoolhouse. He moved in closer, kissing clearly on his mind.

She held up a hand, planting her palm on his chest. "Noah, I can't." No matter how much she wanted to.

"I bet you didn't tell your husband that. I bet you followed your instincts and your heart." There was no sarcasm in his tone. No hurt, no anger, no accusation. "No one in town can see us, not even with binoculars. Follow your instincts, Ella. Follow your heart."

She hesitated, torn. "But what about later?"

"Later?" His hands settled on her waist. "I promise to behave as if we're just good friends."

"Really?" That didn't seem like Noah. He was more of the get-what-I-want type.

"Cross my heart," he murmured, closing the distance between them.

Sentimental, instinctual romantic that she was, Ella welcomed his kiss.

A strong wind whipped behind her and sent them tumbling into a drift.

Ella landed on top of Noah. "Holy mackerel, it's so cold." She tried to get up.

"I'll keep you warm." Noah drew her close and did just that.

CHAPTER ELEVEN

NOAH WHISTLED AS he entered the Bent Nickel.

He couldn't remember the last time he'd whistled or felt like singing. There was just something about Ella that awoke Noah. When they were together, he didn't dwell on his physical deficit or his lost practice. He was too busy staying mentally on his toes. And if Ella had qualms about whatever was percolating between them, she was less intent upon it when their conversations started rolling. And when they kissed…

Noah stopped whistling as the door closed behind him.

There wasn't a schoolkid in sight, not even Ivy's.

Ivy, Mackenzie, Roy and Mitch sat at the counter on stools turned to face Noah, arms crossed, frowns out in full force.

"Well?" Mitch asked, although it sounded

more like a demand. "We saw Ella head out on snowshoes."

"Toward the old buildings," Ivy added.

"With you," Mackenzie pointed out.

Roy shook his head. "I shouldn'ta left her with 'em."

"Why do I get the feeling I might be swimming with the frozen fishes in the Salmon River soon?" Noah crossed the room and filled a mug with coffee, not bothering to shed any of his snow gear since he might be heading back out depending upon what the local tribunal said next.

The foursome exchanged glances.

"Here's the thing." Lately, Noah's patience didn't extend much beyond Ella, Penny and Woof. "I agreed to keep an eye on Ella. I agreed to tell you what her intentions are, but all that ends if you don't confess what's going on here."

Ivy smiled sugar-to-fly sweetly, the way she did at the schoolkids when she wanted them to behave without having to deliver a reprimand. "Harlan wanted his grandchildren to love Second Chance."

Mitch sighed. "He thought their talent and business experience would revitalize the town."

"Harlan also thought buying us out and offering low leases would encourage current residents to stay and invest in their businesses." Mackenzie rolled her eyes.

"I bought a deluxe heating unit for the inn," Mitch said defensively.

Mackenzie placed a hand over her heart. "And I bought a new car lift for the garage."

"I bought me a new drill," Roy said with complete sincerity, as if this accounted for a significant amount of change.

They all turned to Ivy, who was swiveling on her stool.

"Did you put your money in savings?" Noah prompted.

Mackenzie snorted.

"No." Ivy narrowed her gaze at the town mechanic and store owner.

"She took her family to Disney World," Mackenzie said, heavy on the sarcasm, light on the sympathy.

Ivy jerked in her seat. "Which is an investment in itself. My oldest learned firsthand about other cultures at Epcot. He tried sushi. It's not like we have sushi here."

"Oh, please." Mackenzie wasn't cutting Ivy any slack.

"Ladies, please." Mitch held up his hands and then turned to Noah. "*Most of us* used the rest to supplement our income. So if the Monroes decide to sell the town, parceling it out to the wealthy for luxury ranchettes, we'll have to buy our places back at a premium."

"That was a risk you took when you signed your deals." Noah grimaced and set down his coffee, untouched. "You had to know it wouldn't last."

"Maybe," Mitch allowed. "But the same goes with your retainer. You had to know it wasn't going to extend forever."

In fact, his contract expired in six months.

Noah sat down, picked up his coffee and took a sip, needing to consider all of this. He hadn't thought ahead to contract renewal, mostly because he avoided thinking about the future. Ever. "So, what you really want me to do is find out what the Monroes have in mind for the town and then if you disagree, use my influence with Ella—" what little there was "—to change her mind."

"Exactly!" Roy got up and slapped Noah on the back.

Everyone looked relieved.

Everyone, he supposed, but Noah.

THE MONROES WERE hanging out in Sophie's room.

Laurel was lying on one twin bed, complaining of food poisoning. Sophie was supervising a game of Candyland with the kids on the other bed. Shane stood vigil at the window, working on his frown lines.

And Ella?

She sat on the timber footboard and tried hard not to smile, not to glow, not to dream that she and Noah had a future together.

It's just a winter fling. Those kisses mean nothing.

But she felt like laughing, shouting out Grandpa Harlan's favorite saying—*Are you ready, Hezzie?*—and bursting into song.

Since she was a responsible single mom, her song would be something G-rated like "The Wheels on the Bus."

"You and the doctor went out again, I see." Shane pointed out the window toward the church and schoolhouse.

Had he been able to see them kiss?

Ella blushed. "Apparently, there's a safety rule—no snowshoeing alone in the high country." What a big fib.

Shane's expression indicated he wasn't in the mood to buy fibs today.

"Let it go, Shane." Sophie helped Penny roll the dice. "What did you find, Ella?"

"The two of you—" Ella pointed to Laurel and Sophie "—are going to want to poke around some of those buildings."

"They left things?" Laurel perked up.

"What kind of things?" Sophie leaned forward so quickly she nearly upended the game board and lost her glasses.

"An old cash register. A pair of well-used dress forms. Tons of knickknacks. Boxes and barrels of stuff."

"And in your estimation, what are the buildings worth?" Shane cut to the bottom line.

"Honestly?" Ella's enthusiasm waned. "In this sleepy town, not much. The bones are good because Grandpa Harlan paid for maintenance, but everything's outdated. What's the draw to move here or to open a business? There is no clear positive, no sales nugget to say this is where you need to buy and why you need to pay top dollar." Ella paused.

She sounded like... Like the old Ella. Pre-Bryce. Self-sufficient. Self-assured. Savvy.

"I thought so, too." Shane's expression toward Ella softened. "There are shops in the newer buildings, but Mackenzie said their owners go south for winter and from what I can tell, it doesn't feel as if anyone's running a booming business when there's no snow on the ground in spring and summer, either. There aren't any developed ski slopes for winter commerce, no luxury spa to get away to. In short, there's no reason to come to Second Chance any time of year."

"Other than for the fabulous view." Ella sighed, thinking of Noah's smiling face against the snowy Sawtooth mountain range.

"And the decent sledding." Sophie grinned at Ella and adjusted her glasses.

"And the artisan quilter," Laurel added.

The three women looked to Shane, but he had nothing to add.

"To each his own," Ella murmured. And then she straightened, staring at Shane. "*To each his own.* Duh." She thunked her head. "When real-estate developers create new communities, they always create space for businesses they feel people will need or enjoy. From their perspective, you come for a fabulous dinner, a unique shop or quirky theater and you see the great living options nearby, which make you want to move in."

Laurel groaned and cradled her stomach.

"I wouldn't recommend the food at the Bent Nickel."

"But Cam's coming." Sophie waved aside Laurel's complaint. "He's a terrific chef."

"I like the way you guys are thinking, but you're thinking small." Shane paced. "I've been researching the nearby towns that are destinations—Hailey, Sun Valley, Challis. They don't just have fine dining and interesting shops. They have special events, outdoor activities and—"

"No ski slope," Sophie reminded him.

Shane stopped long enough to frown at his twin. "But there's a lake around the bend that freezes over every winter. Visitors could ice-skate or learn how to curl."

"Curling?" Ella touched her hair. "The sport?"

"Yes, not a hair-salon curl." Shane's dark eyebrows lowered in disapproval. "Although I suppose that's important, too."

"Order up one nice warm shopping mall," Laurel said.

Shane chose to ignore her. "Ella's been snowshoeing. There's a huge meadow across the river where people can cross-country ski. This could be—"

"A playground for the middle-aged," Laurel interrupted. "Snowshoeing. Cross-country skiing. That's all tame stuff. What other ideas do you have? Stuff that might appeal to a younger crowd."

"Fairs, concerts, a celebration of spring thaw. There are plenty of festivals of various kinds we could host." Shane frowned at Laurel. "Second Chance used to host a winter festival featuring an ice-sculpture competition."

"How eighties," Laurel murmured.

"But we could up that." Not appreciating his cousin's sarcasm, Shane's frown deepened into a scowl. "Take a new twist on an old theme. Like instead of ice sculpture, we get entrants to build ice and snow castles. There are towns who put on kite festivals with these huge kites that look like fish and dragons and cartoon characters, and rival the balloons in the Macy's Thanksgiving Day parade. I have contacts in entertainment. We could do whatever we want."

"I was thinking more along the lines of mudders, Spartans and iron-man competitions to attract people who wouldn't care their hotel room lacked amenities," Laurel admitted. "But those sound interesting, too, I suppose."

Ella raised her hand. "Just one question. Are you doing all this to help everyone in town earn a better living so you can increase their leases? Or are you going to do all this because you want to increase the value of the property to sell? Which will take years."

Shane leaned against the windowsill. "We've owned this property for less than three weeks. I'm one vote of twelve. We have to keep our options open, but we have to protect our investment, too. All I'm asking is we begin to think beyond the next snowfall."

"Wouldn't those ideas mean we'd have to stay here?" Ella asked.

Shane nodded. "Someone would."

Only Ella met his gaze.

CHAPTER TWELVE

"Mom." Penny snuggled closer to Ella beneath the quilts. When Ella's eyes opened, Penny sat up and pushed off the bedding. "I sed? I schoo? I… Woof?" She coughed once.

Out of recent habit, Ella reached for a tissue, sat up and requested that Penny blow her nose. It didn't escape her that Penny may have been congested, but she wasn't coughing repeatedly anymore.

"Ella?" Sophie knocked on the door. "Gabby says that woman with the three boys is going to snowplow the highway this morning." Which meant they could do more than walk to the diner and back.

Ella gasped dramatically for Penny's benefit. "Do you know what that means?"

"Huh?" Penny asked, wide-eyed.

"School will be in session today."

"Schoo! Schoo!" Penny rolled onto her tummy and slid off the edge of the bed. "Cos.

Want cos. Go schoo-ooo-ooo. Pease. Mom-Mom-Mom."

"All right. All right." Ella was excited, too.

A strip of road to walk on. There'd be more people to talk to. Others who'd found themselves snowbound and in need of human companionship. Like, like… She couldn't think of any, except Noah.

It wasn't long before she stood with Penny on the front porch of the inn and watched Mitch sprinkle salt on the cleared walkway.

A door slammed at the side of the inn.

Gabby walked across the snow toward her father, shoulders bunched up more than a shriveled raisin. "I'm late. I hate tests. I'm going to fail math."

"You're not going to fail math," Mitch reassured her in a tone that said this conversation wasn't a new one. "You worry too much."

"I worry?" Gabby stomped her foot. "Do you know how I can worry less? If I were to know where I'm going to be living next year. You promised that sweet old man you'd watch out for this town and then people come who want to watch out for this town and you treat them colder than a prosecutor would a murderer."

She hurried toward the diner. "I'm going to fail math and next year I'll be homeless."

"Wrong on both counts," Mitch grumbled. "Why couldn't I have had a boy?"

"I heard that," Gabby shouted back, flinging open the door to the diner.

Penny gasped, perhaps realizing where Gabby was going. "Schoo?"

Mitch's head whipped around.

"I thought you knew we were here," Ella said guiltily, coming down the stairs.

He looked from Ella to the diner and back, his discomfort as plain as a spaghetti stain on his face. "I hope you don't think…"

"It's more you and Shane." No sense denying it. "You guys are like two dogs circling the same bone." Ella stopped next to Mitch, ignoring the way Penny kicked her legs like a cowgirl using her spurs on her horse. "I guess Gabby noticed."

"My daughter notices everything." Mitch frowned.

"It's the age." Ella thought back to the time she was twelve. "You're beginning to see the world differently. The stakes and the consequences of your actions. And your parents'." This last came out wistfully.

"She'll get over it. She'll pass her math test and—"

"And she'll still be uncertain about her living whereabouts when your leases are up on December thirty-first."

Mitch's frown deepened.

The rumble of a heavy engine filled the air. And then a gray truck rounded the bend to the north and moved slowly toward them, tunneling a path in the snow. The truck stopped in front of the diner and a familiar trio of boys tumbled out with backpacks and laughter.

The woman driving the local snowplow continued on, waving.

"How does she know where the road is?" Ella wondered aloud.

"There are no trees on the road." Mitch joined them on the porch. "But she's been known to clip a mailbox or a car, so she stays in the middle and then does her wide turn at the crossroads. The sidewalk is icy. Proceed with caution."

Ella did just that. All the way to the diner.

"I'm all out of lettuce," Ivy apologized when Ella and Penny came through the door. "I've put in an order, which they'll deliver as soon as the passes are clear."

"Which should be tomorrow or the next day," Roy said in his perpetually perky tone. "How are you taking to snowshoeing, missy?"

"I do okay." Ella smiled. "Is it bad to admit I've fallen twice?"

"You know what they say about falling?" Roy toasted Ella with his coffee mug. "That's how we learn to get back on our feet."

"Hey, Roy," Ella said slowly, still considering the wisdom of the old man's words. "I noticed the Lees built some of these cabins. Who were they?"

"The *Lees*?" Roy's eyes bulged.

"The *Lees*?" Ivy echoed from the kitchen.

"The Lees." Ella nodded.

"Don't know," Roy said unconvincingly.

Ivy was no longer visible in the kitchen.

The schoolkids had spread out across the booths the Monroes usually sat in and were remarkably quiet and focused, as if they were all taking math tests. They didn't weigh in on the Lees, either.

Ella headed toward a booth near the back. She never sat this far away from the woodstove. It was chillier near the hallway.

Mr. Garland, the nice teacher, brought Penny a sheet to color and some crayons. After Penny was relieved of her snowsuit, she studied the test-taking children with wide eyes for a moment, and then grabbed a blue crayon and leaned over her coloring page with serious intent.

A framed line drawing hung above the booth. The paper was yellow with age and wrinkled, as if it'd been in someone's pocket or satchel before being preserved. It was a map. Ella could make out log cabins and at the bottom of the drawing the artist had noted something and written a date—1919.

"Is this a map of the town?" Ella asked, turning around, but everyone was too busy or preoccupied to answer.

Or perhaps too polite to begin a conversation while the class on the other side of the diner was taking a test. At least now Ella understood why they didn't hold their sessions in the schoolhouse. It was full of junk!

Roy had his nose in a magazine. It sounded like Ivy was moving boxes in the storage room or pantry. Shane was holding up his cell phone to the windowpane, trying to get service. Laurel was slumped at the counter, looking like she hadn't slept well. She hadn't touched the toast that Ella had stipulated she order when Laurel had insisted upon getting out of the inn. Sophie and the boys were in the next booth. The twins were demanding tall stacks of pancakes for breakfast and Sophie was trying her best to get them to order eggs.

"Sophie, you order protein and let the boys have their pancakes." Ella slid into the booth on her knees, hoping for a closer look at the map.

"All that sugar." Sophie poked at her glasses. "They'll be bouncing off the walls."

"And then they'll crash for a nice long nap." Ella squinted at the small, faint writing. *"The most difficult path."* She looked to her daughter. "What does that mean?"

Penny shrugged.

The front door opened. It was Noah. He headed straight to Ella, Woof at his side.

Watching them approach, a warm feeling blossomed in Ella's chest. This was no flutter. No swoon of attraction. Ella felt as if the four of them were meant to be together, to be a family. Maybe lightning had struck twice. Maybe she could fall for two completely different men in two incredibly short amounts of time.

Because the feeling of rightness was almost identical to what she'd felt with Bryce. And to her, that rightness was love. Love for a tall, beautiful, intelligent man who fought to hide his scars and need to be normal harder than she fought to stay in the Monroe family.

I'm in so much trouble.

Ian. Holden. They'd judge. Could they perhaps try to force Penny out of her inheritance?

For the moment, Ella didn't care.

Are you ready, Hezzie?

"Woof! No!" Penny cried, holding out her arms for a hug. "Waffles?"

Noah embraced Penny and then shed his outer gear, revealing jeans and a blue checked flannel shirt. He kept on the gloves, of course. Woof squeezed his big body under the table and laid his head on the bench seat so Penny could pet him. Ella stayed where she was. It was safer not to move, not to glance or reach.

"Waffles for breakfast?" Noah caught Ivy's eye as she returned to the main room and held up two fingers. "What a great idea, Penny." True to his word, cognizant of their audience, Noah didn't hug or kiss Ella in greeting. But the way he looked at her was just as intimate. "What are you looking at?"

"I think this is a map of the town." Ella nodded toward the drawing.

He agreed. And then they continued to stare

at the find in silence while Penny made sweet noises at Woof.

To anyone looking, she and Noah seemed to be appreciating the map as if it was one of those paintings the Monroes owned that was worth millions. Ella could barely see the map for the tension between them. It vibrated along her skin, urging her to move closer, to give in, to admit that there was something here to pursue, something more than simple chemistry.

"I apologize," Noah whispered.

She gave him a sideways glance. "Why?"

"I should have walked in and kissed you good-morning," he murmured with a straight face.

"Perhaps some other time," Ella murmured back.

"Promises, promises."

Ella had to bite back a smile.

It was easy to forget the Monroes when she was with Noah. But they were all here, representing the family she was desperate to hold on to because their love and support justified her love for Bryce.

Laurel lifted her head to glance their way.

Shane looked at them over his shoulder.

Sophie shushed the twins. "What did you say?" she asked Ella.

"The most difficult path." Ella raised her voice. "It's here on the bottom of this old town map. What do you think it means?"

Noah sighed, but played along. "They tell me these passes are the most difficult to traverse in Idaho."

Shane joined them, peering at the framed drawing. "The page is ripped on the bottom. Maybe there's more to it, like a town motto or something."

Ella dug her phone out of her pocket and took a picture. "I feel justified. There's supposed to be four cabins on the other side of those shops on this side of the river and there are only three."

"What if..." Shane's gaze turned speculative. "What if that's Grandpa Harlan's cabin in Philly? People move cabins all the time nowadays."

Ella rejected the idea almost immediately. "I'd need to check the dimensions, but the Philadelphia cabin is as large as the fur-trading post."

"I bet Mitch knows," Shane said, returning to his booth. "He knows everything."

Noah and Ella exchanged quick, private glances and almost-smiles.

Ella was willing to bet Mitch didn't know everything.

MITCH ENTERED IVY'S, dropped coins in the jar on the counter and helped himself to coffee. He immediately sat across from Shane. "How's that plan to save the town coming?"

Shane locked his screen and put his phone down on the white Formica. "You haven't convinced me this town is worth saving."

Mitch tapped his fingers on the tabletop and glanced over at his daughter, whose head was bent over her schoolwork. "What if I could?"

"Start talking."

"Your grandfather loved this town. He…" Mitch faltered. There was something in his expression that nagged at Shane, a mix of emotions he'd seen before.

When Mitch failed to say anything else, Shane sat up and leaned forward. "Do you know what I used to do? What I used to love to do?"

Mitch shook his head.

"I ran a chain of hotels, which meant I had a cadre of employees. I hired men and women who were independent and used to running their own show because I wanted them to operate as if whatever hotel or hotel restaurant or hotel club was their own." It had also freed Shane up to concentrate on special projects and expansion. He gave Mitch a knowing stare. "I recognize the same ability to lead and the desire to run things in you. I can see why my grandfather put his trust in you to watch over Second Chance."

Because clearly, he had. Everyone looked to Mitch.

"I would've hired you," Shane admitted, because after years of managing people he sensed they wouldn't get along until he gave the local man some respect. "Despite the sarcasm and the holier-than-thou attitude. I would have given you a chance to fit in with my style and way of operating." Shane tucked away his cell phone. "But if our situations were reversed, I don't think you would've done the same. I think you took one look at me—*at us*—and came up with some preconceived notion about the Monroes."

Mitch looked taken aback.

"I don't know why I came to Second Chance in the middle of winter." Shane shook his head.

"Was it grief that sent me running here so soon after my grandfather passed? Was it a need to reconnect with him and build upon whatever vision he saw in this place?" Shane shook his head again. "I have no idea."

"Whatever it was, you convinced three others it was the right thing to do." Mitch's dark gaze was even. There was no sarcasm in his voice. It was a compliment from a man who didn't seem eager to give any out.

He'd persuaded two more—Cam and Jonah—but that wasn't the point.

"And now we're stuck," Shane said. In more than just the literal sense. "You and me. Me and my family. My family and this town."

"I appreciate you extending an olive branch when I've been clutching mine so fiercely," Mitch said. "I'm not always easy to get along with. It comes from years spent as a defense attorney."

"Hence the ready sarcasm."

"Like calls to like, they say." Mitch chuckled, and then he sobered. "I wasn't lying when I said I didn't know why your grandfather decided to buy us out. He did want his grandchildren to love the town and help it prosper, but he could have done that in so many different ways."

"My grandfather had the golden touch when it came to business and frankly, Mitch, Second Chance could use a lot of that."

Mitch didn't argue. He got out of the booth. "How about a tour? You, me and Ella. I can't promise it will be snark-free, but it will be informative."

"Great." Shane signaled to Ella to join them. "Sophie, can you watch Penny for a few minutes?"

"I've got her," Noah said with too much familiarity for Shane's liking.

Mitch went over to say something to his daughter.

"What's going on with you two?" Shane asked when Ella was within whispering distance. "Do you need me to say something to Noah?"

Ella closed her eyes briefly, shoulders slumping. "No. We were snowed in together for two days. We're friends. Penny adores him, and he adores her."

The good doctor glanced over to them. It was clear he adored more than Penny.

"Geez, Ella." Shane took her by the arm and

led her out the door. The wind tugged at the ends of his jacket and swept past his cotton layers. "Think this through. There's a reason he's practicing in the mountains and it probably has something to do with the reason he wears gloves all the time."

"Shane."

He zipped his jacket closed. "When Bryce died, some of us made a pact."

"Shane."

The sun was blinding, bouncing off all that white snow.

Where had he put his sunglasses? He patted his pockets. "We promised to watch out for you."

"Shane." Ella spoke his name with increasing annoyance.

"You don't know who that guy is."

"Shane!" she shouted loud enough to be heard inside.

The good doctor got to his feet.

Ella put her gloved hands on Shane's cheeks and lowered her voice. "You worry about other people too much. You worry about this town and what we're going to do with it too much. You need to take better care of yourself." She tugged the black knit cap off her head and put it on his. "I take note of your concern, but—"

"You want me to butt out." How could a knit cap make him feel degrees warmer? As a child of the Las Vegas desert, he'd never had to worry about this kind of cold before. Perhaps there was something to the way Ella and the other residents bundled up. He knotted the scarf at Ella's neck.

"This is hard for me." Ella's eyes looked ready to spill tears. "Finding Bryce... Losing Bryce..."

"Say no more." Shane drew her into a hug because he'd rather do that than witness her cry. "You've got family. That's all you need."

Mitch came outside wrapped up as much as Ella. He took in Mitch's jacket with a smile. "Do you ski, Shane?"

"No."

"Hunt? Fish? Camp?"

"No." Shane was too busy running a chain of luxury hotels to have a hobby. Or he had been.

Mitch gave him the once-over and a wry grin. "Nice shoes."

Shane looked down at his Italian loafers, and then registered the fact that Ella and Mitch had on snow boots. Ella's were a hideous neon pink. "I'll be fine."

"Mackenzie sells snow gear in the store." Mitch led them out to the highway. "Along with scarves and gloves."

"And hats," Ella said, using her outdoor voice.

The wind was rustling the pines, as if they needed the snow cleared from their limbs. Clumps of the white stuff were falling to earth, releasing snowflakes that rode on the wind.

"I'll be fine," Shane insisted. So what if he was cold for a minute or two? In Vegas, he was hot for a minute or two when he went outside in the summer. He'd live.

Mitch stopped in the middle of the highway. Not that there was a danger in that—with the pass being closed there was no traffic. "Second Chance wasn't more than a crossroads and a summer cavalry station until a gifted cabin builder and trapper named Seymore Lee decided this would be a good place to open a fur-trading post."

The cold nipped at Shane's toes. Ella pulled her scarf up higher, covering her nose and ears. He pointed at the knit cap, silently asking if she wanted it back. Ella shook her head.

"He built that big cabin up there," Mitch continued. "And several others. His craftsmanship is why many of the round-log cabins in town are still standing today. Seymore Lee was like Rockefeller in Second Chance. He had a monopoly on land and timber. You had to buy from him to build anything." Mitch pointed to the flat-log building that housed the general store and garage. "His descendants honed their technique and acquired flat-log building skills, and later more traditional carpentry when the sawmill opened in Challis. The Lee family built that church and schoolhouse. They used their influence to bring shopkeepers and service providers to town. They weathered the long hard winters. They designed this stretch of downtown so with a little effort people could traverse either side during the winter."

"Is that why there are paths between the cabins on either end of town?" Ella asked in words chopped by cold. "And the covered sidewalks?"

"Yes." Mitch didn't look like the chill affected him at all. "Although the covered sidewalks collapsed on the high side of the road."

The wind was so frigid, Shane felt as if he didn't have a jacket on. "This is a quaint history lesson, but what does this have to do with my grandfather?"

"He was a Lee."

Shane punched his hands deeper in his jacket pockets. "Say again? I don't think I heard you right."

"Harlan Lee Monroe," Mitch said with a hint of impatience. "Your grandfather was a Lee. He grew up here. None of you knew that?"

Comprehension dawned. The letter. The small-town purchase. The unexpected bequest.

Ella laughed, a sound carried away by the wind. "You don't know how relieved I am to know that Grandpa Harlan's letter had nothing to do with me."

"Why didn't I know he was born here?" Shane looked around the town with fresh eyes, not seeing the run-down buildings that would be so easy to demolish. Instead, he saw his grandfather being taught the value of hard work and community.

"Do you know where your grandmother was born?" Ella asked, peering at Shane's face.

Shane opened his mouth to answer, but then shook his head. "No. I never asked." More concerned with running the family business than in learning about its founder. Shane suddenly wanted to know more about his roots. "Which one was my grandfather's cabin?" It had to be the one that was missing. There was no other explanation.

Mitch shook his head. "He never said."

"The Lees owned the trading post and the mercantile?" Ella asked.

"They owned everything, until they left town and sold most of the buildings."

"Was Harlan the last Lee?" Ella's gaze was intent. She looked like she had hold of a theory, which was more than what Shane had.

"I'm not sure. I'm sorry." Mitch held out his hands. "I only know a little from what I gleaned from Harlan. He didn't talk much about his past."

"That much we'll agree with you on," Shane said, staring longingly at the warm diner and then at the inn. He needed to call his father and ask him what he knew of Grandpa Harlan's past. He needed to call the other grandchildren and pick their brains, too. There was more to discover in Second Chance than bitter cold, a dozen feet of snow and empty log cabins.

Ella was back on point. "If Harlan was the last Lee and he sold the town off when he left, that would explain a lot. How he financed his start in oil. Why the mercantile and trading post look like someone just walked away. Why there is no record of him buying the mercantile and trading post."

"He might never have sold them." Shane was catching on. The cold seeped through his thin jacket. "I think I want to see these cabins."

Ella stomped her feet and nodded.

"Is there a reason we can't have this discussion in the diner, where it's warm?" Shane asked.

"There is." Mitch looked lawyerly grim. "When Harlan bought us out he had us each sign nondisclosure agreements. We weren't supposed to pass on anything we knew about Harlan or anything he said to us individually."

"Harlan loved people." Ella's gaze sought Shane's. "He loved talking. Everyone in town could have a different secret of his."

But that didn't explain why a lawyer was breaking that contract. Shane hit Mitch with a hard stare. "Then why the change of heart?"

"Because Gabby's worried they'll have to move." Ella nodded toward the inn. "I overheard them arguing this morning."

"You can't tell the rest of the town that I told you anything." Mitch turned and began walking along the path they'd created, making Shane feel as if Mitch hadn't spilled all of his sworn secrets. Mitch paused, glancing back as if realizing Shane and Ella weren't following him. "I've given you a lot to think about. Let's get you inside where it's warm."

Shane's phone buzzed. It was Cousin Holden, the leader of the six Monroes who wanted to challenge the will. He was asking for an update. Shane shoved his phone back in his pocket and headed for the diner. It was going to take awhile to figure this out. There was more to discover here than just the town's market value. There was family history and something else profound Shane couldn't quite name.

CHAPTER THIRTEEN

"EVERYTHING OKAY?" NOAH asked Ella when she returned to their booth.

While she'd been gone, he'd buttered and cut Penny's waffle and drizzled it with hearts the way Ella had done during their snowed in days. The sweet little toddler had kissed his cheek as a thank-you. She kept herself busy eating and chewing, humming happily to herself.

"I think you know the answer to that particular question." Ella unwrapped herself like a present on Christmas morning—gloves, scarf, jacket, smile. "I'm fine."

Her smile spread when their gazes connected. That smile... It was a gift, the same as Penny's kisses.

Soft! Dr. Bishop proclaimed from the corner of Noah's mind, where he stewed on a stool in surgery scrubs.

So what?

Ella's quick wit and big heart soothed the

restlessness inside him, made the fact that he could no longer be a superstar in medicine more bearable. She'd be gone soon, taking Penny with her. His chest ached at the thought, but it was for the best. Eventually, Ella would discover how deep his wounds went. She'd find a place where the staunch Dr. Bishop drew a line she couldn't smile her way across. And then she'd realize he couldn't be changed.

Mitch's deep voice rumbled from across the room. He was talking to Shane. They were playing nice with each other—in the same booth, no less.

Noah and Mitch's gazes connected. There were no exchanged smiles. No sense of peace. There were expectations. Ones that made Noah's neck stiff.

Noah turned back to Ella. "What was that all about?" He nodded toward Mitch, who looked as if he was getting more information out of Shane than Noah ever would out of Ella.

"It was…" Ella's gaze caught on the men in the booth and her smile lost its carefree feel. "Unexpected." Her attention returned to Noah. "I may have to rethink my plans. How would you feel about me staying in town longer than a few weeks?"

Dr. Bishop fell off his stool in a dead faint.

Noah's reaction was equally shocking. His mouth dropped open and his waffle-loaded fork hung in midair. It wasn't immediately clear to Noah if he was more shocked that his snarky alter ego had keeled over, or that Ella had brightly presented the idea of staying longer. Just yesterday she'd told him what they had on the down-low could only stay on the down-low. He'd been relieved. Eventually, if she stayed longer, she'd discover his darkness went on forever. Her smile would disappear. She'd gather Penny close, turn her back and walk away, never looking back because she'd know Dr. Noah Bishop was hideous inside and out.

"You're staying longer?" he murmured, placing his fork deliberately on his plate. "That's great."

But what if she didn't leave? What if she never realized that he and the cranky Dr. Bishop were one and the same? Ella wanted to see where things between them would lead? Fantastic. He enjoyed her company and her kisses, except...

It might lead to her staying in Second Chance permanently.

shop sat up and groaned.

ke it here," Noah said firmly. He was
n. He had his independence. No medical
ners to answer to.

He did have to answer to Mitch. He'd agreed
o keep his eye on Ella and try to sway her to
Mitch's way of thinking.

Stay here forevermore? Dr. Bishop tugged
off his scrub shirt and tossed it in the trash.

Noah frowned, glancing up at Ella. "If you
stayed, it'd be great. I'd feel great." The words
echoed in his ears like the hollow beat of a re-
ceding drum.

He hadn't sold his enthusiasm. He could tell.
Ella blushed to the roots of her hair. His frown
deepened. He could feel it etching its way between his eyebrows.

Noah cleared his throat. "That came across
the wrong way. I have a lot on my mind this
morning."

"No—no." Ella's elbows were on the tabletop. Her hands clasped. "I presumed too
much."

"I done." Penny waved her artwork in the
air. It took her an inordinate amount of time
to chew, minutes she'd used to color. The two-

year-old didn't color within the lines. The entire page was blue.

The toddler climbed over Noah, gave him a kiss and slid over his thigh to the floor. She hurried to Eli Garland with self-important steps that made Noah want to smile, except…

Ella wouldn't look at him and he had a sneaking suspicion that if he stayed in Second Chance he'd lose a key part that made up Noah. Or Dr. Bishop.

He cleared his throat again. "I'm happy you'll be here a while. It makes it more bearable." The loss of his ability to perform surgery. The loss of his sense of self.

The loss of adulation, Dr. Bishop muttered.

"I'm not your Band-Aid." Ella crossed her arms over her chest.

"I was thinking more like my teddy bear." He tried to smile. It seemed harder to smile than it used to be with her.

"You have Woof for comfort," she pointed out.

Her voice was so cold, it made him want to shiver. He didn't like her bringing Second Chance weather indoors. "I didn't mean to offend."

I've never groveled before, either.

"You could make it up to me." Ella volleyed her words across the table and speared a bite of waffle from his plate with her fork.

"What did you have in mind?" Noah could think of many ways he'd like to make it up to her, but he doubted she'd made the same list.

Ella's gaze didn't waver. "Take off your gloves."

Noah fell back in the booth as hard as if he'd been hit with life-giving defibrillator paddles.

There were children in the diner. Kids, who'd cringe and pull out their photo-taking tablets. Roy, who had a way of never dropping a topic he was fascinated with. Shane, who felt the Monroes deserved the very best of everything. He'd point out all Noah's flaws to Ella. He'd make her see Noah wasn't worth her time or her heart.

Noah's hands remained in his lap. His mouth remained closed.

Ivy rushed up to their table with moment-saving news. "Ella, I know we're out of greens, but I was rummaging in the cupboard and found the ingredients for a three-bean salad. Does that sound good for breakfast?"

"How nice of you." Ella gushed. "But I'm going to eat Noah's waffle. He's lost his appetite."

"LET'S TAKE THE kids outside." Sophie peered through the inn's front window at the midday sunshine. "I don't think we can hike up to the trading post, but we can walk down the road."

Past Noah's cabin? Ella made a soft noise of acknowledgement, not consent.

She slouched in a straight-backed chair, as spent as a wrung-out cleaning rag. She'd been so sure her feelings for Noah would be reciprocated. But his interest seemed more on the physical end of the relationship spectrum. Not love.

Not yet.

Ella's temples pounded as she remembered the panicked way he'd looked at her in the diner.

Maybe not ever.

The news that Grandpa Harlan's family had built Second Chance sparked Ella's interest in remaining behind. Here was a story. One that could make the town an interesting tourist destination and increase the local economy or increase the town's value for sale.

Maybe she'd blindsided Noah with a question about staying. Maybe he hadn't thought beyond a diverting few weeks of companionship. He'd said relationships needed to take a natural course. Was he the type of guy who needed to ponder how a woman fit into his life? He hadn't pondered that first kiss.

The kids ran around the couch, made the turn and then ran the length of the room near Sophie.

Shane sat on the sofa and frowned at the fireplace, a pad of paper on his knee. He'd told Sophie and Laurel what they'd learned from Mitch, which had made the two women excited, not because part of the mystery regarding why Grandpa Harlan had purchased the town had been solved. Based on what they were told, they believed the contents of the mercantile and fur-trading post were the property of the Monroes.

"Think of the inspiration that authentic hundred-year-old fashion and design could bring," Laurel said.

"Think of the historical treasures we can save and restore," Sophie chimed in.

Laurel was curled in the corner of the couch opposite Shane. "Is there anything interesting to see down the road, Sophie?"

"Just more snow." Sophie didn't quite look at Laurel and didn't quite not. There were still hurt feelings there regarding Sophie's little-heathens comment. "Maybe the snow will give you inspiration to design a new dress. Is white still in?"

"No." Laurel settled deeper into the cushions. She had the brown-and-blue quilt over her.

Ella pulled the cowl collar of her lime sweater up around her neck. The top was a few years old and a comfy favorite of Ella's on cold winter days. It was like wearing a much-needed hug. "Why can't women wear clothes until they wear out instead of replacing them with the latest trendy color or pattern?"

"Because wearing something new is exciting," Laurel said defensively. She longed for a career in fashion, after all. "It makes you feel good inside. And isn't that the point to life? To feel good?"

"What if you feel good with what you have?" Ella murmured. *What if it was scary to reach for something new?*

The three kids turned and ran back the length of the room, their little feet echoing on the wood.

"The wind has died down. The sun is out. It's a shame to be cooped up in here." Sophie leaned against the windowsill, watching the kids pass by like a train that didn't stop at her station. "There's got to be more to see at the end of the road than I'm seeing now. What do you think, Gabby?"

Mitch's daughter sat at the inn's check-in desk with her laptop open. "Odette lives up the road. Last cabin before the bend. Otherwise, there's not much different to see than what's out here."

Laurel perked up. "Odette the quilt-maker?"

The girl nodded. "She knits, too."

"Let's go." Laurel's feet hit the floor. She'd exhibited more energy in that one moment than she had in days. It was infectious, bringing Ella and Sophie around to the idea. "Kids, get your boots and coats. We're going outside." She stared down at an unmoving Shane. "You coming?"

"No." His brow was wrinkled as if he was pondering the heaviest of issues. "I'm thinking."

"Would you like me to stay?" Ella asked, lingering nearby. "Sometimes it helps to talk things through."

"That's okay," he said absently.

Ella refilled his coffee cup before she left. Once outside, the twins chattered excitedly about building a snowman. Penny tried to say "snow angel." That all changed when they walked past the general store. It had to have been just this morning that Mackenzie had put bright, colorful sleds in the window. They hadn't been there when they'd walked back from breakfast.

"A sled!" Alexander dropped to his knees and held out his arms toward the wares in the window.

Not to be outdone, Andrew collapsed beside his twin. "I would be so good if I had a real sled. I'd be one of Penny's snow angels."

Penny slowly got onto her knees, a slight frown on her face, as if she wasn't sure if she should make a snow angel or ask for a sled. And then her gaze landed on a blue plastic sled that looked identical to the one she'd ridden with Gabby. She gasped and pushed herself back to her feet, pointing. "Mom. Sed. Mom. Peas."

"That Mackenzie is a sneaky one." Sophie adjusted her glasses and gave Ella a look that was half annoyance, half respect. "She knew there were three new kids in town who didn't have sleds."

"Brilliant," Ella admitted.

"Who cares? They're cheap and they wear kids out." Laurel led the charge toward the store. "And while you're picking out a sled, the kids will enjoy running up and down the aisles." She opened the door for the rest of the clan. "That's the point, right? Burning off energy."

"That's the point." After a moment's hesitation, Sophie corralled the boys and they all went inside. Sophie then let them loose.

Ella held Penny's hand until they'd wiped their boots on the big all-weather mat. Penny broke free and set off to roam the sled display. Sophie was right. These beauties must have been in the back the day before.

Mackenzie greeted them with a nod since she was on the phone behind the counter. She thanked someone on the other end and hung up. "Hey, Noah. I ordered some precut salad bags for you. They'll be on the next delivery truck."

He'd ordered salad? Ella fought the urge to back out the door.

Boots echoed on linoleum. And then Noah appeared carrying a box of waffles and a bag of frozen grilled chicken strips. He saw Ella and stopped near a display of gloves.

Not that he needed any more of those, although she wouldn't put it past Mackenzie to keep a big supply in stock to entice Noah to buy extra pairs.

His eyebrows were slanted low, the way they'd been the day they'd first met. But the look in his eyes wasn't haunted. It was apologetic.

Ella didn't want his apologies.

"No!" Penny greeted him enthusiastically.

Ella grabbed Penny's hand, not wanting her to toddle over to give Noah a kiss. "I'll pay for this gentleman's waffles." She turned away from Noah and entered the aisle with the sleds. "But I didn't bring my wallet."

"I'll start you a tab," Mackenzie said brightly.

The twins were fighting over the only red plastic saucer among the sled options.

"Do you have another saucer?" Sophie called to Mackenzie and then turned to Ella. "Why do my boys always see the one thing that there's only one of?"

Noah moved past Ella and plucked a longer plastic sled from a hook near the ceiling. "This is what you need." He must have dumped his purchases on the counter first because his hands were otherwise free. "The boys can double up on this one." He handed Sophie the sled and bent down to the twins' level, looking them each in the eye. "Or ride solo flat on his back if you're old enough to take turns nicely." He glanced up at Sophie. "Don't let them ride face first. It's a safety hazard."

"As are coat sleds," Ella added, earning an inscrutable glance from Noah.

"Thanks." Sophie looked from Ella to Noah, brown-eyed curiosity amplified behind her glasses.

"Don't ask," Ella muttered.

"'Cause we won't tell," Noah added, straight-faced.

The twins gasped, having spotted something behind Sophie. They tumbled over each other to reach a yellow plastic water cannon. Shouts of "I saw it first" preceded their tug-of-war.

"Boys!" Sophie moved quickly, but Noah moved faster.

He captured the summer toy and held it out of their reach, disappearing into the depths of the shop before returning empty-handed. A stern look on his face. "That was over the line, Mack," he called out.

"Well, now I know where the line is," the

shop owner called back to him from behind the safety of the cash register.

"This is why I no longer have nice things at home," Sophie said on a half sob. Holding each son by the hand, she thanked Noah profusely. "After my ex-husband was downsized he became a stay-at-home dad. And by stay-at-home, I don't mean he cleaned house and watched out for the boys, although that was our agreement. He let them run around like…like…like *heathens*." Her thin shoulders drooped. "I'm going to have to apologize to Laurel for the fallout of my ex-husband's identity crisis." After yelling for Laurel and ordering the boys not to touch anything else, Sophie gathered the sled and vacated the aisle.

Noah's eyes had widened when Sophie used the term "identity crisis."

Ella felt sorry that he'd lost the skill needed to continue his dream, but he was an adult— not to mention he hadn't been ecstatic about her decision to stick around longer. He needed to get over it, just like she needed to get over her feelings for him.

"Noah, from what I can see behind that beard, you look pale." She'd meant her comment to be a dig, but her hand had somehow landed on Noah's arm. "Don't worry, your identity crisis won't impact the behavior of any growing toddlers, like Penny." But it had caused a bruised heart for one single widowed mother.

She reached over all the other stock on display for the blue sled Penny wanted that was in the window, but her arms weren't long enough. "Shoot."

"No-No-No." Penny tugged on Noah's injured hand and pointed to the window crowded with sleds. "Want sed."

Ella sighed and stepped back, vowing this would be the last time Noah helped her with anything. "Please. She wants the blue one."

One long-armed extension later and Noah was handing the sled to Penny. "The perfect choice for the perfect princess."

Penny grinned from ear to ear. "Sed-sed-sed." She dropped it to the floor and sat in it, scooting her bottom as if trying to make it go.

"Are you going to Sled Hill?" Noah's voice was deep and rich and promised things that Ella knew he didn't want to deliver on.

Her heart panged with unrequited longing.

"Ella?" he asked, because she hadn't answered. "Are you?"

"If you ask me if I'm all right, you know I'll have to say I'm fine." Her frustration was getting the better of her and she hated herself for it. Ella drew a breath and tried again. "I meant what I said about paying for your waffles. I'll buy you a tray of frozen lasagna, too."

"Stop. You're spoiling me."

She would not smile or look at him. "Penny, the sled needs snow to make it go."

"Technically, it needs an incline or a strong hand to drag it along."

Pressing her lips together, Ella picked up Penny and set her on her feet.

"Penny needs to hitch her wagon to a beast who will do her bidding," Noah continued. "I gallantly offer my services."

"If you don't take him up on that," Sophie called back to them, "I will."

Ella felt something suspiciously like jealousy pinch her jaw. She scooped up the sled and headed for the checkout.

"Going…" Noah said in that dangerously deadpan voice of his. Ella refused to smile. "Going… Gone. One beast is now at the beck and call of one Sophie Monroe."

Ella's jaw ticked.

"Were these quilted hot pads made by

Odette?" Laurel had been in the gift-shop part of the store and held up some of the items for Mackenzie to see.

"No. Those are from the quilters guild in Hailey," Mack said.

"We wanted to pay Odette a visit." Laurel rehung the hot pads. "I'm a huge fan of her work."

"Having seen one quilt," Sophie said under her breath, and then shouted, "No chocolate, boys, since you misbehaved!"

"Actually, Odette made every quilt at the inn," Mackenzie said. "If she kept everything she made, she'd need a bigger cabin. She makes things for people. Even I can't convince her to sell anything."

"Interesting." Sophie leaned across the counter to whisper to Mackenzie, "I'll be by later for that Hershey bar." And then she said to Ella, "Don't judge. You ate the last of my emergency supply."

"Gabby said Odette knits." Laurel held up a red-and-green knit cap made with thick yarn. "Did she make this?"

"No." Mackenzie barely looked up to see what Laurel held. "Odette doesn't sell her knitting, either."

"She made me an afghan," Noah said, standing too close to Ella. "She likes me."

Mackenzie snorted.

"I'm also buying the doctor's waffles and a tray of frozen lasagna," Ella insisted when it was her turn to pay.

"I'll spring for dessert," Noah offered, trying to goad Ella into an exchange. "I like how women nowadays want to go halfsies."

Ella pressed her lips together once more. Oh, but it was hard not to quip back at him.

"Are you guys almost ready?" Laurel moved to the door. "I want to see Odette." She said it like Odette was a local attraction, like the hot springs or the world's biggest ball of yarn.

"Odette lives across the highway." Mackenzie had Ella sign a form agreeing to pay for her purchases. "Third cabin down. She's got a wooden rocker sitting on the porch. But she's not always open to visitors."

"Not always?" Noah murmured. "More like not ever."

"But I'm sure if you show up with her very good friend, the doc here, she'll welcome you in for sure." Mackenzie was almost as good at sarcasm as Noah. She grinned at him.

The Monroes stomped back out into the

cold, sunny day. The kids climbed into their sleds, grinning with excitement.

Ella smiled at them all, but her chest ached. She'd lost all enthusiasm for their outing.

Laurel's blue eyes sparkled with mischief. "This is a good hike to Odette's, not to mention the sledding the kids will do. I'm sure we'll all love a nap when we return to the inn."

Sophie gasped. "You said a bad word."

"No nap! No nap!" the boys chorused.

"No nap," Penny said without much gusto. She liked her naps.

Laurel laughed and slung an arm around Sophie's shoulder. "On to Odette's!" It was the first time since they'd arrived in Second Chance that Laurel looked like herself.

They set off down the road, Laurel leading the way, setting a pace Noah probably appreciated. Sophie claimed she could pull the sled for the twins, so Noah only had to carry his grocery bag. The snow had been plowed to either side with an island of powder in the middle.

"Go, Mom. Go." Penny giggled as she and Ella pulled away from Sophie and the twins. "We win!"

They waved at Roy in the diner window as they passed. Ella looked but couldn't find the

"Peas," Penny added.

"Last one to Laurel has to eat frozen lasagna for dinner." Ella took off, determined Noah would eat alone.

Her head start meant she was able to cut in front of Noah. The only way for him to pass her was to take his former lane, the one next to the snowdrift. Predictably, the twins couldn't resist sticking their arms in the snow and creating drag, which slowed Noah down. Ella and Penny won, barely.

"Is that the one?" Laurel turned and asked Noah. "Odette's cabin?"

"Yes." Noah set his groceries down and gently tipped over the boys' sled, tumbling them into the snow and eliciting peels of laughter. He took the sled and drove the end into a snowdrift. "You climb from here."

"Me, No. Me." Penny squirmed in her little blue sled, anticipating Noah tumbling her into the snow.

He didn't disappoint, although it was less a tumble than a slow slide. He parked Penny's sled in the snow, as well.

The round log cabin was a forty-foot climb above them. Someone—Noah?—had made a snowshoe path from Noah's cabin to hers, but there was no path down to the road.

"Are you coming with us?" Ella asked.

"No. I've got someone coming in for a follow-up appointment soon." Noah picked up his bag and walked backward.

Ella forced herself to smile. "I was hoping you were going to blaze our trail uphill."

"Oh, heavens, yes." Sophie's smile looked more natural than Ella's felt. "Or we'll all be floundering in the snow."

Penny had already flopped onto her back to make a snow angel, sinking deep into the white powder.

"It's better than any city gym workout," Ella said. "Or so I hear."

Noah's retreat hit reverse. He stalked back to Ella, stopping close enough to wrap his arms around her and deliver one of those heart-melting kisses, although he did neither. "What do I get in return?"

A kiss.

Surely, not that. But Ella's mouth was too dry to say anything.

"Dessert!" Sophie cried. "At the inn."

"Dessert…" His gaze dropped to Ella's lips.

"With my family," Ella croaked.

Noah's free hand landed on her upper arm. *Or you can just kiss me.*

Instead of administering a lip-lock, he guided Ella out of his way, and then began the climb up the slope to Odette's house, followed at a much slower pace by two boys.

To her right, Sophie put both hands on one of Ella's shoulders and whispered, "I think I might swoon."

"What was that look in his eyes just now?" Laurel came to stand at Ella's other shoulder. "Those weren't kind eyes."

"Or haunted ones, either." Sophie laughed.

"If either of you say *kissing eyes*, I'm going to push you in a snowbank." Ella bent to help Penny from her sinking snow angel while the two women laughed.

"Done." High above them, Noah sent them a jaunty salute. "Enjoy your visit. I'll see you for dessert tonight."

The two women laughed again, chortling when they noted Ella's blush.

Following Noah's footsteps, the Monroes reached Odette's one-story cabin and stomped onto the wood porch like a herd of restless horses.

"Do you hear that?" Laurel held up a hand.

"Is that a sewing machine?" She had the same dreamy expression Sophie did when anyone mentioned nap.

"Or a washer." Ella couldn't tell.

"Who's there?" a spindly voice called from inside.

"It's Sophie." She grinned at Ella. "And Alexander and Andrew and Penny and Ella and Laurel."

The kids giggled.

The door opened.

An older woman peered through the crack. Her short gray hair stuck every which way, but her lips were drawn in a disapproving pucker and her faded brown eyes fixed on Ella. "Did your bus break down?"

Laurel peered unabashedly past the elderly woman. "Is that a Husqvarna quilting machine?" She gasped. "Look at the way those colors on your quilt block blend. It's so beautiful... I could just die."

"Normally—" Odette smacked her lips and studied Laurel "—that's my line."

"Taking fabric and turning it into something breathtaking is what I do every day," Laurel gushed. "But when I look at your work—"

"A couple of quilts," Sophie muttered to Ella.

"—it steals my breath."

The old woman's expression softened, if only a little. "Are you a quilter?"

"No. I'm a costume designer." At the woman's frown, Laurel added, "A Hollywood seamstress." And when Odette still seemed unmoved, she offered the pièce de résistance. "For the movies."

Odette's nod indicated she was unimpressed. "I expect I should let you in or I'll be heating the whole out-of-doors."

They trundled into her cabin, which was as well-preserved as Noah's cabin. But Odette's must have been double the size of Noah's. She had a large living room, a sewing nook and a galley kitchen. A small dining table was pushed beneath a front window. Two doors were closed and made Ella wonder what was on the other side. She wouldn't have been surprised to find a covered breezeway and more than one bedroom.

Although the cabin was occupied, her professional side captioned Odette's home as *Historic and charming cabin featuring open concept living!*

"Come see this." Sophie's glasses had slid down her nose, a product of her grasping each curious boy by the hand. She was tilting her head back and to-and-fro, trying to see through her glasses as she looked at a framed quilt hung on the wall above the fireplace. It had various hand stitches around irregularly shaped blocks of faded fabric. "It's a crazy quilt. The date in the corner says nineteen twenty-five. That was the year Grandpa Harlan was born."

"Are you Monroes?" Odette's brow lowered, as if being one was a negative mark against them.

"Yes." Laurel was busy admiring Odette's stacks of folded quilts and missed the nuances of the conversation. "Did you know my grandfather?"

"We all knew him." Odette was a prickly one.

Ella wondered what secrets she hid between the lines of a nondisclosure agreement. And then her gaze was drawn to a framed cross-stitch on the wall. *The most difficult path is finding the truth in your heart.* It was the second half of the sentence written beneath the old map hanging in the diner.

Ella faced the old woman, barely able to contain her excitement. "Odette, where did this saying come from?"

Her eyes narrowed, although it was unclear whether her displeasure was due to Ella being nosey or because she'd struck upon something she shouldn't have. "It's a saying folks used to have around here."

"It's lovely," Ella murmured, wondering if it was a saying the Lees had or a motto adopted by the town. She'd never heard Grandpa Harlan say anything like it.

"Want dat." Penny pointed to a chunky, pink knit cap that was hanging on a hook near the door.

"It's not ours, Penny. You have to ask if you can touch it." Ella gave Odette a reassuring smile.

The elderly woman made a low sound in her throat, eyeing Ella suspiciously.

"Peas." Penny tugged on Ella's pant leg.

"You have to ask Odette if you can touch it." Ella pointed to the cabin owner. "This is her home."

Penny rushed up to the older woman. "Peas." She pointed to the knit cap, then pulled off her own and held it toward Odette. "Give you."

"She's offering a trade," Ella translated, which was good, wasn't it? Since Odette didn't sell anything.

A smile might have made a fleeting pass across the old woman's thin lips. "That cap's too big for a pint-sized girl like you, but…"

Odette removed it from its hook and placed it on Penny's blond curls.

Penny curled her fingers into the pink yarn and tugged it deeper on her head. "Petty."

"Don't stretch it, honey." Ella reached for her daughter's hands.

"Let her." Odette patted Penny's head. "That hat has been waiting for someone to love it for years."

"Knitting always takes the shape of its owner," Odette and Laurel said at the same time.

"Jinx," Ella murmured into the ensuing silence.

Penny glanced up at Ella, her hands still fisted at her ears.

The two textile-loving women stared at each other—Laurel with adoration, Odette with assessment.

Laurel recovered first. "Did you make everything in here?" She moved around the room, touching fabric and yarn creations reverently.

"Is this for sale?" Sophie was still admiring the framed baby quilt, her two boys anchoring her to the hearth like little cleats.

"I don't sell my work." Cranky Odette was back.

Sophie turned to look at the elderly woman. "Could you—"

"No." Odette cut off Sophie with a swipe of her hand.

Laurel came to stand near Odette. "Could you—"

"No!" Odette grabbed the doorknob and yanked open the door.

"Could you teach me?" Laurel blurted, a look of desperation on her pale face.

"Teach you what?" Odette shook the doorknob just as a gust of wind whipped into the cabin. "You say you already know how to sew."

Sophie brought the boys over to stand near Ella and Penny.

"There's an imprint every master seamstress makes in her work." Laurel approached Odette and gently eased the door closed. "Like a fingerprint."

"That doesn't answer my question." Odette's gaze was measured. "What can I possibly teach you?"

"I…" Laurel's gaze bounced across Sophie and Ella. Her voice fell to a whisper. "I haven't found my imprint yet."

"And you want to steal mine?" Odette huffed. "Just like a Monroe."

Ella moved to Laurel's side and put her arm around her. "Laurel wouldn't do that."

"No, I…" Laurel placed a hand on Odette's forearm, stalling the inevitable reopening of the door. "I want you to help me find mine."

Odette's expression ran the gamut—disapproval, disbelief and, finally, acceptance. "All right. But no more talk of buying or selling." She scowled at Sophie and opened the door.

The boys broke free of Sophie's hold, charged through the door and tumbled down the hill toward the parked sleds, shouting about going to Sled Hill.

"But…" Sophie pushed her glasses up her nose, glancing back at the framed baby quilt.

"No *buts*." Laurel grabbed her cousin's hand and tugged her out the door. "Can I come by tomorrow?"

"No. I'll come to you."

Ella and Penny were the last ones out the door and probably the only ones to hear Odette's parting whisper.

"If I decide you're worth it."

CHAPTER FOURTEEN

"NOAH!" ELLA HURRIED up the hill to Noah's cabin carrying Penny with her hand pressed to her forehead. "Noah! Are you there? Noah!"

From his window, Noah could see there was blood on Ella's navy jacket and Penny was crying.

Noah's heart dropped to the floor.

It seemed as if he'd just seen them leave Odette's and head for Sled Hill. His only appointment for the day hadn't even shown up yet.

Noah flung open the door, making a quick assessment. "Head wound?"

"Yes," Ella sobbed as she reached the porch, apparently at the limit of a mama's bravery. "There's so much blood."

"There always is for head wounds." He took Penny from Ella and instructed her to wash the blood from her hands. "Hey, baby girl. What's all the fuss?"

Calm her down. Clean and sanitize the wound.

That was the calm Dr. Bishop. Calm because he hadn't thought ahead to the challenge of stitches. Noah's stomach triple-somersaulted to join his heart on the floor, freezing him in place. He'd seen men who were broken, bones and sinew not where they were supposed to be. He'd endured their pleas and threats and cussing. But this...

"Ow-wee!" Penny wailed, clinging to Noah when he tried to put her on the exam table.

He knew this child. He cared for this child. He didn't want to hurt this child, even to help her heal.

Just say it, Dr. Bishop sniped. *You love her. Love?*

Penny was bleeding on him. Noah didn't care. He quit trying to put her on the table and held on tight. "Have a little faith, Penny."

Let's hope it's not misplaced. You could disfigure the kid when you close that wound.

Noah's gaze connected with Ella's. She looked as small as Penny without her big jacket on. Her eyes were huge. He wanted to wrap his arm around her, too, and reassure her that everything was going to be all right.

Penny continued to wail. His stomach somersaulted again.

Woof hopped onto the table and its crinkly paper. Penny leaned toward the dog, big drops of blood coming from her forehead. With Noah's help she dropped into a sitting position. Woof put his big head in Penny's lap.

The dog did what Ella and Noah couldn't. Penny's sobs subsided. She snuffled and buried her hands in Woof's fur, her lower lip trembling.

In that moment, Noah knew three things. He wasn't giving up Woof. He wasn't giving up Penny. And he wasn't giving up Ella. He loved them all.

Yes, love.

Extremely poor timing, Doc. As usual.

Who cared about timing? Noah was in love!

The feeling coursed through his veins like a thundering waterfall—*love-love-love*—roaring past his ears and filling his empty places.

If you spread your arms, spin around and break into song, I'll be sick, Dr. Bishop grumbled.

Woof stared up at Noah with sad eyes, as if to say: *Maybe you should think about love later—after you fix my little girl.*

"Pet the nice doggy," Ella said from Noah's side, her presence grounding him.

"Woof." Penny clutched the big dog's neck as if he was a pint-sized stuffed bunny. The tears continued to fall, but the soul-crushing sobs subsided.

"Everything's going to be all right. Tell me what happened." Noah cleaned Penny's wound while Ella recounted events in a quiet voice.

"She went down Sled Hill and the twins couldn't wait until she was clear to go down after her. They caught up and heads collided. I swear, I could hear the thud from the top, louder than cars colliding."

Penny's skin had split open above her brow. The gash was nearly an inch in length and there was a contusion forming beneath it. Noah pressed a fresh piece of gauze on the opening. He needed to stop the bleeding before he closed it up.

"Ow-wee," Penny whispered, touching Noah's hand.

"Yes. But it's going to feel better soon, Penny." What a lie that was. Her head was going to pound for hours. "Can you keep your hands on Woof while I make it all better?"

The little girl nodded.

He glanced at Ella. "I'm not steady enough to stitch her up." Her skin was thin, and he didn't want her to have jagged scars. "But I have skin glue and a butterfly bandage."

"Do it."

He hesitated. "It might not seal well."

"So?"

"She might get a scar."

"My daughter isn't going to go into acting like her father's cousin, Ashley. If she goes to Hollywood, she'll be a stuntwoman. Glue her back together, Noah."

A few minutes later, Penny was cuddling with Woof on the couch with drowsy eyes, a small icepack on her head.

Noah felt like joining them. "I wish everyone's injuries could be glued as easily," he said, flexing his fingers.

Slender arms came from behind to hug his chest. Ella wiggled around to slip under one of his arms and sighed. "Penny's really going to be all right?" Dried blood streaked the side of Ella's neck. Tears stained her cheeks. She'd never looked more beautiful to Noah.

"I think so." He kissed Ella's nose, and then got a wet cloth and gently wiped her clean so he could kiss her properly. When he was done, and she still looked shaken, he laid his palms on her shoulders, aiming to reassure. "Kids get bumps and bruises all the time. We'll need to watch her for signs of a concussion."

Ella laid a hand over his, much as Penny had done earlier. "Thank you. I was—"

"Cool as ice." He appreciated that in a medical assistant.

She laid her forehead on his chest. "I yelled at the boys."

"Any parent would." Noah enfolded her in his arms, not wanting to let go, not ready to tell her he loved her. She deserved candles and flowers and moonlight.

"Sophie's feelings were hurt."

Ella was compassionate to a fault. "Sophie needs to give those boys more discipline. I'm sure she'll understand once everything calms down."

"Yes, but—"

"*Help!*" Someone yelled from outside.

Woof's ears perked up, but he didn't move from Penny's side.

"Doc, help!"

For the second time that day, Noah hurried to the window.

A woman wearing a fleece-lined jacket

and a cowboy hat stood next to a large truck with the Bucking Bull logo on the side. "Doc! Help!" It was Francis Clark. "It's Zeke. He's bleeding. Come quick."

On autopilot, Noah leaped into heart-thumping action. He thrust his arms into a jacket and put on his snow boots without slowing to lace them up. He ran through the powder to get to the truck.

Shane was running toward them, having left the Bent Nickel across the street. "Do you need an extra pair of hands?"

Francis, standing near the open driver's door, looked near tears. "Zeke's inside the cab."

Noah opened the rear passenger door.

Zeke was one of the Bucking Bull's ranch hands. He was half lying down, half sitting across the back seat. His jeans were torn on one leg, revealing an open fracture. His tibia bone was protruding through the skin. He was pressing a blood-soaked T-shirt to the wound, but weakly, as if he might pass out. His face was pale. "Hey, Doc. Can you squeeze me in?"

"You cowboys are always trouble." Noah glanced into Zeke's eyes. The pupils were normal. "What happened?" Noah carefully examined the wound, and then took a toolbox from the floor and carefully elevated Zeke's foot. For once, he and his internal critic were on the same wavelength.

The cowboy wiped sweat from his brow with the back of his hand. "I skidded on black ice coming down the road from the Bucking Bull. A tree jumped out in front of me."

"I was right behind him." Francis spoke in the mournful tones of the guilty and gripped the steering wheel as if she needed something sturdy to keep her balance. She had a bruise rising on her cheekbone and panic in her eyes. "I rear-ended him. About fifteen minutes ago."

"Now, boss, I told you not to take it personal." Zeke tried to smile, but it looked more like a grimace.

Noah caught Francis' eye. "Are you okay?"

She waved a hand, as if her condition didn't matter. "I hit the steering wheel when I hit him." Her truck was too old to have an airbag. Her eyes misted, and she said quietly, "I'm so sorry."

"It was an accident," Noah said firmly.

"What he said," Zeke seconded.

Shane skidded into the driver's side of the truck and swore. He threw open the cab door.

"Shane," Noah said calmly, checking his

watch to note the time. "Call nine-one-one. Tell them we have an open fracture and need a medevac ASAP."

Shane didn't say anything or move.

Noah glanced up.

Shane was staring at blood and bone, his face nearly as pale as Zeke's. Or perhaps he was staring at Noah's scars. Noah's hands were in the same region and he hadn't put on his gloves.

Noah's stomach did a slow churn, but the damage was already done. Shane knew Noah wasn't able-bodied.

"*Now*, Shane." Noah put more authority in his tone and repeated his instructions.

Shane nodded and moved away to make the phone call.

"Zeke, when was your last tetanus shot?" Noah asked.

"I can't remember." Zeke frowned.

He'd need one. "Are you allergic to anything? Any meds, like penicillin?"

"Nope."

Antibiotics were a priority if Zeke's leg was to be saved.

"What can I do to help?" Ella appeared at Noah's side, wearing one of Noah's black hooded sweatshirts. She'd brought a blanket, which she draped over Zeke's lap and chest without flinching at the sight of his injury. She produced a bottle of water from the sweatshirt pocket, opened it and handed it to Zeke. "Tell me what to do, Noah."

She'd done plenty, just with those two gifts. He introduced her to the cowboy. "Keep Zeke talking and warm while I get what I need." Noah was already making a list in his head. A shot of antibiotics, a tetanus booster, saline solution, sterile wrap, a splint, ice packs. He was more in his element with Zeke's injury than he'd been with Penny's.

"Although I like the doc," Zeke said with a strained smile that tried to be pickup worthy. "I enjoy talking to pretty ladies more."

"Flatterer," Ella quipped, proving she was more than capable of handling an emergency with grace. She would have made a fantastic ER nurse or doctor. She waved off Noah, but not before their gazes connected.

He nodded at her and she nodded back.

Another connection. Albeit a simple one. A quick one. Still, it confirmed for him that she was the one for him. He climbed back through the snow to his cabin and threw what he needed into a plastic tub, running on the good kind of adrenaline.

Woof followed him with his eyes, still acting as Penny's pillow. Her eyes were closed.

Noah spared a moment to pry open Penny's eyes and flash light in them. Still no sign of concussion. She swiped his hand away and grumbled something unintelligible.

Noah returned to the truck and Zeke, sending Ella back to the cabin to watch over Penny. His pulse was pounding with excitement. He was alert and engaged in the challenge, knowing exactly what to do, knowing what Zeke would need when he reached a hospital.

Thirty minutes later, a helicopter touched down in the middle of the crossroads. Noah helped Zeke into a flight gurney. And then he watched as Zeke and Francis were carried away.

"You were good," Shane said from his position nearby. "You probably saved that guy's life."

Noah nodded once and thrust his hands in his jacket pockets, the feelings of relevancy and elation draining. He climbed the path to the cabin.

Ella met him on the porch. She was still

wearing his black hooded sweatshirt, probably because her jacket was stained with her daughter's blood. "You were in your element with Zeke."

"In a way." Noah was happy to see her, grateful she'd come out to meet him. But that didn't change the almost numbing letdown. Zeke's future was in someone else's hands.

"What happens next?"

"Surgery. He'll need surgery." Noah replayed a scenario in his head where he was the one to perform the procedure. Irrigating the wound, making sure flesh and bone were clean, implanting metal in both ends of the bone, stitching him up, praying there'd be no infection.

"I bet Zeke wishes you were doing the surgery, too." Ella slipped her arm around Noah's waist, trying to draw him inside, where it was warm.

Noah hesitated in the doorway. He stared down at the top of Ella's head and then drew his right hand from his pocket to stare at his scars. He turned to take in the broad flat valley covered in picture-perfect snow and then the crossroads where the helicopter had touched down.

He loved Ella. He was growing to love the people who lived in this valley.

But there would always be a hole in his heart where his dreams once resided.

One that no one and nothing could fill.

He drew Ella closer, splaying his ugly hand across her back, but lingering in the doorway.

He loved her. And she loved him. He could sense it in the way she'd accepted him.

They went inside and he closed the door behind them.

Love. He tried to tell himself it was enough.

Never, jeered Dr. Bishop.

"I NEVER MADE s'mores before." Ella wiped Penny's hands with a damp paper towel. "A couple more of those and I won't fit in my jeans tomorrow."

She sat in the corner of the couch in the living room of the inn, Penny—wearing her butterfly bandage—nestled in her arms. Penny's sledding accident and resulting tears had worn out her daughter, but it had drawn Ella and Noah closer together in those brief minutes after he'd stopped the bleeding and sealed her wound. But then Zeke...

Noah had been amazing with the injured cowboy. He'd stood tall. He'd given orders with precise authority. He'd tended to Zeke's wound without gloves. There was an energy to his every breath that said this was what he was meant to do.

And then the helicopter had taken off and he'd been quiet. She'd left him to his thoughts and hadn't asked anything of him when he'd shown up after dinner with chocolate, marshmallows and graham crackers for their promised dessert.

"You've never had s'mores, Ella?" Gabby turned from her place on the hearth, pale red hair in a ponytail. She'd been roasting marshmallows for the twins, who knelt on a rug a safe distance from the fire. "Seriously? How can this be?"

"I've never been camping," Ella admitted.

Gabby gasped. "Then you have to have another one."

Had Noah known she'd never had the treat when he'd brought over the makings of s'mores? If given a guess as to what he'd bring, she'd have chosen a box of frozen cheesecake from the general store's freezer. Ella's gaze searched for Noah and the chance to ask him about it, coming up empty. He'd disappeared with Mitch shortly after arriving at the inn and she hadn't seen him since.

"Grandpa Harlan took us camping once when we were little." Laurel was tucked into the other corner of the couch covered by the quilt she coveted, the blue-and-brown one made by Odette. "All twelve of us. Remember?" She glanced toward her cousins.

"I do." Shane shuddered dramatically from his seat in the corner. "Grandpa Harlan was a brave man."

"You can't call that camping." Sophie snorted, pushing her glasses with the back of her s'more-filled hand. "He rented a tour bus with bunks in it."

"It *was* camping," Laurel insisted. "We parked in a campground."

A familiar wave of longing swept through Ella's chest. "I went fishing once." With one of her foster dads. "I didn't catch anything." But Aaron had taught her how to skip rocks. It was the first and only trip they'd taken together. A few weeks later, he'd lost his job and was forced to give up Ella. She still had one of the small flat rocks from that trip.

"How much more snow do you think we'll get this winter?" Shane asked, the same as he'd asked every hour since dinner.

As one, Ella, Sophie and Laurel groaned.

Laurel kicked out her feet. "The last time a man talked so much about the weather, he used it as a pickup line." She pitched her voice low. "How much longer do you think it'll rain?"

"What an original opener." Sophie chuckled. She'd accepted Ella's apology regarding her harsh words toward the boys earlier, and had offered an apology of her own.

"Did it work?" Ella asked.

"Of course it worked." Laurel sat up, eyes twinkling. "Do you know what it's like to live in Hollywood and be the identical twin of Ashley Monroe? Anyone who doesn't ask me if I'm Ashley has a leg up on the competition."

When Sophie's laughter died down, she admitted, "I once went on a blind date with a man who couldn't remember my name. Turned out he was someone else's blind date." She rolled her eyes. "I should have taken that as a sign."

"Why's that?" Ella snuggled Penny closer.

Sophie sighed. "I married him."

Ella gasped, but Laurel found this hysterical.

"Did your husband not want to be a father?" Gabby handed Ella another s'more. "That's why my dad divorced my mom. She figured out early on that she didn't have the mommy gene." At Ella's offended noise, she added,

"Not that I take it personally. I was just a baby." By the slant of her eyes, Ella could tell her mother's disregard did hurt Gabby.

"It was her loss," Ella said.

That earned her a small smile from the girl.

Shane reached for a marshmallow roasting stick, finally enticed to join the binge. "I once accepted a date with a pop star who was doing a six-month concert residency at our resort in Vegas. She took me to a bar in our hotel, ordered a drink and seemed to be interested in me until she got a text and left with another man."

"I don't believe you." Sophie called his bluff. "Women adore you."

"Family doesn't count," Shane chided gently. "I was being used. She knew her ex-boyfriend was going to be there. She needed a man to make him jealous and get him back."

"Oh, that's sad. And it makes you a little bit more human, brother dear." Sophie patted his arm.

Shane speared a marshmallow. "And you deny you're the evil twin."

"You couldn't play nice? Just this once?" Sophie heaved a dramatic sigh, one that elicited a giggle from Penny, which brought Sophie's attention to Ella. "What about you, Ella? What's your bad-date story?"

"I don't have any bad-date stories because—"

"She's just like Bryce," Laurel muttered. "None of his relationships ever ended badly."

Ella paused, wondering once more if Bryce had loved her as deeply as she'd loved him. Her stomach churned, but that might have been because she'd eaten three s'mores. "My romantic life hasn't been all wine and roses."

Noah's silhouette appeared in the doorway behind the check-in counter.

"Prove it," Laurel challenged. She hadn't had anything but graham crackers, having decided her stomach woes were either from bad sushi she'd had at the Boise airport, or the turkey-salad sandwich she'd eaten at the Bent Nickel when they'd arrived. She claimed she was going to cleanse her system by only having water and crackers.

Ella didn't have the heart to tell Laurel graham crackers weren't part of a mild diet for upset tummies.

"See?" Laurel sighed as if Ella's silence had proven her point. "Sunshine and rainbows."

"Hang on." Ella suddenly remembered

something from her past. "There was the time a guy in high school asked me to prom."

"Keep going," Laurel prompted. "It doesn't sound bad so far."

Noah was still in the doorway, lingering on the outskirts of Ella's life. She feared the distance between them might end up as relationship fodder the next time the Monroes brought up the topic of failed romance.

Ella plunged ahead with her story. "I was ecstatic. But the next day he withdrew his invitation."

"Oh, now that is bad." Sophie shook her head. She picked up a chocolate bar and tried to foist it on Ella. "You need a dose of sugar to make it all better."

"Really, really bad," Laurel agreed, taking Sophie's cue and trying to force a graham cracker on Ella.

Noah didn't comment.

"Did this loser have a reason?" Shane demanded, blowing out the marshmallow he'd set on fire. "I might have to look him up and tell him how to treat a lady."

"He said he'd decided going to prom was too expensive." Their sympathy enveloped Ella. This was what it was like to be part of a family. To be a Monroe. "While he was counting pennies, I'd already dived in and purchased a prom dress." From the secondhand store.

"Stores frown on prom-dress returns," Laurel said, in her voice of experience.

Sophie nodded, unwrapping the candy bar.

She'd still had it in her closet when she'd married Bryce. She'd told him the story behind it and he'd asked her on a grown-up prom date, insisting she wear the dress. When the night of their date arrived, Bryce wore a tux, dinner was a catered affair at their place and they'd danced in their living room. With her expanding curves, the dress hadn't been a flattering fit. But it hadn't mattered—not to Bryce or Ella.

Shane swiped the candy bar from Sophie and the graham cracker from Laurel, using them to make a s'more. "Seriously, though. It's going to stop snowing tomorrow, isn't it?"

They all groaned.

"Don't you know this is one of the coldest, snowiest places in the United States?" Gabby gathered the marshmallows and the roasting forks. "It's January. Winter has barely begun. Suck it up, Shane."

"Yeah," Laurel agreed with a grin. "Quit complaining."

"Oh, come on." Shane struggled to sandwich his marshmallow between layers of chocolate and graham cracker. "You all feel the same way I do. Admit it."

"Never." Ella set Penny on the floor and stood. "I'm going to bed. It's past someone's bedtime."

Boots scuffed behind the front desk. Noah stepped into the light, hands thrust in his jacket pockets. "How's Penny doing?"

"Good."

Penny toddled to Noah and wrapped her arms around his leg.

"Good night, Penny." Noah patted her head with a gloved hand, his gaze finding Ella's. "You'll wake her every hour to make sure she doesn't have a concussion?"

If I say no, will you stay the night with us?

"I can handle it," Ella said instead. What she wasn't sure she could handle was falling off the ledge they were dancing across.

"What's the latest on Zeke's condition?" Shane asked Noah.

"He came out of surgery with flying colors.

It's just a waiting game to make sure there's no infection inside the bone or tissue."

"Or he could lose his leg?" Sophie's glasses had slid down her nose.

Noah nodded.

"But he won't. Because Noah was here." Ella picked up Penny. "Dessert was lovely." *I wish you would have joined me.* "Thank you."

That sparked a round of appreciation for Noah's originality and the deliciousness of s'mores.

Their words barely registered in Ella's head. What was registering was the distant look in Noah's eyes. Between her rushing the natural course of things and Zeke's accident today, she'd thrown Noah off-balance and he hadn't yet recovered.

And if he never recovered?

My heart will break.

Noah left without a look of longing or so much as a kiss on Penny's cheek or Ella's lips.

"I bet he wouldn't get a blind date's name wrong," Sophie murmured.

"Or renege on a prom," Ella added.

CHAPTER FIFTEEN

"LAUREL DIDN'T COME down to breakfast this morning." Shane paced the living room of the inn. "And she didn't answer when I knocked."

"I'll go check on her." Ella left Penny eating Cheerios with Shane and went upstairs to Laurel's room. She knocked on the door, which had a Do Not Disturb card hanging from the handle. "Laurel? It's Ella."

She thought she heard the rustle of bed-sheets, but the door remained closed.

Ella knocked again. "Laurel? If you don't open up, Shane might break the door down... or worse—ask Mitch to open the door with his pass key."

There was a groan and a shuffle. The lock clicked and the door opened an inch.

Laurel flopped back on the bed, the one advantage of having supersmall rooms. "I'm sick."

"Stomach bug or food poisoning?" Ella entered the room. Laurel's suitcase was on the floor, surrounded by every stitch of rumpled clothing she'd worn since they'd arrived. On top of the suitcase, her cosmetic case sat unopened.

"I thought it was bad sushi or that turkey-salad sandwich from the Bent Nickel, but it must be a bug. Every afternoon I feel better and I eat a little. And then I feel fine until morning." Her red hair was in a tangle. She wore gray leggings and a baggy green tank top. "I ate too many graham crackers. Can graham crackers spoil?"

"I don't think so." Ella placed a hand on her forehead. "You don't feel like you have a fever." And those symptoms didn't sound like any flu Ella was familiar with.

"Could you do me a favor and bring me some toast?"

"Of course." Ella returned a few minutes later with some of Penny's crackers, dry toast and a big mug of tea. "I told Shane you weren't feeling well."

"Thanks."

Ella helped Laurel sit up. She took a wet washrag and cleaned her face. And then she put her hair into a ponytail. When Laurel was done eating a little toast, Ella handed her the toothbrush along with a cup to spit into.

Laurel sighed. "You're good at playing nursemaid."

"Having Penny has given me lots of practice in anticipating comfort."

"I appreciate it." Laurel sank into the pillows.

"I also brought you a bucket in case you get sick again." She'd asked Mitch for one.

"This place is the lap of luxury." Laurel's eyes closed.

Ella slipped out with Laurel's key, determined to find Noah. Laurel was looking gaunt. There was more than bad sushi in her system.

Noah wasn't in the store or the diner. Ella climbed the path to his cabin, passing by Roy, who was on his way down.

"Beautiful morning," Roy said in the super-cheery tone of his. "The passes are open. But enjoy it while it lasts, because we're getting a doozy of a storm tomorrow night."

Another storm.

Ella glanced toward Noah's cabin. He stood in the window, watching her.

She wouldn't be snowed in with him this time.

What a pity.

Noah opened the door when Ella reached

the front porch and ushered her inside. Woof danced around her in that slightly awkward way of his, bumping her legs with his shoulder until she committed both hands to pet his neck and face.

And then she and Noah stood staring at each other, much as they'd stood staring at each other the day she'd made a tunnel in the snow. His expression was warm and interested, and yet the look in his blue eyes was cool and reserved, as if he didn't want to face an unpleasant truth.

She recognized that look. She'd worn it often after Bryce died.

"Is Zeke okay?" Had he taken a turn for the worse? Was that why Noah seemed so standoffish?

"No infection. He's good." Short. Sweet. To the point. Noah wasn't even trying to be clever.

There was definitely something wrong here.

"Are we good?" she asked, feeling like she was standing on unsteady ground. "I can't always tell what you're thinking past that beard of yours."

He ran a hand down the sides of his black beard as if he'd forgotten it was there.

Speaking of slips, Ella had almost forgotten why she came. "I need a favor."

His eyes flashed with interest and his gaze dropped to her lips, making hope flutter in Ella's chest.

"I need a house call." Ella rushed on before Noah decided now was the time to start with the quips and innuendo. "Laurel hasn't been holding down food very well since we got here. At first, she thought it was food poisoning or the lingering funk of car sickness, but now—"

"I don't want to cast stones," Noah said in a voice better suited for undertakers. "But it sounds like she's pregnant."

"Having been pregnant myself, I concur, Dr. Bishop."

He drew back at her use of his title—not a lot, but a noticeable amount.

Ella refused to let the sinking feeling take hold, the one that said whatever connection they'd made during the blizzard had broken. "But I also know that being unable to eat anything is a warning sign that something might not be right or that Laurel needs a little something to set her back on a less stomach-upsety path." Ella nodded at the exam room. "What do you need? Stethoscope? Blood-pressure cuff?"

He heaved a sigh. "A little black bag. A pair of thick spectacles. Gray hair." He may have been complaining, but at least he was moving in the right direction. Grabbing a backpack, opening drawers, stuffing it with equipment. When he'd finished and had put on his boots and jacket, he turned to Woof and told him to stay.

"Is he in time-out?" Ella patted the golden dog on the head. Woof hadn't come to the inn for dessert last night, either.

"Bed rest." Noah's tone lightened. "He refuses to take it easy. That brace makes him more confident and then he tries leaping in the snow and stresses his ACL once more."

"Sorry you're in rehab, Woof." Ella walked out the door, expecting Noah to build on her comment.

He said nothing as they walked down the hill to the road.

With each step, Ella felt more certain Noah had decided there was no more need for a natural progression where their attraction was concerned.

When they were both on level ground, she stared up into his face. "I guess we're at the end of the natural course of things." She had to say it out here, where they were alone, where her heart could break, because it hurt to acknowledge her love had been misplaced.

He scowled. "Even a river has to learn to flow around a rock."

"Am I the rock in this metaphor?" Standing in his way of... Ella was stumped.

"I have a lot on my mind." Noah started walking. "Ignore me."

He'd said as much when he'd fumbled in their conversation about Ella staying in town longer. And he'd spent last night's dessert hour with Mitch, not her.

She hurried to catch up to him. "Whatever it is, you can tell me about it." She and Bryce had talked about everything.

Noah gave the usual grunt and continued toward the inn. His long stride outpacing hers.

Ella scurried after him, until she was struck by a memory of following one of her foster fathers down the hall to her social worker's office. Larry had told her in the car that they couldn't keep her anymore because his wife had been diagnosed with cancer.

"Don't let me go," thirteen-year-old Ella kept saying. "I can help."

But Larry had kept on walking at a speed designed to leave her behind.

Ella stopped near a gas pump and watched Noah walk away. Seeing his broad back. Seeing Larry's. Seeing Bryce's casket being lowered into the ground. Seeing Ian look at her with regret. Seeing her mother dressed to party as she walked out the door one last time.

I can't run after love anymore.

She couldn't go after Noah. She couldn't hold on to what wasn't hers. Loving someone wasn't enough to make someone stay. Love wasn't an insurance policy. It didn't guarantee anything, not even that Ella would be loved in return.

Someday she'd be watching Penny walk away. Walking off to college. Walking down the aisle. Walking to a home and a family she made with a man who loved her.

And it would just be Ella. Alone. With her glass bowl of mementos and her head full of memories.

The most difficult path is finding the truth in your heart.

The truth was Ella was alone.

What could she take from this man to remind her of the love she'd felt? He hadn't taken her to a baseball game and caught a fly ball as Bryce had done. Or put a silver dollar in her Christmas stocking as Larry had done. Or pinned a turquoise tie tack on her sweater when he'd heard her whisper the knitted hand-me-down was too plain as Thomas had done. Or skipped rocks as she'd done with Aaron.

There was only snow and cold. And now the inevitable loneliness.

She'd think of Noah during a snowfall, but snow always melted. Was anything ever permanent?

"Ella? Are you coming?" Noah stood on the inn's porch, frowning slightly.

She nodded and moved on. She didn't say anything to him. Not when he opened the door to the inn for her. Not when she led him up the stairs. Not when she unlocked Laurel's door and told her she'd brought the doctor.

"I don't need a doctor," Laurel insisted, having not taken a look at her emaciated face in the mirror and not acknowledging that she'd thrown up into a bucket while Ella had been gone. "I just need to watch what I eat."

"You can't keep anything down," Ella pointed out from the bathroom, where she was rinsing out the bucket. "Not even toast and crackers."

Shane hovered behind Noah. "Sophie's watching Penny. What's the diagnosis, Doc?"

Noah hadn't officially entered the room. He'd been standing in the doorway listening to the women talk. "Laurel, is there a possibility you might be pregnant?"

"Show some class." Shane scowled. "That's not a possibility."

But Laurel's face went from pale to white. She hung over the edge of the bed and dry-heaved.

Ella rushed back with the bucket. When it wasn't immediately used, she retrieved a damp washrag and wiped Laurel's face.

"I'll take that as a yes." Noah sat on the edge of her bed. He gently pinched the skin on Laurel's arm and then released it. Frowned. Reached into a compartment of his backpack and handed her a pregnancy-test stick. "This isn't one-hundred-percent accurate, but it's the first option to explore."

Shane made annoyed noises from the doorway, mostly mumbled negatives about Laurel's feminine state and how it couldn't be true since she was a costume designer, behind the scenes only, not a Hollywood starlet going to flashy parties and…

He continued, but Ella tuned him out, helping Laurel from the bed.

"I thought it was food poisoning," Laurel said weakly when she got to her feet. "But… My mom said she was sick as a dog when she was pregnant with my sister and I."

"Let's not jump to conclusions." Although Ella already had. She helped Laurel toward the bathroom.

"How could you be pregnant?" Shane demanded. "You don't even have a boyfriend. Don't tell me the father is that weatherman?"

"It was a line, Shane." Laurel gripped the bathroom door frame, resisting entry. "He wasn't a weatherman."

"Can we talk about the parties involved some other time?" Noah waved away Shane. "We need to keep Laurel hydrated and get some food in her to stay down."

"How can you be so calm?" Shane wagged a finger at Laurel. "She's unemployed and pregnant!"

Her cousin's astonishment must have given Laurel strength. "At least let me take the test before you go shouting it to the world," she shot back. She entered the bathroom and closed the door, shutting them out.

The test was positive, surprising no one.

"Mitch just told me the pass was open."

Shane stood in the doorway, ready for action. "I'm taking you down the hill to a hospital."

Back in bed, Laurel seemed to shrink at the thought. "I don't want to go to the hospital heaving all the way." She looked to Noah. "At least let me stay until I'm not throwing up all day. That is… If my doctor says I can stay."

"I can give you an IV to help with fluid depletion," Noah said. "But I urge you to eat a mild diet, lay flat in bed and see a specialist as soon as possible to make sure everything is progressing as it should be."

"I just want to stay here," Laurel said. "For a little while longer."

"You can't deny your situation forever." Ella squeezed Laurel's hand, but she was looking at Noah when she said it. He was denying his situation, too. "You owe it to your baby to seek care."

Laurel's blue eyes filled with tears. "But…"

"We'll make a decision in the morning," Noah said gruffly, giving Laurel the freedom she wanted.

ELLA WAS AVOIDING NOAH.

He knew he'd said the wrong thing. Many times. Always before, she'd forgiven him. Always before, she'd coaxed him out of his funk.

But then she'd said she was staying, he'd reacted badly, he'd realized he loved her, and Zeke had been injured, and nothing had felt right since.

Noah stared out at the valley from Laurel's window. He was waiting for the IV to finish. He'd consulted with the staff ob-gyn at the hospital in Hailey about Laurel's condition—gynecology not having been an area of interest in Noah's official studies at med school. She'd agreed that Noah should reevaluate Laurel after awareness of her pregnancy made her wiser about what she ate and the IV had a chance to return her body to a healthier level of hydration. She'd recommended a clinic in Ketchum for a follow-up since it was closer to Second Chance.

This is what it's come to. Other doctors used to call you for a consult.

Noah wavered in a state between annoyance and despair. He clenched his right hand, hating that he was no longer a revered expert.

"This is done," Laurel said from her bed. Her color was better and her spirits up.

Noah checked the IV bag. It hung from a clothes rack Mitch had brought in from another room. "There's more." He squeezed the bag.

"It needs to be done. All that liquid went straight to my bladder."

"You can wait a few more minutes."

Laurel heaved a sigh. "How did you blow it with Ella?"

"What are you talking about?"

"She's mourning your loss. I recognize that look on her face from after Bryce died."

Noah didn't have to ask Laurel to describe which expression. He'd seen it when he'd reached the inn porch earlier and had turned to see Ella standing in the grocery-store parking lot next to a gas pump. Her face had been drawn. Her gaze filled with sadness.

He'd chalked it up to a mood of hers, a reaction to the dark mood of his. A lot of people were moody. Just because she'd never been moody in the few days he'd known her previously hadn't registered.

Yes, he'd had a lack of serious relationships because he'd been so focused on his career and on the need to excel. But that was no excuse for his lack of basic human kindness. The breed of kindness that Ella brimmed with.

He stared at his gloved hand—the hand she'd touched without cringing—and reminded himself he loved her.

He glanced up and caught his reflection in the bathroom mirror. A scruffy beard and eyes with dark circles. He didn't look like a successful doctor. He looked like a lumberjack at the end of the logging season. And he was just as surly.

No wonder Ella had given up on him.

Sparkle in the corner of the bathroom caught his eye. "Is there a reason you have a formal dress hanging from the shower curtain?"

"Yes. The closet curtain rod is too low." Laurel kicked her feet beneath the covers and blew out a breath. "Seriously, can't you call the IV bag empty?"

"Yes."

The hydrating liquid had done its job. Laurel's eyes were less sunken. Her skin bounced back into place when he gently pinched it.

Laurel was bouncing back. It was time for Noah to do the same.

NOAH AND WOOF entered the diner that afternoon just as the schoolkids were dispersing.

Woof made the rounds with his usual ambling hobble, spending too much time sniffing out what Penny had eaten and spilled on her shirt for lunch, and then settled down in front of the fireplace, keeping his eye on Noah. Noah knew the dog's leg needed flat ground and rest, but Woof had cabin fever and Noah needed a wingman.

No one noticed Woof. Everyone stared as Noah stacked his wood near the fire. Everyone, that is, but Ella.

Ella and Penny sat at the booth in the corner beneath the hand-drawn map of Second Chance. Ella's back was to Noah.

"Hi, No." Penny waved to him, and then wiped ketchup-stained fingers on her shirt before reaching for another potato fry.

"Look at that-there face of yours." Roy stood up and blocked Noah's path. "Finally unpacked your razor, did you?"

"It was time," Noah said, shedding his jacket, knit cap and scarf on what should have been his way to Ella's side. "If you'll excuse me." He sidestepped Roy, only to run into Mitch.

"What are you doing, buddy?" Mitch rubbed his own clean-shaven chin in an implied question between friends: *Why did you shave, and should I worry about you?*

Noah gave his head a small shake. "Someone thought I'd look better with more like a five-o'clock shadow." Ella had mentioned twice that she couldn't tell what Noah was feeling because of his beard.

Franny Clark's sister dodged past them with a travel mug in hand. "I'm driving down to Boise to visit Zeke and bring one or both of them home. I need to gas up the truck and myself." Emily stopped in front of the coffeepot.

"Don't rush off." Ivy poked her head out of the kitchen. "I made cookies last night. Those will perk Zeke right up."

Emily began her caffeine pour. "Can't rush anywhere at the moment. I backed my trailer that's got Zeke's truck attached into Mack's service bay. She needs to clear out a couple things before we can get it on the lift."

Noah moved past Mitch, only to be brought up short by Shane.

"Buddy." Shane held up his hands and sent a half glance over his shoulder at Ella. "What are you doing?"

Annoyance at the multiple distractions and anger that Shane would presume to know what was good for Ella had Noah coming forward into Shane's space. "I'm minding my own business." His voice dropped. "I suggest you mind yours."

Woof appeared between them, sitting on Noah's feet.

"Shane." Ella spoke without her turning around. "Stand down."

Her softly worded command silenced everyone in the diner.

Shane gave Noah one more hard look. "I'll be right over here if you need me, Ella."

"She won't need you," Noah muttered, nudging Woof forward toward his goal. Ella. He was lucky that Sophie and Laurel weren't in the diner.

Noah finally reached her table. Ella's face looked as strained as it had this morning when they'd walked to the inn.

This does not bode well.

Particularly with an audience.

"Hey, can we go outside and talk?" Without waiting for an answer, he scooped up Penny, ketchup fingers and all.

Ella stood and plucked Penny from his arms. "No." She sat Penny back in the booth. "Penny hasn't finished eating."

"But—"

"No."

Noah glanced at his very large, very interested audience.

Just get it over with.

Noah hesitated. But he loved Ella, so he got down on one knee.

A collective gasp rose. Everyone shifted in their seats. Everyone, that is, but Ella.

Ella didn't move. She wasn't even looking at him.

Noah wanted to check her pulse to make sure her heart was beating. But the floor was cold and hard and if he didn't get down to business soon the whole town would get involved.

"Ella, I love you and—"

Across the diner, Gabby dropped her schoolbooks. They scattered on the floor. The sound sent Woof scurrying beneath Ella's table. The preteen cringed. "Sorry."

"It's okay," Noah lied. Nothing was okay. But maybe if he proposed things would turn out all right. He took a deep breath and started over. "Ella, I love you and—"

"I wuv No." Penny giggled.

"I love you, too, sweetheart." Noah's pulse was pounding way too fast. The cold from the linoleum attacked his legs. "Ella, I love you and—"

"No." Ella's face was white.

"But… I haven't asked you anything yet." And everyone was staring at them.

Ella turned sideways in the booth, swinging her feet to the floor. She wore neon-pink snow boots that nearly blinded him. She leaned forward and framed Noah's face with her palms. There was love in her eyes.

He looked deep into her blue eyes and smiled, waiting for her kiss. Things were looking up. There was no way this could end badly.

Ella swallowed thickly. "I love you, Noah, but—"

"No." Noah shook his head. He didn't want to hear what came next.

Ella's gaze softened. "You're not ready for me. You might not ever be ready for me." Those words came out in a pained whisper, but there wasn't a sound in the rest of the diner. Everyone heard what she'd said.

"No." Noah shook his head once more. This was not happening to him. He was a world-renowned surgeon. He'd extended the careers of athletes with million-dollar contracts and endorsements with the likes of Nike and Gatorade. The woman he loved… The woman he was sure loved him back couldn't be rejecting him.

"Shh." Ella placed a gentle finger against his lips. Her touch soothed, the same way it always did. It was her words that cracked Noah's foundation. "You weren't meant to be a general practitioner. You should have seen yourself when you were treating Zeke. You came alive."

Noah wanted to deny it—if he didn't deny it, he'd lose her—but he couldn't speak. He could only give a halfhearted shake of his head. The cold crept past his waist, reaching into his chest.

"It's why you couldn't get excited when I told you we might stay longer. A relationship here… Roots here… Where you'd have to give up specialized orthopedics… It would kill your spirit. It's killing you now."

"We can move somewhere else." He loved Ella. He loved how she made him forget he wasn't perfect. How she made him feel whole. But he needed a backup plan and his brain was stuck in the epic failure that this proposal had become. Dr. Noah Bishop, he of the sharpest tongue in the New York tristate area, had nothing up his sleeve. "I could become a… Become a…" He couldn't think of anything he wanted to become except an orthopedic surgeon and that was impossible.

"No. We can't." Ella's hands moved to his hands.

His gloved hands.

"Until you're comfortable with who you are—inside and out—you won't be ready to give yourself to anyone." Her voice dropped to that pained place where just a whisper had the power to wound. "Not even me."

Not the woman who'd accept him, scars and all.

Noah tightened his grip on Ella's fingers. What she said couldn't be true.

But it might be, whispered Dr. Bishop.

"I'm sorry, but…" Ella slipped her hands free.

Or maybe Noah let her go, because Dr. Bishop was a part of him, a part of Noah he'd been trying to ignore for six months, the cocky, egotistical part that resented the loss of his dreams and tried to convince himself that love was enough to make up for it. Ella had known it wasn't.

"We've got to go." Ella rose to her feet, gathered Penny, their coats and her diaper bag, and walked to the door with steadfast steps, as if her heart wasn't breaking the same way his was.

Penny waved to Noah over Ella's shoulder. "Bye, Woof. Bye, No."

Bye.

CHAPTER SIXTEEN

ELLA PUT ONE foot in front of the other.

She could see the inn and its hulking logs ahead, but the rest of her surroundings were a blur of tears. She balanced Penny in her arms, the diaper bag on her shoulder, her jacket dragging behind them through the icy sidewalk.

She'd been so heartbroken, she hadn't put either of their jackets on and the temperature was below freezing. Penny's snowsuit hung from her small head like a thick pink cape.

Ella was sure she couldn't hide out in her room for long, not with so many Monroes in attendance. And she was doubly sure that it would be difficult to avoid Noah completely until she left town. But she'd manage. She always managed when things didn't work out.

"Are you okay?"

Ella sucked in a sob and looked up.

The woman who'd come in for coffee was pumping gas.

Ella didn't trust herself to speak. Heartbreak crowded her chest and made it difficult to breathe. But she could nod.

The woman hesitated before nodding back. "I'm Emily Clark, from the Bucking Bull Ranch." Her sister had been the woman who'd driven Zeke into town after his accident. Emily had an understanding smile. "If there's anything I can do, just ask."

Ella put her feet back in motion. The woman was leaving town. How could she possibly help Ella?

She's leaving town.

Ella stopped and turned back to this smalltown stranger. "Can I get a ride to the Boise airport?"

"Sure."

Ella sucked in more air. "I need a few minutes to pack." That would be the deal breaker—delaying her. Everyone had a schedule to keep.

"I'll wait," Emily said with just the right amount of casual reassurance.

"Thank you." Ella hurried back to her room, throwing clothes in her suitcase without folding a thing. She had to sit on top of it to get the zipper closed, but close, it did.

The door to Laurel's room was ajar. Laurel

was buried under the covers. Instead of waking her to say goodbye, Ella moved on.

"What are you doing?" Shane met her at the top of the stairs.

"Leaving. You'll be fine without me." She rolled her suitcase to him. "Take that down for me, will you?" She didn't wait for him to agree. "I need Penny's car seat from your SUV."

"You can't leave." But Shane carried the bag, anyway.

Sophie came through the inn's front door with the twins just as Ella reached the ground floor, carrying Penny, their jackets and the diaper bag. The threesome was pink-cheeked and smiling, even Sophie. The twins went to the hearth and each unwrapped a bar of candy. Penny squirmed to be let down, hurrying to plead for a piece of the chocolate.

"What's happening?" Sophie demanded, handing Penny a candy bar from her pocket.

"Noah proposed," Shane blurted. "Ella shot him down and now she's leaving."

"But why?" Sophie grabbed Ella's shoulders. "If you're upset, you need to be with family. Here. With us."

Ella's body went numb and she wavered. But then it all became so clear. Grandpa Harlan had wanted his loved ones to come to Second Chance and find a path in life, one not dictated by the Monroes.

The most difficult path is finding the truth in your heart.

The truth was it wasn't just Noah who wasn't ready for love. Ella had to be comfortable loving him unconditionally.

Are you ready, Hezzie?

She may have been heartbroken, but she was ready for sure.

"All my life, I wanted a storybook family." Ella dropped her room key on the counter. "And you and you." She gestured to Shane and Sophie. "And Grandpa Harlan. And *Bryce*." Her voice cracked. "You all gave that to me. But the truth is… I need to be comfortable being alone before I try to fit into anyone else's family."

"You fit in," Sophie argued.

"Legally, you're a Monroe," Shane added, scowling. "No one can take that from you."

"But maybe…" It killed Ella to admit it. She had to swallow twice and hug Penny tighter to get the words out. "But maybe I don't want to be a Monroe."

Sophie gasped.

"Maybe being a Monroe means I have to meet expectations and be someone I'm not." She pressed a kiss to Penny's forehead. "Maybe I need to accept who I am and where I come from first." She'd always be the impoverished daughter of a waitress, saving ketchup packets and bundling up at the first snowfall.

Shane swore. "There's no arguing with that, Soph. I'll get the Hummer keys." He took the stairs two at a time.

"Don't listen to my brother." Sophie gave Ella another shake. "I can't let you go like this."

"You can. You have to." Before Ella collapsed into a blubbering mess on the floor and lost her nerve.

There must have been something in Ella's eyes that convinced Sophie, because she hugged Ella fiercely. "You will always be a Monroe. Always."

Shane returned to them, keys in hand. In no time, he had Penny's seat in Emily's truck and Ella was buckling her daughter in for the trip.

"You stay in touch." Shane hugged Ella just as fiercely as his sister had done. "And take care of Penny 'La Pew' Monroe?"

Ella nodded, blinking back tears. "Tell Laurel I said goodbye. I'm not dropping off the face of the earth." Just getting into a truck with a complete stranger.

"Well," Emily said when Ella closed the door and the truck was in gear. She gave Ella a searching look. "Last chance."

"To stay in Second Chance?" Ella shook her head.

NOAH STAYED AWAY from the window in his cabin.

He sat in the desk chair in the shadowy exam room with Woof where he couldn't see what was happening in town and where Odette couldn't see what was happening with him—the beast.

Woof had his big shaggy head in Noah's lap.

"I thought you were my ace in the hole, buddy." Noah stroked the dog's soft fur.

Woof sighed, as if he'd thought so, too.

How had everything gone so wrong? Noah felt about as gutted as he'd felt when he'd woken up in the hospital after his accident.

Woof's ears swiveled toward the door. Someone climbed his porch steps and knocked.

"Go away!"

A key fit in the lock and the door opened.

"Odette, I've got no patience for your drama today." He'd had enough of his own.

Mitch stood in the doorway. He spread his arms. "Not Odette."

"Not happy to see you, either," Noah snapped.

Mitch closed the door. Too bad he remained on Noah's side of the door. "I've been thinking. Maybe this arrangement between you and Second Chance isn't working out."

"You're firing me?" Could this day get any worse? "Is this because I wasn't willing to milk information out of Ella about the Monroes and their plans?"

"No." Mitch produced a folded piece of paper from his pocket and ripped it up, letting the pieces fall to the floor. "That was your contract."

Noah's mouth dropped open. "But… Why?"

Mitch shoved his hands in his jacket pockets. "Because Ella's right. You aren't cut out to be a country doctor. And I want you to be happy." That was so not like Mitch.

"Happy?" Noah hung his head. "I don't know what that means anymore." How could he be happy if he couldn't practice the branch of medicine he loved or be with the woman he loved?

"It's not hard to discover happiness." Mitch gestured toward the bits of paper at his feet. "Especially when you have nothing tying you here. You're free to follow Ella if you want. Maybe you can figure this happiness thing out together."

Noah's head whipped up. "Ella's gone?" The day just got worse.

Mitch nodded, looking like he wished he could take that news back. "She's on her way to the Boise airport."

Woof laid his head on his big paws.

For whatever reason, the bearer of bad news didn't leave. "Do you remember when we first met?"

Noah wasn't in the mood for a trip down memory lane. "Vaguely." It had been a frat party. "We were both questioning why we'd ever considered pledging." They decided Greek life wasn't for them.

"You introduced yourself as Noah Bishop, future surgeon general."

He'd forgotten that. "Not to be outdone, you introduced yourself as Mitch Kincaid, future attorney general." How bright and shiny the future had looked back then. "We were full of ourselves, weren't we?"

"We were." Mitch sighed. "I loved the law,

but the legal system sickened me. As mayor I found a way to bring justice and peace to this tiny corner of the world."

"I love practicing orthopedics."

"You just used the present tense," Mitch pointed out. "If I were to introduce myself to you today, I'd say something like, 'I'm Mitch Kincaid, mayor of Second Chance.' And you'd say…"

Noah drew a blank. He knew what he wanted to say—Chief of Orthopedic Surgery—but that no longer applied.

"And that's the problem, isn't it?" Mitch sighed. "Look, buddy. I'll never be attorney general and I'm okay with that, but…" He fixed Noah with a hard stare. "You can still be the surgeon general. Or at the very least, an orthopedic doctor."

Noah reached down to pat Woof. "Just not an orthopedic surgeon."

"Yeah. But life is always about compromise and trade-offs." Mitch laid the remains of Noah's contract on the exam table. "I'll see myself out."

And he did, locking the door with that spare key.

What was it Ella had said to him in the Bent

Nickel? It was hard to remember anything but the bitter taste of rejection. But the gist of it had been he shouldn't be a general practitioner.

He'd been ecstatic treating Zeke, in his happy place. It was wrong how much joy he'd derived from that poor man's misfortune.

Maybe Mitch was right. Maybe Noah needed to find his happy place in the world.

Without Ella.

Noah thought he might be sick.

Someone else braved the steps and knocked.

"Unless you're gushing arterial blood, go away!"

Whoever it was had the firm walk of the healthy and the courage to weather Noah's horrible mood.

A key slid in the lock and the door opened once more.

"Doc, I'm dying." Odette didn't bother taking off her jacket or boots. She tracked snow across the floor and hopped onto the exam table without using the stepping stool.

"You're not dying." Noah didn't get out of his chair.

"How can you tell?"

"Because I couldn't get so lucky."

Odette cackled. "You're the first doctor to tell me that."

"Points to me." The phrase made him think of Ella, which made the room feel claustrophobic. He stared at his gloved hands.

"Do you want to hear a secret?" Odette asked.

"No."

She hopped off the table. "Someone I loved deeply left me here."

"I can't imagine why."

"Because I loved him, but not near enough. I loved him within the comfort of my boundaries, which happened to be the Second Chance city limits." She leaned down until they were eye-to-eye. "You have to ask yourself how far you're willing to go and how much of your pride you're willing to swallow to love another soul. And when you think about that answer, think about old Odette and ask yourself one final question." Odette walked to the door, digging in her pocket for the key. "How much are the two of us alike?"

CHAPTER SEVENTEEN

NOAH RANG ELLA'S doorbell and stood back, straightening his tie and gripping the bouquet of flowers tighter. It was March, but it was Southern California and the late-afternoon sun was warm on his back. Ella had fled snowy Second Chance and snowy Philadelphia for a place where he understood she'd never feel cold and relive her childhood nightmare.

In the two months since Noah had seen Ella last, he'd done the opposite. Instead of running away from his past, he'd faced it, beginning with a long-overdue conversation with his father about practicing medicine and accepting imperfection.

At Noah's feet, Woof's ears perked up, an indication that Ella was home.

"Let's hope she lets us in." Noah shifted on his feet. He couldn't remember the last time he'd been this nervous. But then again, he could.

It'd been the day she'd rejected his marriage proposal.

The door to the condominium opened.

"Noah?" Ella's sun-streaked blond hair was a mess, twisted and held up with a pencil. Her eyes were glazed over, but they brightened at the sight of him. "How did you find us?" She glanced down at her wrinkled blue tank top and white capri leggings. "I'm a mess. I was studying real-estate regulations."

"I should go." He'd come at a bad time. Maybe there would never be a right time like they'd had when they'd been snowed in in Second Chance.

"Oh, no. You're a welcome distraction." She drew him into the foyer and after a moment's hesitation kissed his cheek.

"Woof! Woof-woof-woof!" Penny ran to the door. Noah noted she'd gained new skill as a runner, although Sophie's twins would still be faster. "No-ahhh." She hugged the dog first, giggling when Woof licked what looked like spaghetti sauce from her face. And then she raised her arms to be picked up. "Petty fowers."

"Yes, pretty flowers." Noah handed them to Ella and then scooped Penny into his arms.

"White roses." With the thorns trimmed off. "They're for your mom."

"Fowers for me," Penny said staunchly.

"I'm sure your mother can share."

Ella hustled them down the hall, closing the door behind them.

The condominium was cozy with French doors that opened to a small patio area. There was light and there was color, but Noah couldn't have told you later what kind of furniture Ella had or what pictures hung on her walls. He only had eyes for Ella and Penny.

"Look at Woof." Ella scratched him behind the ears. The act of leaning over sent her blond hair spilling around her shoulders and the pencil tumbling to the tile floor. "He doesn't have a limp."

"His surgery was successful." Like Penny, Woof's mobility was still improving, and those improvements made Noah happy. "Although we're sticking to flat ground for another four weeks."

"Woof," Penny called to the dog, holding the bouquet. "My fowers. See how petty."

Noah chuckled. "A three-word sentence. I didn't think her vocabulary would get that good in such a short time."

"She goes to preschool a few mornings a week." Ella moved into a small kitchen with white shaker cabinets. She got down a vase and filled it with water, placing it on a white granite counter next to a glass bowl with an odd collection of things, including a scuffed baseball, a smooth river stone and a small photograph of the hand-drawn map of Second Chance that hung in the Bent Nickel. "How did you find us?" She sounded curious, not angry.

A good sign? Noah had no clue.

"Shane told me."

"That just proves you can move out of the Monroe compound but not out of the Monroe universe." She faced him. "What brings you to Southern California? Dressed so nicely." She hadn't stopped moving since she'd opened the door. Now that she had, he could see she was nervous. Her smile wavered, and her gaze kept dropping. "I've missed you. We both have." But she didn't throw herself into his arms and kiss him.

"I missed you both, too." More than he could put to words. "I got a job at a sports clinic in Los Angeles." Contingent upon him getting his license to practice in the state of California.

Dr. Noah Bishop's reputation opened many a door in orthopedics.

"You got a job here?" She frowned. "As a surgeon?"

"No. As an orthopedic staff doctor and consulting physician." A practice that served several professional sports clubs in the city and was glad to have an experienced former surgeon on staff, one who was interested in researching new techniques and treatments. "You were right."

"About what?" Her gaze dropped to the floor and then popped right back up.

"Everything. Me not being ready for you. Me needing to find the right career path." Seeking out a way to pursue his once-lofty dreams. Noah held up his hands. "Me needing to be comfortable in my own skin." He no longer considered himself a beast.

She blushed. "Are you happy about that? I hope you're happy, Noah. You deserve to be."

Was that blush a good thing? Since he'd left Second Chance, Noah hadn't heard from his snarky alter ego. He was alone or perhaps unified in his own head.

He cleared his throat. "You told me once

that you fell in love with your husband at first sight."

"Yes. I know it's hard to understand, but it's true." She laughed self-consciously. "My father-in-law never believed it."

"I believe it." Noah rushed on before she could say anything more. "Because I fell in love with you the moment you walked into the Bent Nickel. And I shamefully fought the inevitability of that love until the day you left me." He held up his scarred right hand. He'd been working on strengthening and stretching the muscles and tendons with some success, but wouldn't ever regain his full dexterity. "Because of this. Because I didn't think a woman like you would be able to love a man with one ugly hand."

"Your so-called ugly hand doesn't make you ugly to me, not on the outside or the inside." Her voice was soft. Her gaze misty. "I tried to tell you that. Many times."

She had. "But I wasn't ready to listen." He took Ella's hands. He'd only been bare-skin-to-bare-skin with her palms one other time. "Your words finally sunk in. I was hiding in Second Chance and I was unhappy. I wanted to stay in Second Chance so I could stay hidden.

But you forced me to acknowledge there's life beyond what can be found inside a one-room cabin. Being a country doctor can be rewarding. It has been for me in a way. But if I want it, I can be more than a country doctor. I can be a superstar in the medical field, hurt hand and all. Most importantly, I can be a superstar to my family, meaning you and Penny." His voice lost its strength, became a whisper. "If you let me." If she gave him a second chance. "If you don't run from me again."

"Oh, Noah." Her words were taut with emotion. "I left Second Chance and you for many reasons. I didn't just turn you down because you weren't ready." She drew a deep breath. "I wasn't ready either. I fell for you fast and yet I couldn't trust those feelings because I was judging them by the Monroe standards. I couldn't be a Monroe without doubting what my heart was telling me, because…you know… ice cream."

It took Noah a moment to catch on. "I'm not ice cream, Ella. I'm going to be here every day because that's what makes love special. Love may come on like a lightning strike, but true love…true love is still standing after the storm." Their separation had been a storm, of sorts.

"It took a little time," Ella said ruefully. "But I'm comfortable being Ella Bowman Monroe."

Noah's heart swelled with love.

"Woof." Penny giggled. She'd been feeding the dog her garlic bread.

He realized this was his moment. Noah got down on one knee, which attracted Woof to his side, followed by Penny.

Ella gasped, clasping her hands over her heart.

"Sit," Noah said to the dog.

Both Woof and Penny sat next to him on the floor.

"I love you, Ella. I love you so much I crawled out of my cave to be with you."

"I wuv you, No-ah." Penny stood and kissed Noah's cheek. "Kiss-kiss."

Noah drew Penny closer with one arm and Woof with the other. "Marry me, Ella." The words were gruff with emotion. "You can have a long engagement if it'll make you feel better about what people think, but our love is real and ready to blossom. All you have to do is say one word."

Yes.

"I wuv you. I wuv you." Penny hopped like a bunny out of his arms, until he drew her to him once more, pressing a kiss to her sweet cheek.

Noah sought Ella's gaze. Her insightful, loving, patient gaze. "Aren't these the three faces you want to wake up with every morning?" His, Penny's and Woof's.

Ella turned away abruptly, moving into the kitchen, opening the refrigerator door.

Was she rejecting him again?

But then she stood before him, holding a tub of ice cream.

Noah wasn't sure what the ice cream meant. "Is that a yes?"

"Yes." Smiling, Ella dropped to her knees for a group hug. "Yes, I'll marry you. I love you so much. I love you whether we're having an ice cream moment or not."

"Ice cream!" Penny cried.

"This is definitely an ice cream moment." Ella pressed a quick kiss to his lips. "I want to be with you, Noah, forever. I'll marry you today or tomorrow or a year from now."

"Well, I really thought you should pick." Noah grinned. "But if you're letting me pick,

I say we get married in Second Chance on the hill overlooking the river come spring."

Her smile widened. "The hill I slid down?"

Noah nodded. "The one you slid down." Having taken his heart with her.

* * * * *

*The next romance in
The Mountain Monroes will be coming in
June 2019 from award-winning author
Melinda Curtis!*

*Don't miss it and other great titles
available now at www.Harlequin.com.*

Get 4 **FREE REWARDS!**

We'll send you 2 FREE Books
<u>plus</u> 2 FREE Mystery Gifts.

Love Inspired® books feature contemporary inspirational romances with Christian characters facing the challenges of life and love.

FREE
Value Over
$20

Get 4 FREE REWARDS!

We'll send you 2 FREE Books <u>plus</u> 2 FREE Mystery Gifts.

Love Inspired® Suspense books feature Christian characters facing challenges to their faith... and lives.

FREE Value Over **$20**

MUST ♥ DOGS COLLECTION

SAVE 30% AND GET A FREE GIFT!

Finding true love can be "ruff"— but not when adorable dogs help to play matchmaker in these inspiring romantic "tails."

YES! Please send me the first shipment of four books from the **Must ♥ Dogs Collection**. If I don't cancel, I will continue to receive four books a month for two additional months, and I will be billed at the same discount price of $18.20 U.S./$20.30 CAN., plus $1.99 for shipping and handling.* That's a 30% discount off the cover prices! Plus, I'll receive a FREE adorable, hand-painted dog figurine in every shipment (approx. retail value of $4.99)! I am under no obligation to purchase anything and I may cancel at any time by marking "cancel" on the shipping statement and returning the shipment. I may keep the FREE books no matter what I decide.

☐ 256 HCN 4331   ☐ 456 HCN 4331

Name (please print)

Address   Apt. #

City   State/Province   Zip/Postal Code

Mail to the Reader Service:
IN U.S.A.: P.O. Box 1867, Buffalo, NY. 14240-1867
IN CANADA: P.O. Box 609, Fort Erie, Ontario L2A 5X3

Get 4 FREE REWARDS!

We'll send you 2 FREE Books plus 2 FREE Mystery Gifts.

FREE Value Over **$20**

Both the **Romance** and **Suspense** collections feature compelling novels written by many of today's best-selling authors.

STRS19R

YES! Please send me 2 FREE novels from the Essential Romance or Essential Suspense Collection and my 2 FREE gifts (gifts are worth about $10 retail). After receiving them, if I don't wish to receive any more books, I can return the shipping statement marked "cancel." If I don't cancel, I will receive 4 brand-new novels every month and be billed just $6.74 each in the U.S. or $7.24 each in Canada. That's a savings of at least 16% off the cover price. It's quite a bargain! Shipping and handling is just 50¢ per book in the U.S. and 75¢ per book in Canada.* I understand that accepting the 2 free books and gifts places me under no obligation to buy anything. I can always return a shipment and cancel at any time. The free books and gifts are mine to keep no matter what I decide.

Choose one: ☐ **Essential Romance**   ☐ **Essential Suspense**
                        (194/394 MDN GMY7)   (191/391 MDN GMY7)

_____

Name (please print)

_____

Address   Apt. #

_____

City   State/Province   Zip/Postal Code

Mail to the **Reader Service:**
IN U.S.A.: P.O. Box 1341, Buffalo, NY 14240-8531
IN CANADA: P.O. Box 603, Fort Erie, Ontario L2A 5X3

Want to try 2 free books from another series! Call 1-800-873-8635 or visit www.ReaderService.com.

STRS19R